**Nicholas dropped to the floor. "Move over,"
he whispered to Charlotte.**

He attempted to squeeze himself into the confined
space and she gave him a look as if she wanted
to kill him. But at least she wriggled farther back,
giving him a bit more room to maneuvre. He edged
himself as far into the underside of the desk as he
could, his knees tucked up to his chin. He had been
amused by Charlotte's ungainly appearance, but his
was even more absurd.

Charlotte was about to speak, but he put his finger
to his lips to indicate silence and pointed toward the
door. He was so close the action almost resulted
in their arms becoming entangled. This was most
certainly not where he had expected to spend
the first evening of this weekend party, crammed
under a desk with Charlotte FitzRoy while they
hid from the dowager duchess and two relentless
debutantes. If he'd known the evening was going
to become this entertaining, he would have shown
more enthusiasm about attending the party.

Author Note

Charlotte FitzRoy and Nicholas Richmond first appeared in *Beguiling the Duke*, where they were already fighting their attraction for each other. Now, in *How to Avoid the Marriage Mart*, they have their own story.

Charlotte is a feisty, opinionated young woman. She is typical of the type of woman who emerged in Victorian England sometimes disparagingly referred to as the New Woman. They were independent, educated and determined to change society and improve the lives of women.

Charlotte's plan to change the world does not include falling in love with a notorious rake, but sometimes the best-laid plans can go decidedly wrong.

I enjoyed writing Charlotte and Nicholas's story and hope you enjoy reading it. I love hearing from readers and can be contacted through my website at www.evashepherd.com.

EVA SHEPHERD

How to Avoid the Marriage Mart

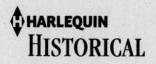

HARLEQUIN
HISTORICAL

HARLEQUIN®
HISTORICAL™

Recycling programs
for this product may
not exist in your area.

ISBN-13: 978-1-335-50592-7

How to Avoid the Marriage Mart

Copyright © 2020 by Eva Shepherd

This edition published by arrangement with Harlequin Books S.A.

For questions and comments about the quality of this book,
please contact us at CustomerService@Harlequin.com.

Harlequin Enterprises ULC
22 Adelaide St. West, 40th Floor
Toronto, Ontario M5H 4E3, Canada
www.Harlequin.com

Printed in U.S.A.

After graduating with degrees in history and political science, **Eva Shepherd** worked in journalism and as an advertising copywriter. She began writing historical romances because it combined her love of a happy ending with her passion for history. She lives in Christchurch, New Zealand, but spends her days immersed in the world of late Victorian England. You can follow her on evashepherd.com and Facebook.com/evashepherdromancewriter.

Books by Eva Shepherd

Harlequin Historical

Breaking the Marriage Rules

Beguiling the Duke
Awakening the Duchess
Aspirations of a Lady's Maid
How to Avoid the Marriage Mart

Visit the Author Profile page
at Harlequin.com.

Chapter One

Somerset, England—1893

It was just a kiss. Just one kiss. It had meant nothing to Lady Charlotte FitzRoy—or at least it should have meant nothing to her. After all, she was sure it would have meant less than nothing to Nicholas Richmond, the Duke of Kingsford. Charlotte doubted he would even remember what had happened between them five years and one month ago.

She glared at him across the drawing room. Leaning nonchalantly against the marble fireplace, his legs crossed at the ankle, his arm resting on the mantelpiece behind him, he was surrounded by a gaggle of simpering debutantes and was quite obviously thoroughly enjoying himself.

She looked him up and down with disdain, taking in those long, muscular legs, clearly delineated under the fabric of his black trousers, his slim waist and wide shoulders encased in his formal swallow-tailed evening jacket, and sniffed her disapproval.

How Charlotte could ever have been attracted to such a reprobate she would never know. Apart from his good looks and masculine physique the man had nothing to recommend him. Now that she was no longer a foolish girl of eighteen attending her first Season she could see him for what he really was. She was now far too mature to be dazzled by his charm or his handsome appearance.

Unlike those other young women, she would not be batting her eyelids at him and acting the coquette. Instead, she would treat him with the contempt he deserved. She added what she hoped was a disapproving sneer to her already disdainful expression. She expected him to look away, to turn his full attention back to the prattling pack of women gazing up at him with adoring eyes. Instead, he continued to look in her direction.

Why on earth was he doing that? It must be because she was the only unmarried woman in the room who wasn't vying for his attentions. The man's conceit knew no bounds.

No, that was unfair. Nicholas had many faults, but he wasn't conceited, nor was he vain, although he had plenty of reasons to be.

As a naive eighteen-year-old she had waxed lyrical in her diary when describing his good looks. Blue eyes the colour of the ocean on a summer's day, or sapphires sparkling in the candlelight, were among her absurdly poetic descriptions. And his hair—hadn't she described his tousled blond hair as being the colour of a wheat field moving in a gentle breeze, or the spring sun shining in a cloudless blue sky? And how she had loved the contrast between his blond hair and his dark brown eyebrows and eyelashes. She had even gone as far as to say they gave his face the look of a romantic poet, or a dashing hero from a mythical tale of dragons and damsels in distress.

And as for his lips, what ridiculous imagery had she used when describing them?

Fire erupted on her face at the memory of what she had written about his lips. She had dedicated multiple pages of her diary to how desperate she was to feel the touch of those full, sensual lips on her own. Then, when the opportunity had arisen, she had all but thrown herself at him. And he had rejected her. She forced herself not to look away from him in shame, despite the humiliation that was engulfing her like a raging inferno. She just had to remember she was no longer that foolish, fanciful girl and Nicholas Richmond now meant nothing to her. She had absolutely nothing to be embarrassed about.

'Why on earth have you turned that unbecoming shade of beetroot?'

Charlotte groaned inwardly. While she had been wallowing in the agony of her past, she hadn't noticed that her mother had sidled up to her.

'The room is a bit warm and stuffy, that's all, Mother.' She turned her gaze from Nicholas to the older woman, who bore that familiar disapproving look of flared nostrils and pinched lips.

'Well, you look like a peasant girl who has spent all day working in the fields. You'll never get a husband looking like that. And can't you at least try to smile? You're at a party, for goodness' sake, not a funeral.'

Charlotte was unable to suppress a sigh of exasperation. It was her mother's fault she was here at all. She did her best to avoid balls and other social occasions during the Season and she most certainly never attended shooting parties. Yet here she was, at the Marquess of Boswick's Somerset estate, having to endure a weekend of complete boredom, while the other guests entertained themselves during the day by slaughtering as many pheasants and partridges as they could.

Once the Season was over, the shooting and foxhunting parties that had started on the twelfth of August, some weeks ago now—known as the Glorious Twelfth—gave all those debutantes who hadn't made a conquest during the Season a second chance at finding a husband. If they weren't pretty enough, charming enough, rich enough, or with a high enough status to attract a beau during the Season, they could try to impress a future husband with their riding and shooting skills. And then there were the endless card evenings, musical evenings and dinner parties they could attend, all designed for the men to enjoy themselves while the leftover girls attempted to shine.

At twenty-three Charlotte was almost officially on the shelf and that was exactly where she wanted to be. She had more important things to do than search for a husband and had no interest in becoming a married woman, effectively giving up her independence and becoming little more than a man's possession. She released another exasperated sigh, looked over at Nicholas, then back at her mother.

'How many times do I have to tell you, Mother, I am not here to find a husband? The only reason I let you drag me to this pointless event was so that I could try to get the Marquess of Boswick to act as patron for the charity hospital I'm raising funds for.'

Charlotte had also been hoping that the Prince of Wales would be in attendance. The Marquess was part of the Prince's set, a group commonly known as the fast set because of their gambling, parties and other disreputable activities. But one good quality the Prince did possess, he could be philanthropic towards any charity he believed deserved support. Unfortunately, the Prince was reported to be shooting deer up in Scotland, so she would have to make do with the very wealthy Marquess of Boswick.

Her mother flicked her fan in Charlotte's direction. 'Oh, pish posh, you and those pointless social causes will be the death of me. No one ever found a suitable husband by indulging in so-called worthy causes. Indulging in a nice little charity can be attractive in a woman, it shows she cares, but you take it too far and get too involved. And why you want to actually mix with those people in the London slums I'll never know.' She shuddered slightly, then took Charlotte's arm. 'But let's not talk about that now. Let's go for a walk outside so those unflattering red cheeks can calm down. It will also give us a chance to discuss our strategy.'

Charlotte was reluctant to go anywhere with her mother and certainly had no interest in listening to her latest husband-hunting plans, but it was that or remain in the drawing room, watching Nicholas and his coterie of flirtatious young debs all fighting for his attention. So, she let her smiling mother lead her across the room, through the crowd of men dressed in formal black evening wear and elegant women in an array of colourful silk and satin evening gowns, talking politely in small groups.

A liveried footman in purple and gold opened the doors and as they stepped out on to the balcony the cool air stung Charlotte's burning cheeks, the nip in the air signalling a frost was on the way. The September day had been warm and sunny, but the evening air suggested it wouldn't be long before they were in the grip of winter.

The French doors closed behind them and the sound of voices died, along with her mother's smile. She was all business now as she pulled two pieces of paper out of her beaded reticule, along with her pince-nez spectacles.

'I've made a list of all the eligible men here this weekend and placed them in order of acceptability.' She looked at Charlotte over the top of her spectacles to make sure she was listening, then looked down at the paper clutched in her bejewelled hands. 'And I've made another list of those who you've got the most chance with. Hopefully, the fact that you're the sister of a duke from a prestigious family with a long and noble history will help with some of the men with lower titles or no title at all, even if…you know.' That familiar pinched look returned to her mother's face. 'Even if our fortune is not quite what it was. So, you might want to start with them.'

Charlotte would have once been surprised by her mother's determination and calculated approach to marriage, but not any more. She'd endured the agony of five Seasons and each Season her mother had become worse, until she now approached husband-hunting like a military campaign she was determined to win despite the overwhelming odds stacked against her.

'I've also made notes on each man's areas of interest, so you'll have something to talk about, and I've written out a few conversation openers for you.' She shook her head, her face the epitome of a disappointed mother. 'For someone who reads as much as you do I would have thought you'd be able to find something to talk about other than the plight of the poor, or why women should have the vote or any of that other nonsense you insist on spouting. But as you can't, I'm sure you'll appreciate my assistance in this area.'

Charlotte sighed loudly, which her mother ignored by flicking the paper, then commenced reading out the list of supposedly suitable men that even someone as inept as Charlotte might have a chance of winning. Charlotte only heard the first name on the list, a widowed baron who was old enough to be her grandfather. Instead of listening, she did what she often did when her mother was lecturing her: she let her mind drift off.

Her mother's voice fading into the background, she looked out at the topiaries in the formal garden, which were bathed in the lights coming from the countless sash windows at the back of the Marquess's extensive country home. The grounds surrounding the house were magnificent and rivalled any in the country, including those at Charlotte's home, Knightsbrook.

He was an immensely wealthy man and would

hopefully give generously towards the charity hospital. But his wealth paled in comparison to that of Nicholas Richmond. Nicholas was one of the wealthiest men in the country. When his father died, he had inherited the title of Duke of Kingsford, along with the vast family estate in Cornwall, and homes and other estates throughout the country. It was no wonder that so many women were after him. He was undeniably an excellent catch for any aspiring young lady. But Charlotte had never been interested in his title or his wealth. She drew in a strained breath. And he had made it quite clear he wasn't interested in her.

Her mother was looking at her expectantly and Charlotte realised she had stopped talking. 'Thank you, Mother,' she said, trying to keep the facetious note out of her voice. 'I'll remember all your excellent advice.'

Her mother raised her eyebrows, not convinced in the slightest by Charlotte's acquiescence. 'Right, now to the list of the men who are most eligible, but also the most in demand. If you get a chance to talk to one of them, then you must do everything you can to impress them, but the competition is going to be tough. There are some desperate young women here this weekend and even more desperate mothers.'

And you're the most desperate of them all, Charlotte wanted to add. Instead her gaze returned to the garden, to the fountain sending plumes of water high into the evening air and the statues standing guard along the winding walkways. Once again, she was determined to ignore every foolish word her mother uttered.

'Nicholas Richmond, the Duke of Kingsford,' her

mother read out. Charlotte's attention immediately snapped back to her mother, her stomach clenching, her heart doing the seemingly impossible and skipping a beat.

Her mother paused and glanced up at Charlotte. 'I didn't expect him to be here this weekend, but I've added him to the list and put him at the top as he's by far the most eligible man present. But that also means there will be some fierce competition for him and some of the young women present only came out this Season, so I'm afraid he's a bit out of your reach, really.'

She tilted her head in question. 'Charlotte, dear, you've gone bright red again. You can't blame it on the stuffy room this time. You don't harbour ambitions in the Duke's direction, do you?'

Charlotte refused to answer. She would not be discussing Nicholas or any other man with her mother.

'Oh, my dear, I think you've missed your chance there.' Her mother placed her hand gently on Charlotte's arm. 'You should have tried to capture him during your first Season, before his older brother's unfortunate passing. Now that he's inherited the title, he can have his pick of any unmarried woman he wants. I'll do my best to help, but all the other mothers at this shooting party will also be making a concerted attempt to secure him for their daughters.'

She removed her hand from Charlotte's arm and tapped her forefinger against her chin. 'I suppose I do have the advantage of being friends with his mother, so I can try to exert some influence there. It won't be easy, but there's no harm in trying.'

Charlotte drew in a deep breath and exhaled slowly, fighting to keep calm and to still her now furiously pounding heart. 'I do not need your help, Mother,' she stated slowly and emphatically. 'Do not talk to his mother and do not talk to him.'

Turning to look back at the garden, she hoped that would be the last word on the subject of Nicholas, but, knowing her mother as she did, she knew it would not be.

'If you insist, I'll leave it all to you to gain his attention, but when you do make your play, remember to ask him about his time in Europe. And make sure you let him do all the talking. You have an unfortunate habit of talking too much and being too quick to give your own views. It's much better if you let the man do the talking. All you have to do is look interested in everything he says, smile, laugh at his jokes and try not to sound too clever. And for goodness' sake, do not mention that charity hospital or any of your other silly social causes. You don't want to bore the man rigid. But we're still going to need to think about what we'll do when… I mean, in case you fail to attract the attentions of the Duke of Kingsford.'

Her mother resumed reading out her list of the most eligible men. Charlotte knew she would most certainly not be making a play for Nicholas. Nor would she be smiling at him or laughing at his jokes. And as she already had her suspicions about what he had got up to in Europe, she certainly would not be asking him about that.

'Right,' her mother said, coming to the end of the list, removing her spectacles and placing them back in her reticule. 'Chin up, Charlotte, shoulders back. Let's return to the drawing room and find you a husband. And for goodness' sake, smile.'

Life would be so much less complicated for Nicholas Richmond if Lady Charlotte FitzRoy was happily married with scores of children. And life would be even easier if he wasn't the Duke of Kingsford and the target of every young woman who wanted to elevate her position in society. He smiled politely at the blonde debutante as she twittered on about something. What was she talking about now? The weather for tomorrow's shoot, or was it the state of the grounds and how it would affect the pheasants? He was unsure. All he knew was that he'd rather be anywhere else than this infernal shooting party, but the Marquess of Boswick had insisted he attend.

The Marquess had about as much interest in shooting as Nicholas did—his younger, more athletic brother had arranged this party. For the Marquess this weekend would be all about gambling and that was why he had demanded Nicholas's presence. He had taken a sizeable amount of money off the Marquess during their all-night gambling sessions at their London club and Boswick was hoping to recoup his losses with some serious card sessions this weekend.

The brunette debutante interrupted her friend, causing the blonde to sneer momentarily before she remembered herself and beamed another smile up at Nicholas. She then laughed lightly as if she was having the most delightful time. Nicholas smiled back at her and stifled a yawn. It was going to be a long weekend, that was for certain.

Charlotte and her mother, the Dowager Duchess of Knightsbrook, re-entered the room. The Dowager Duchess was smiling and nodding to various guests as they moved through the crowded room, while Charlotte followed on behind, a look on her face that suggested she was as excited to be here as he felt. She sent a quick glance in his direction, then looked away.

Despite that look of annoyance that was distorting her pretty lips, she was undoubtedly the most attractive woman in the room. An unconventional beauty, her skin was lightly tanned and even from this distance he could see the row of dark freckles that dotted her straight nose and high cheekbones. Most women moved heaven and earth to ensure their skin was never touched by the sun, desperate to maintain their alabaster complexion. But not Charlotte.

He smiled to himself as he remembered the arguments she had had with her mother over her appearance. Charlotte loved to be outside in all types of weather. Her mother was constantly trying to get her to stay indoors, or at least to wear a hat, or carry a parasol, but every argument fell on deaf ears.

Nor could her mother get her to take an interest in fashion and it looked as though the Dowager was still failing in that pursuit. Unlike the other women in the room, who were dressed in flowing, embroidered gowns of satin and lace, Charlotte wore a plain dark blue skirt and an equally plain cream blouse. Nor was she adorned with jewellery or wearing fashionable flowers and feathers in her chestnut-brown hair.

Instead her hair was pulled back tightly into a simple bun at the back of her neck.

And she looked beautiful. The most stunning woman he had ever seen. She had taken his breath away when she was eighteen and the years had only improved her appearance. She was no longer a young lady, but a woman, and she was even more enchanting for it. The slight figure had filled out and she was now all womanly curves, slim waist, full breasts and lusciously rounded hips.

Damn her. Why did she have to be even more beautiful?

She flicked another look in his direction and he couldn't help but remember how she had looked when she had gazed up at him with those dark brown eyes on the night they had kissed. The colour of her eyes had such depth to them, just like the woman herself. He sighed lightly. She would never look up at him like that again, with such passion, such fervour. He pushed that memory away. He had made the right choice five years ago and there was no point questioning his decision now.

Instead, he looked back down at the young blonde debutante, who was still laughing and chatting happily. He stifled another yawn. Charlotte was one young woman who had never bored him. He had always enjoyed her company, her wry humour and the unique way she looked at the world.

And, unlike the young women surrounding him now, she could not be accused of chasing after a man with a title. During her first Season he had been merely the spare, his brother the heir in line to inherit the title. Despite his lack of status, she had made her interest in him clear. Too clear.

Her behaviour had sorely tested his determination to act the perfect gentleman when she had kissed him. They should never have kissed—even that was taking more liberties than a man ever should take with an unmarried young lady. But they had and he'd had to fight hard not to release the passion that had been building up inside him like a capped volcano. And then, in her naivety, she had said she wanted more than just his kisses. In her unique, no-nonsense manner she had told him she wanted him to show her what lovemaking between a man and woman was like. She had matter-of-factly told him that she had no intention of marrying, but also had no intentions of remaining a virgin.

That was five years ago. It seemed as though it was both yesterday and a lifetime ago. The temptation to do as she asked had been all but overwhelming, but for once in his life Nicholas had done the right thing. He had untangled her arms from around his neck and told her no. It had been bad enough that he had kissed a debutante, but he would do nothing else to ruin her reputation. It had taken a level of self-control he had not thought he possessed and it was a decision he was both proud of and bitterly regretted. He had fought every impulse in his body and put the need to preserve a young woman's reputation ahead of his own physical needs. And he had been rewarded for his gallantry with an outburst from Charlotte that had cut him to the quick then and still smarted.

'What use are you to me, then?' she had said, her face burning, her fists clenched at her side. *'Why else*

do you think I'd be interested in a man like you if it wasn't so you could teach me about physical love? It's not as if I'd be interested in you for your sparkling conversation, your wit or your intelligence.'

With that she had left and had refused to speak to him again.

Not long after that he had left for Europe. As the spare son of a duke his family expected him to either join the army or the church, neither of which suited Nicholas's temperament. The prospect of barking out orders to subordinates, or, even worse, being expected to follow orders, filled him with disdain. As for the church, the thought of him becoming a pious country vicar would be comical if it wasn't horrifying. It took Charlotte FitzRoy to force him into making a decision on what his future would hold. Escaping to Europe enabled him to put some distance from Charlotte and he could bury all memories of her in the time-honoured fashion of a young aristocrat on the Continent. He'd indulged himself in every vice he could, with an emphasis on gambling, drinking, women and wild parties. He had become the man Charlotte accused him of being, a rake with no conscience, who thought only of indulging in pointless pleasure.

And the European gambling dens and houses of ill repute were where he would have stayed if his brother's untimely death from consumption and his father's passing hadn't meant he inherited the dukedom. He'd been forced back to England to reluctantly take up his title and the responsibilities of running the estate. But even that, it seemed, was not enough. His mother now wanted him married and producing the heir and the spare as soon as possible.

He looked over at his mother, who was smiling at him encouragingly while talking to the mother of the blonde debutante. As soon as she had heard he was attending this shooting party at the Boswick estate, his mother had insisted on accompanying him. The reason for that was obvious. As she never tired of telling him, he was twenty-eight now and it was high time he settled down with a suitable wife.

Unfortunately, on that, his mother was going to be disappointed. He had resolved not to marry many years ago, when he was still just the spare second son, when ambitious mothers steered their daughters away from him and on to more advantageous targets. Becoming the Duke had changed his mother's attitude to him, but had not changed his attitude to marriage. He was determined to remain unmarried and without an heir. After all, it hardly mattered. The title could just as easily be passed on to some other branch of the family, but remaining single would ensure he would not have to endure the torturous marriages that his parents and so many others were forced to suffer through.

He looked over at Charlotte. She was now standing beside her mother and staring into space, while an elderly man looked her up and down as if assessing a thoroughbred horse that had just come on the market. The elderly gent was so obvious in his inspection. Nicholas almost expected him to ask Charlotte to open her mouth so he could check the quality of her teeth.

As bad as these marriage mart parties were for a man, they were far worse for a woman. He looked down at the growing group of debutantes surrounding him and could see the desperation behind their smiles. Women had so few choices in life. If they didn't make a good marriage, they had to throw themselves on the mercy of their family and hope they would support them. If their family was unwilling, then they'd have to find work as a governess or companion to some wealthy woman, or risk ending up living in poverty, with all the dangers that presented for a woman.

And often marriage was not much better for them. His own mother was testament to that. She had married the man her family deemed suitable because he had a good title and substantial income. No one cared that her marriage was a misery right from the start and only got worse with each passing year. At least he had the option of remaining single, an option he was determined to exercise. Yes, life could certainly be hard for a woman.

He sent the debutantes sympathetic smiles, to let them know that he understood how difficult this was for them.

Big mistake.

Their faces lit up as if they'd been illuminated by modern electric lightbulbs. Their smiles grew wider. Their eyelashes batted faster. The blonde opened her fan, flicked it in front of her face and gave him a coy, encouraging look. The other women instantly followed her example, their fans moving in front of their faces at a rapid rate.

Nicholas's reassuring smile died slowly. If he was going to survive this weekend, he was going to have to remember at all times—do nothing to encourage the debutantes. The pheasants were not the only prey at this shooting party. He, too, was being mercilessly hunted down and, if he was to avoid being trapped, cornered and potentially bagged, he was going to have to adopt some stringent survival tactics.

Chapter Two

Charlotte swallowed down the scream that was welling up inside her. She was tempted to yell at her mother to stop. She did not want to marry Baron Itchly or any other man, so her mother could just stop right now in this relentless, fruitless pursuit of a husband.

She wanted to grab her mother by the shoulders, shake her and let her know in no uncertain terms that the only reason she was standing in this drawing room was because she wanted to ask the Marquess of Boswick to donate money to the charity hospital. That was it. Nothing else. She was not in pursuit of a husband, she was in pursuit of a patron.

As the second richest man in the room the Marquess would make an ideal patron for the hospital. Nicholas Richmond was the richest, so he would be even better. But there was no way she was going to ask *that* man for anything.

She looked over at the Marquess of Boswick, chatting and laughing with a group of young women. As soon as possible she would ask him about donating money to the hospital, then she would leave this wretched weekend party. But it looked as though he, too, was enjoying flirting with a group of admiring young women. She had enough diplomatic skills to know that interrupting a man when he was flirting with a pretty girl would not be to her advantage.

So, until she could get the Marquess's undivided attention she was going to have to continue to endure this ongoing horror.

Charlotte tried to block out her mother's voice as she itemised her daughter's supposed virtues and accomplishments to Baron Itchly, but found it impossible, particularly now that her mother's behaviour had descended to a deeper, even more desperate level. She had moved on from praising Charlotte to denigrating all the other young women present, causing Charlotte's raging temper to flare up several more degrees. To make matters even worse, this particularly elderly gent was on the bottom of the list of potential conquests. He was the one her mother had listed as the easiest catch in the room. Charlotte hated to think what her mother was going to say to men further up the list, the ones who presented more of a challenge. And if she actually made it to the top of the list of eligible men, to Nicholas, the possibilities of what her mother might do or say were too horrendous to even contemplate.

A groan of despair escaped Charlotte's lips.

Please, please, Mother, do not speak to Nicholas, she silently begged.

Fighting hard, she tried not to look in his direction, but her eyes seemed incapable of following that one simple instruction and, as if under their own volition, they moved to where he was so nonchalantly leaning against the fireplace. It was just as she expected. He was still surrounded by his group of adoring young women, all primping and preening, their fluttering fans making their intent all too obvious. And Nicholas was still smiling at them, basking in all the adoration.

Like some sort of Roman god surrounded by infatuated nymphs, he was in his element. Although this god was thankfully not dressed in a toga. The last thing she needed to see was Nicholas's naked muscular chest and shoulders. But, damn him, even in formal evening wear he still looked god-like. Charlotte did not usually use words like *damn*, but in this instance, it was the only word that would suffice. Damn him for being so handsome. And damn him for looking so good in his evening suit.

While the women were wearing embroidered gowns of every colour and were adorned with sparkling jewels, coloured feathers and delicate lace, the men were all attired in the same identical black suits with white shirt and tie. But Nicholas wore it so much better.

He gazed in her direction, forcing Charlotte to flick her eyes back to her mother, her teeth gritting together so tightly her jaw was starting to hurt.

Damn him, she did not want him to make her feel even more uncomfortable than she already was, but all he had to do to raise her discomfort level from barely tolerable to completely insufferable was to look at her with those captivating blue eyes.

It was bad enough having to put up with her mother

marketing her to any old eligible man as though she was a prize cow, but having to do it in the presence of *that* man was more than anyone should be expected to endure.

Charlotte simply could not put up with this torture a second longer. If she couldn't speak to the Marquess of Boswick tonight, then there was no point staying in this drawing room and continuing to subject herself to this ordeal.

'Will you excuse me for a moment,' she interrupted the Baron, who was describing his estate to her mother. It seemed she had passed muster and they were already getting down to politely discussing financial arrangements.

They both looked at her and smiled. 'Yes, you run along, dear,' her mother said. 'The Baron and I have much to talk about.'

Charlotte glowered at her mother. How could she possibly think that her daughter would even consider marrying this elderly man with a tobacco-stained, grey walrus moustache and red watery eyes? As soon as she was alone with her mother, she would tell her in no uncertain terms.

Why her mother would want her to marry at all was something Charlotte could never understand. Her mother's own marriage had been a misery, as were the marriages of so many members of the aristocracy. They were negotiated like business transactions and had little or nothing to do with whether the couple were compatible. And once married, the woman had just one role, to produce children, while the man continued to have complete freedom and could do as he pleased. And men like her father took full advantage of that freedom. Throughout her childhood her father had hosted countless drunken gambling parties at Knightsbrook that sometimes went on for weeks at a time. He either did not know or did not care what effect such debauchery was having on his wife and children. Charlotte would think a caring mother would want to save her daughter from that unhappiness, rather than trying to foist her on to any available man, no matter how unsuitable.

She crossed the room, her body rigid with pent-up anger, desperate to escape the stultifying atmosphere of the drawing room. She nodded her thanks to the footman as he opened the door for her and, as the door closed behind her, she breathed a sigh of relief, the tension starting to lose its tight grip on her shoulders.

She looked up and down the long black-and-white-tiled hallway lined with its statues, oil paintings and large ornate displays of flowers in enormous vases. She was still too agitated to retire to her bedroom, but she had no idea where she wanted to spend the rest of the evening. All she knew was she had to get away from her mother and her relentless matchmaking. With no destination in mind she strolled down the hallway, admiring the artwork on the walls.

Coping with her mother's behaviour was getting harder and harder with each passing Season. It didn't matter how many times she insisted she had no interest in marrying anyone, ever, her mother refused to listen.

She knew her mother still harboured hopes that she would marry a wealthy man, one who would ensure Charlotte would be able to live in the level of luxury that the FitzRoys had once seen as their birthright. Thanks to her father's and her grandfathers' gambling the formerly prosperous Knightsbrook estate was all but bankrupt. Her brother, Alexander, the new Duke of Knightsbrook, and his wife, Rosie, were working hard to modernise the estate and pay off the mountain of debts, but it would be many years, if ever, before the family returned to its once prosperous state.

Charlotte's mother's answer to their financial problems had been to try to marry Alexander off to an American heiress. But all her plans had been thwarted when Alexander had married for love, not money, and chosen a penniless orphan for his bride. Charlotte smiled at the memory of how horrified her mother had been when that matchmaking plan had gone disastrously awry.

But with Alexander married, Charlotte's mother had been free to turn her full attention to finding a husband for her only daughter. She shuddered at the memory of her mother's lists of eligible men. A bigger group of wastrels she was unlikely to ever meet. And she had put Nicholas at the top. That was appropriate. He was the biggest wastrel of all.

Charlotte's cheeks once again burst into fire as she remembered the embarrassing way she had all but thrown herself at him. She had wanted to prove herself to be free and progressive, and all she had done was prove herself to be a fool.

When she had met Nicholas, her mind had been full of fantasies of living a bohemian lifestyle, just like Mademoiselle LeBlanc, her art tutor. Her mother had hired the flamboyant Frenchwoman to try to teach

Charlotte to paint. She was about to have her debut and her mother saw her as sadly lacking in the skills a young lady was expected to possess. Mademoiselle had been a revelation, particularly as Charlotte was already starting to have her doubts about what Society expected of a young woman of her class.

Mademoiselle had been so carefree and happy, a stark contrast to Charlotte's mother and her miserable married friends, and the few months they had spent together had been full of fun and laughter. Instead of occupying their time talking about colour, form and painting techniques, Charlotte had bombarded her with questions about her lifestyle, and her time among the artistic circles of Paris. Charlotte had revelled in tales of women who had thrown off the strict rules of society, who had taken lovers just like men did, and cared nothing for what so-called respectable people thought of them.

It had all sounded so romantic and liberating. She was dreading her first Season, where she would be expected to marry as quickly as possible and spend the rest of her life with a man her mother deemed suitable, but Mademoiselle had presented her with an alternative.

Charlotte knew she did not want to be like her mother, forced into the horror of an unhappy marriage. She wanted to be like Mademoiselle LeBlanc, single, happy and free.

When she had met Nicholas, he had seemed like the perfect candidate for her to launch her new bohemian lifestyle. She could take this handsome rake as her lover and live a wild, carefree existence.

What a mistake that had been. Nicholas had destroyed all her romantic illusions. His rejection had left her shattered and seeing him again brought back the full force of her humiliation.

This weekend, the Earl of Uglow would not be the only man she would be avoiding—not when every time she looked at Nicholas she was reminded of just what a fool she had made of herself.

She rounded the corner and saw the Marquess's library, the door wide open. No one else was likely to venture in there. She glanced back down the empty hallway, then entered the room and breathed in the comforting scent of leather from the books lining the walls.

Charlotte suspected the Marquess, like many members of the aristocracy, had never read a book in his life. He had probably inherited all these books from some more learned forebear, when he took possession of this estate and his title. She pulled a book off the shelf and settled down in the comfortable leather chair in front of the large mahogany desk.

Smiling to herself Charlotte began reading. Her mother was forever berating her for constantly having her nose stuck in a book, but this was how she enjoyed spending her time. Being surrounded by shelves full of books was infinitely preferable to being bored to death at a social gathering, surrounded by the idle rich and being forced to listen to the gossip and fripperies of the aristocracy. If only she could spend the rest of the weekend in this private sanctuary, this horrible shooting party might be almost tolerable.

* * *

Nicholas looked discreetly over his shoulder at the clock ticking on the mantelpiece. It was an antique, Georgian, he guessed, and he was sure time must have moved more slowly in the Georgian period, because the hands seemed to be ticking at a painfully slow pace. The card game didn't start till eleven o'clock and it was still only ten. Could he endure another hour of these debutantes' company? A set of redheaded twin sisters had joined the group and were gazing up at him with identical, imploring blue eyes. Now he was hemmed in against the mantelpiece by a circle of women, all laughing at everything he said as if he were the star act at the Gaiety Theatre, and the relentlessly flicking fans were now creating quite a breeze.

He looked around the room for a means of escape and accidentally caught his mother's eye. She was talking to yet another debutante. She smiled, took the debutante's arm and began leading her across the room in Nicholas's direction.

Please, no, not another one.

Despite the constant agitation of the air from the debutantes' fans, the room was becoming increasingly stuffy. Nicholas pulled at his starched collar and took another look at the clock. He was sure the hands were now moving backwards.

His mother introduced the latest debutante and then, smiling to herself, departed, presumably in pursuit of more debutantes to round up and add to the growing corral.

If the entire weekend was going to be like this Nicholas was unsure how he would survive. The newest debutante started telling him a supposedly amusing story about the daughter of a duke who had run off to America with her footman. He could see the group of young women relishing their outrage over something so scandalous.

Nicholas's mind drifted off and he looked around the room. The Baron and the Dowager Duchess of Knightsbrook were still deep in conversation, but Charlotte had departed. Sensible woman. He had watched her leave, envying her ability to escape. Unlike him, she had the luxury of retiring early.

While he was enduring this tedium, she was presumably relishing the pleasure of being alone, probably reading a good book. There was little chance of him achieving that state. As soon as the clock struck eleven, he would be ensconced in the card room until the small hours of the morning, with no chance of escape.

Another yawn rose up inside him. Gambling— that, too, was becoming a bore. It no longer served its purpose of distracting him and relieving his growing sense of tedium. If it ever had. All it did was pass the endless hours, nothing more. Unlike his fellow gamblers, it did not give him a thrill to win money and he cared even less when he lost, although that rarely happened.

While gamblers like the Marquess of Boswick grew more impassioned with every hand, win or lose, Nicholas could not get excited and reacted with the same level of languor no matter how the cards fell. His fellow gamblers thought he was exhibiting coolness under pressure, but that wasn't the case. He just didn't care. And, ironically, this lack of passion meant that he often won. He had taken excessively large amounts of money off the Marquess over the last few months and tonight Boswick was hoping to regain his losses. The Marquess could certainly afford to lose, but Nicholas knew that was not the point. Unlike Nicholas, he took losing personally and was desperate to prove himself the better card player, which in the Marquess's mind also meant proving himself the better man. Nicholas was almost tempted to just let the man win and have done with it, but just as card players were adept at spotting a cheat, they could just as easily spot someone who was deliberately playing against form.

He took another look at the clock. Only five minutes had passed since he last looked. In fifty minutes the gambling would begin. Fifty long minutes of this tedium, to be replaced by the tedium of the card table. The debutantes had moved on from discussing the scandal of the lady and the footman to talking about how it was typical of a servant and how none of them could be trusted.

He had been polite for long enough. It was time to make his escape. He'd retire to the card room early, order a glass of brandy and spend some luxurious time in solitude before the other men joined him and the all-night session began.

Making his apologies, he was met with a row of disappointed frowns, which he managed to assuage when he told them how much he was looking forward to seeing them tomorrow after the day's shoot. It was a lie, but a small white lie, and the truth would only hurt their feelings.

He nodded to the footman as he opened the door and, when the door closed behind him, for the first time since he had arrived at the Boswick estate he breathed easily. Striding down the hallway, he took the familiar route to the card room.

He passed the open door of the library and something drew his attention. It was Charlotte. Sitting at the desk, a book in her hand.

He should keep on walking. He should leave her to her solitude, but he didn't. Instead he stood at the door, watching. It wouldn't hurt to secretly observe her for just a few seconds, would it? After all, she was engrossed in her book and had no idea of his presence.

He smiled to himself. It was so pleasant to see her looking so relaxed. In the drawing room she had looked so angry, petulant, strained. Now she just looked like her beautiful self. It was just as he remembered her, his stunning, outspoken, earnest Charlotte. A woman like no other he had ever met. She was one woman who would never be caught simpering and smiling or behaving coquettishly in order to attract a man's attentions. But she had certainly caught his attention the first time they met and she had caught it again tonight. And one thing he could most definitely say about Charlotte, she was never boring.

He turned away, still smiling to himself. He should move on. In the past she had made it perfectly clear to him just what she thought of him. She would not want to talk to him. After all, she saw him as nothing more than a rake, a man who lacked wit, intelligence or sparkling conversation. Despite that, he turned to take one last look at her before departing. Charlotte was staring back at him over the top of her book and she didn't look happy to see him.

Chapter Three

'Hello, Charlotte,' he said quietly, almost to himself. She lowered her book, her eyes still fixed on him, her look one of disapproval. He cursed himself. He should not have spoken. He should not have interrupted her. He should have merely nodded a greeting and moved on. The tension had returned to her face. She clutched her book tightly to her chest, but said nothing in response.

'I'm sorry to disturb you. I was looking for the card room.' He looked around the room as if expecting it to magically transform itself into the room he was searching for.

'Well, *this* is a library.' Her voice was terse, implying that he was unlikely to know what a library was. 'I have no idea where the card room is.'

He remained standing at the door. He should leave, spend some time alone before the gambling began. So why was he still standing at the library doorway? And if he wasn't going to leave, he needed to say something rather than just staring at her like a tongue-tied idiot.

But what do you say to a woman who saw you as little more than a dim-witted rake, whose only redeeming quality, if it could be called that, was his reputation in the bedroom?

– You don't say anything. You just walk away. And that's what you should do. Right now.

The bustle of silk and satin behind him drew his attention from Charlotte to the hallway.

'Have you seen Charlotte?' the Dowager Duchess of Knightsbrook called to him from the end of the corridor. 'She seems to have disappeared and the Earl of Uglow is desperate to meet her.'

The Dowager was approaching at a rapid rate, her black satin gown billowing out around her, like a warship in full sail. The Dowager's husband had died several years ago, but like Queen Victoria the Dowager had chosen to continue to wear widow's weeds long past the requisite two years of mourning. It seemed strange that she had chosen to do so, because, unlike Queen Victoria, Nicholas doubted the Dowager's decision to remain in black was due to ongoing grieving, considering what a reprobate the old Duke of Knightsbrook had been. Although from what his mother had said, since the old Duke's death, the Dowager had almost elevated him to sainthood status, and now claimed that they had had an idyllic marriage. Why this should surprise him, Nicholas did not know. After all, the Dowager wasn't the only person he knew of who was capable of deluding themselves that marriage and happiness went hand in hand.

While the Dowager was occupied opening doors, Nicholas quickly glanced into the library. Charlotte's expression was no longer tense. She now bore an uncanny resemblance to a cornered fox facing a pack of hounds.

Nicholas turned back to the Dowager. 'No, I'm sorry, Your Grace, I haven't seen her. Perhaps she's decided to retire early.' He pointed towards the stairs at the end of the corridor. 'You should check her bedroom. I'm certain that's where you'll find her.'

'No, I've already looked in her room and she's not there.' The Dowager opened another door and peered in, then expressed her disappointment at not finding her daughter by shutting the door with a resounding slam.

He took another swift glance into the library. Charlotte was rapidly flicking her hands in his direction, as if indicating that he should do something, anything, to stop the Dowager from finding her there. But apart from tackling the Dowager to the floor, he suspected there was little he could do to halt her relentless progress. Poor Charlotte was going to be caught and dragged back to be inspected by the Earl of Uglow, and he was going to be caught in a lie.

Nicholas looked back at the Dowager. 'Perhaps she's already returned to the drawing room. I think you should go back there. That's certain to be where she is.'

But the Dowager kept coming, opening and closing doors, each one slammed firmly behind her as she made her way down the corridor. As discreetly as possible he closed the library door and leant against it, his body filling the frame.

She arrived at the library, stood in front of him and

sent him an imperious look. They held each other's gaze for a moment and Nicholas knew he had lost. Charlotte was right. He was completely dim-witted. He was unable to think of a single reason why he would bar the Dowager's entrance to the library. 'Let me get the door for you,' he all but shouted so Charlotte could prepare herself as best she could for her inevitable discovery.

The Dowager huffed her annoyance at his delay and continued to frown at him as he fumbled with the doorknob.

He opened the door slowly and reluctantly stepped aside.

The Dowager leant forward and peered inside. 'Hmm, the library, that would be the most likely place for her to be, but she's not here. Perhaps you're right and she has gone back to the drawing room.'

Nicholas looked over the top of the Dowager's head at the now empty library. Charlotte was nowhere to be seen.

Giving one more irritated *hmmph*, the Dowager turned, then looked up at Nicholas as if seeing him for the first time and smiled. 'Nicholas, it's so good to see you again. Or should I call you Your Grace now that you're the Duke of Kingsford?' She bobbed a small curtsy. He returned her greeting with a formal bow, then shook his head. 'To you, Duchess, I will always be Nicholas.'

She sent him a smile that would be called coquettish if it came from a younger woman and Nicholas inwardly groaned. There had been a time when the Dowager had hardly spoken to him, unless it was to order him about. But now that he was a duke, she was suddenly acting in a deferential manner. He should be getting used to this change in the way people spoke to him and behaved in his presence, but he wasn't.

'That's so gracious of you, Your Grace... I mean, Nicholas.' The Dowager tapped him lightly on his arm with her fan and gave a small laugh. 'Charlotte and I were only a few minutes ago discussing you and wondering about your time on the Continent. I know Charlotte is anxious to hear all about it. I'm sure she'll find everything you can tell her about your adventures absolutely fascinating. Perhaps you'd like to visit Knightsbrook some time soon so you can enthral us with all your tales of travel.'

Nicholas heard a low groan emerge from behind the curtains, which he covered with a loud cough. He tapped his chest with his fist. 'Excuse me, Duchess, I believe I might be coming down with a slight cold.'

'Oh, that is unfortunate. You must talk to Charlotte about that. She's such a compassionate young lady. Whoever marries her will be so fortunate to have such a caring, tender wife. Plus, she's not just caring. She's also talented and accomplished as well. Do you know she speaks four languages fluently, is a wonderful piano player, has a beautiful singing voice, creates exquisite pieces of embroidery and her watercolours are much admired?'

Nicholas coughed again to cover the even louder groan.

'No, I didn't know any of that. And, yes, I promise you I will make some time to talk to Charlotte this weekend. But as she's obviously not in the library, perhaps you had better find her first.'

The Dowager took another look around the library, frowned, then smiled up at Nicholas. 'I'll tell her you're anxious to talk to her. Perhaps I'll have a word with the Marquess and make sure she's seated next to you at tomorrow night's dinner. Charlotte is much sought after as a dinner companion because she's such a wonderful conversationalist, as I'm sure you know, but don't worry, I'll be able to pull some strings to ensure you're seated together.'

Nicholas coughed again, covering the expected groan once more. 'Yes, that would be delightful. Now, if you'll excuse me, Duchess, I have a card game to attend.'

'Yes, yes, you go off and enjoy yourself. But you're on a promise now, Nicholas... I mean, Your Grace... I mean Nicholas.' She giggled girlishly. 'I'll make certain of tomorrow night's dinner arrangements.' The Dowager sent him another smile, even broader than the last, turned and bustled back down the corridor.

Nicholas waited till she had turned the corner, then entered the library. Smiling to himself, he took hold of the curtains and pulled them back with one dramatic flourish.

She wasn't there.

The large sash window was wide open so he placed his hands on the windowsill and looked out. Then he looked down and laughed out loud at the sight before him. In the light spreading out over the garden from the well-lit library was Charlotte FitzRoy, hiding in the shrubbery, her skirt and petticoat caught up and twisted on the branches, her lacy white undergarments exposed, along with a rather delightful expanse of silk stocking.

She looked up at him with narrowed eyes, then went back to frantically pulling at her skirt, seemingly oblivious of the fact that she was further entangling it in the branches and, as a consequence, further imprisoning herself.

'She's gone now,' he said. 'So may I offer you some assistance?'

'I'm perfectly all right, thank you.' Her voice sounded anything but thankful.

She gave the white fabric of her petticoat a firm pull, winced at the sound of ripping fabric, then sent him a withering look that suggested he was somehow responsible for the torn undergarment.

'If you don't accept my help, I suspect you're going to be stuck there for some time. So maybe you can pass the time by listening to tales of my European travels. Your mother says you're anxious to hear them.'

The disdain on her face increased. 'My mother also said I'm an accomplished piano player, have a beautiful singing voice and that my watercolours are much admired. Being truthful has never been one of my mother's virtues.'

'And I assume being an escapologist is not one of your accomplishments. So perhaps you should let me help you out of that tight spot.'

'I said I do not need your help.'

Nicholas shook his head slowly. Women's clothing could do many things. They could accentuate a woman's curves, diminish the size of their waistline and give them a floaty, feminine appearance. All things that Nicholas was appreciative of. But one thing their clothing didn't allow for was ease of movement and they were definitely not designed for climbing trees, or escaping through windows.

How she had been able to jump out of the window so quietly dressed in a long gown and layers of petticoats he would never know. It must have been the motivating factor of desperation. He suspected Charlotte could scale the tallest mountain in a long dress and petticoats if it meant getting away from her mother.

But now that desperation had passed and she was stuck. Without his help she would be unlikely to free herself any time soon.

He smiled as he continued to watch the performance, which was more entertaining than any vaudeville show. It was a fruitless endeavour, but that wasn't stopping her from trying.

That was the stubborn, proud and independent woman he had been so attracted to when he had first met her. And only Charlotte could maintain such a haughty expression, even when stuck in such an embarrassing predicament.

'Charlotte, just admit it. You need my help.'

She ignored the hand that was reaching out towards her and continued to pull at her skirt, cringing each time she heard another ripping sound.

'You're going to destroy your clothing if you carry on this way. And you can hardly go back into the house with your skirt in tatters. What would your mother think then? Just admit…'

His attention was drawn from Charlotte to the rustling of silk behind him.

'He's in here somewhere,' he heard a woman's familiar voice.

'He wouldn't be hiding from us, would he?' another young woman responded. The swishing of silk indicating they were walking down the hallway towards the library.

It was the blonde and the brunette debutantes who had been the first to corner him this evening. It seemed leaving the drawing room hadn't been enough to put them off their relentless pursuit of their quarry.

While trying not to laugh, Nicholas vaulted over the windowsill and landed with a crash of branches beside Charlotte.

Charlotte was about to speak, but he put his finger to his lip to indicate silence and pointed upward, towards the open window. While she glared at him Nicholas stifled his laughter. This was most certainly not where he had expected to spend the first evening of this weekend party, hiding in the shrubbery with Charlotte FitzRoy while they were pursued by the Dowager Duchess and two determined debutantes. If he'd known the evening was going to become this entertaining, he would have shown more enthusiasm about attending the party.

But the stern look on Charlotte's face suggested she did not see the funny side of their predicament. And the way she was breathing in rapid gasps, with her cheeks and neck flushed, suggested she was having a strong reaction to being imprisoned with him. Either it was annoyance or, perhaps, just maybe excitement at being so close to him. He hoped it was the latter, because he was painfully aware that her lovely body was so close they were almost touching.

He was also acutely aware that her skirts were hoisted up and her legs exposed, but that was something he most certainly should not be thinking about.

'No, he wouldn't be hiding from us,' he heard the other debutante say. The response was louder this time. They must be in the library.

He ducked down so his head would not be seen above the windowsill and flattened himself against the cool stone wall.

'Mother says that he's anxious to wed and produce an heir, that's why he's here. After all, why else would a man who doesn't own a gun attend a shooting party if it wasn't to find himself a wife?'

They both giggled and the sound of swishing silk came closer. Nicholas closed his eyes and said a silent prayer that they would not think to look out of the open window. He could think of no logical reason to explain why he and Lady Charlotte FitzRoy would be hiding behind a large bush in the garden of the Marquess of Boswick.

'And not just any wife,' the debutante continued. 'Did you see the way he was smiling at me? I think you might as well give up now, because this one is most definitely mine.'

'Nonsense,' came the annoyed response, followed by an angry rustle of silk. 'It's me he's interested in and it's me he'll be proposing to before the end of this weekend.'

'How can you possibly think that?' the blonde debutante said, her voice rising. 'It's me he'll be marrying.' She giggled lightly. 'I'm going to love being the Duchess of Kingsford. I'll not only have a title, but I'll be married to a man who's as handsome as sin and has a reputation that's just as sinful. Oh, I'm going to enjoy experiencing every bit of that sinning and you're going to be ever so jealous of me.'

'You'll be the jealous one,' the brunette fired back, her voice rising. 'Just you wait and see. But we've got to find him first and he's obviously not here.'

The sound of rustling silk started again, indicating that the huntresses were on the move.

Charlotte frowned and shook her head. 'Well, aren't you the popular one.' She pulled her face into an exaggerated imitation of coyness. 'He'll be proposing to me before the end of the weekend. Oh, no, he won't be. It was me he was smiling at.'

Nicholas smiled at her mocking voice. 'If I didn't know better, I'd almost think you were jealous.'

Her face registering her contempt, she tried to turn away from him, but was stopped by her entangled skirt. 'Jealous? Of you? Of them? Don't be ridiculous.'

He laughed lightly at her outrage. 'As I said, *if* I didn't know you better. But it's not me that's popular. It's the title Duchess of Kingsford that those young women are attracted to. And if you were jealous…'

Her glaring eyes grew wider.

'I said *if* you were jealous, which I know you're not, you've got nothing to worry about. I'm obviously not planning on proposing to anyone this weekend, otherwise I wouldn't have jumped out of that window. I'm here to play cards with the Marquess, no other reason.'

'I am most certainly not worried.' She gave her skirt another sharp pull. 'I neither care nor am interested in who you are or aren't going to propose to.'

He suppressed a teasing smile. 'And according to your mother you're certain to get a proposal before the end of the weekend as well, either from Baron Itchly or the Earl of Uglow.'

As expected, her glare intensified until it became an angry glower. 'If anyone is foolish enough to propose to me, I'll be responding with a firm no. I told you that five years and one...'

Even in the subdued lighting he could see her cheeks turn an intriguing shade of pink. It seems she, too, remembered exactly how long ago it had been since they'd kissed. Interesting.

She tilted up her chin and crossed her arms, her affronted body language a contrast to her blushing cheeks. 'I believe I've already told you I have no intention of marrying. Unfortunately, my mother refuses to believe me.'

'So, if you're not here for the matchmaking, are you here for the shooting?' That was something he found hard to believe. Shooting parties always appalled him and he was sure Charlotte felt the same way. He could not see the sport involved in standing in a field while servants scared every bird in the vicinity into the air, making it as easy as possible for the guests to slaughter as many of the frightened creatures as possible, before retiring to a lavish lunch. If Charlotte now found that a fun way to spend a weekend, she had changed a lot from the young woman he had once known.

'I am most definitely not here for the shooting.'

Nicholas smiled at her emphatic reply. 'The only reason I'm here this weekend is because I'm raising money for a charity hospital in the East End of London. I'm hoping the Marquess of Boswick will become the patron.'

She continued to challenge him with her stare. 'That's nothing to smile at. The charity hospital is not a source of amusement. Life for the people in the East End is a daily struggle and, if they get sick or injured, it often means they can no longer work and that means families go hungry. I don't see why that should make you laugh.'

'I'm not laughing, Charlotte. I've always found your commitment to helping those less fortunate than yourself an admirable quality. And I'd like to help. If money is all you need, then why didn't you just ask me? I'd be more than happy to donate as much money as you need.'

'I'd prefer to ask the Marquess,' came the immediate, terse response.

I don't want your money and I don't want you.

Her message couldn't be clearer. She still saw him as nothing more than a self-indulgent rake who cared only about enjoying himself in frivolous pursuits. It was the view she'd held of him in the past and something he was going to have to continue to accept. After all, wasn't her opinion of him correct? Unlike Charlotte, who never wasted her time, who was always busy helping others, didn't he spend most of his time trying to decide how to spend his days, to while away the endless hours of boredom?

He tried to ignore the sense of guilt nagging at him over the way he lived his life and began untangling the fabric of Charlotte's petticoat. 'Getting money out of the Marquess of Boswick is not going to be easy. He isn't known for his generosity when it comes to charitable institutions.' He broke off a piece of branch with a decisive crack to get to another piece of twisted fabric. 'The only time he parts with money is when he's settling gambling debts. You're going to have your work cut out for you if you try to get him to give you a donation.'

She sighed with dejection. 'Unfortunately, that is something I've discovered over and over again. It seems the richer the man is, the less likely he is to part with his money to help others.'

Nicholas was about to repeat his offer and remind her that some wealthy men could be generous—all she had to do was get down off her high horse and accept his help. Then he had a better idea, one that would help her and keep those guilty pangs at bay.

'But that doesn't mean we can't work together to get him to finance your hospital. You won't take my money, but will you take the money I win from him at cards?'

Her forehead furrowed and she gave him a wary look. 'What do you mean?'

'I'll be playing cards with him this evening. If I win money from the Marquess, it can go to the hospital. If I lose, I'll absorb the losses.'

She stared at him for a moment, considering his

proposal, then slowly nodded in thought. 'And are you likely to win?'

He smiled. 'Gambling is the other thing I'm reputed to be good at.'

With satisfaction he watched the blush on her cheeks deepen to a delightful shade of red. It seemed the kiss was not the only thing she remembered. She was maybe also remembering what she had said to him about the one and only thing he was reputed to be good at was his prowess in the bedroom.

'Well, that's one problem solved. It's unfortunate we can't come up with a solution to the marriage problem just as easily.' He went back to untangling her petticoat. 'We can hardly spend the entire weekend hiding in the garden.'

Although that was a prospect Nicholas had no real objection to. As Charlotte was now waiting patiently while he untangled her clothing, rather than resuming her own attempts to free herself, maybe, just maybe, she had no objections either to being in such intimate surroundings with a man she had claimed held little interest for her.

He dismissed that idea. She'd probably just realised that letting him help was the fastest way she was going to get away from him.

She sighed loudly. 'My mother is getting very worried. I've only got to get through this Season, maybe the next, and I'll officially be on the shelf, then I can be left alone to live my life the way I want to. But my mother is in a state of near panic and it's starting to show. I'm practically thrown at every eligible man who crosses her path. If I was the sort of person who cared what society thought of me, it would be embarrassing. Fortunately, I don't care.'

Nicholas remembered well her claim that she did not care what society thought and cared even less for its rules. It was his turn to feel uncomfortable as her words came back to him when she had kissed him all those years ago.

Just because I choose not to marry doesn't mean I should be denied the experience of knowing what happens in the marriage bed between a husband and wife. Will you show me, Nicholas?

It had been said in such a matter-of-fact way, as if taking a debutante's virginity, ruining her reputation and making her all but ineligible as some man's future bride was something he would be willing to do. She had claimed it was what she wanted, but he had been older than her, more experienced than her, and he knew how society treated a woman who was no longer chaste. He had said no and, before he could explain why, she had turned on him and claimed that the only reason she had shown him any interest was because she had expected a man of his reputation would have no objections to deflowering a virgin.

She gave him a thoughtful look as if registering his discomfort. 'But what about you? Why haven't you married and sired an heir for the Kingsford dukedom? Is your mother not just as determined to marry you off as mine is to get me to the altar?'

He attempted to shrug in a display of nonchalance but was thwarted by the low-hanging branches surrounding him. 'Yes, my mother is becoming somewhat relentless in her desire to find me a suitable brood mare to produce the requisite heir and a spare.'

She snorted. Whether that was in disgust at the way young women were married off then expected to breed in exchange for their position in society, or at the disagreeable prospect of some unfortunate woman being expected to marry him, he didn't know.

'You should be grateful my mother hasn't set her sights on you as the future Duchess of Kingsford. She seems to have approached every other unmarried young woman present this weekend.'

She adopted that familiar haughty pose, which was contradicted somewhat by her blushing cheeks. 'Surely your mother doesn't expect me to join the pack of young debutantes chasing you around the estate and driving you to jump out of windows in desperation.'

Nicholas was tempted to point out that he was not only *not* hiding from her, he was hiding *with* her, in a very intimate space. A space so intimate that her exposed legs were almost touching his and her scent, one that had always reminded him of flowers after a spring rain, was filling his senses, and her soft lips were close enough to kiss.

He swallowed, looking away from her beautiful face, and concentrated on unravelling the fabric, determined not to think about the close proximity of her very kissable lips. 'It seems our mothers are equally intolerable.'

She nodded slowly. 'This shooting party is going to be impossible for both of us. I'm going to be spending the entire time hiding from my mother, you're going to spend the entire time fighting off a bevy of debutantes.' She sighed again. 'Why can't society just accept that some people don't want to marry? If you don't produce an heir, what will it matter? Another strand of the family will inherit, and no harm will be done. And it matters even less for me. I just wish they'd leave us alone.'

'Indeed.'

They sunk into silence, which was just as well, as they heard the sound of the pursuing debutantes swishing along the corridor, still discussing where he might be, followed by the bustle of satin and the Dowager calling Charlotte's name.

The sound of voices died out and he shook his head in dismay. 'We really do need to think of a way to stop your mother from trying to marry you off to men like Baron Itchly and the Earl of Uglow and to keep those relentless debutantes at bay.'

She drew in a deep breath and slowly exhaled. 'Believe me, I've tried everything and, so far, climbing out of windows has been the most successful tactic.'

'But unfortunately, it's not the most practical in the long term.'

He unwound the last bit of material, freeing her petticoat. She brushed it down, covering up her legs, and pulled her skirt into order.

'You're right.' She nodded her thanks. 'We can't hide here all night. I think we should return to the house.'

Reluctantly, Nicholas pulled back the branches of the shrub, then paused as a thought occurred to him. 'We could help each other, you know.'

She looked up at him, nodded and began pushing back the branches. 'Yes, all right.'

'No, I mean we could combine forces and fend off all this infernal matchmaking.'

She let go of the branches, furrowed her brow and tilted her head in question. He had her full attention.

Chapter Four

Nicholas was unsure whether this was the best idea he had ever had, or the most foolish, ill-conceived… dare he think it, even dim-witted one he had ever come up with. But she was looking at him with such expectation he couldn't back out now.

'It would serve them right if we pulled the wool over all their eyes and told them we were courting. Then our mothers would be happy and the debutantes would leave me alone.'

Her eyebrows drew together and he watched the shadow of doubt cross her features.

'It would only be for this weekend,' he quickly assured her. 'Then we could come up with some excuse as to why we've decided to call things off.'

The doubtful look left her face, to be replaced by a pinched expression of disapproval. 'And we won't have any trouble thinking of lots of reasons for that, will we?'

Nicholas winced. Could her opinion of him be any lower? He was offering her his assistance, a way to save her from her mother and the attentions of unsuitable beaus like Baron Itchly and the Earl of Uglow, and all she could think of was that he was a man of disrepute.

Her face relaxed slightly and she gave him a long, considered look. 'I suppose it could work, but we'd need to just tell our mothers, no one else, and tell them we don't want anyone else to know. That way when it's called off it won't become a major topic of gossip.'

She tilted up her head. 'Not that I care if people are talking about me.' Her brows once again knitted together. 'But you're right. This might work. If our mothers think there's even the possibility that we might get married, between them they'd move mountains to fend off the competition. All my mother would see would be your title and your wealth. You'll be safe from the debutantes and I'll be safe from Itchly, Uglow and most of all my mother.' She nodded slowly and smiled. 'Yes, this might just work.'

Nicholas's annoyance at her rebuke dissolved. It was lovely to see that warm smile once again, the one that lit up her usually serious face, like the sun coming out from behind a cloud. He had once so enjoyed making her smile and laugh. Their friendship had ended so abruptly when they had kissed, then they had parted with such acrimony that he had almost forgotten the times when they had been comfortable in each other's company, had laughed and talked together with such ease.

'We'll just need to think of a good excuse we can tell our mothers why we need to keep things quiet and not let anyone else at the shooting party know that we're courting,' she continued.

'I could say there is another woman involved and I need to sort that out before our courtship becomes public.'

That lovely smile disappeared. 'Yes, that is something they'd believe,' she responded promptly.

Why had he said that? Was he deliberately trying to remind her of the sort of man he was? And why was he so offended that she had agreed with him so quickly? After all, she was right, it was something that *would* be believed. He stifled his chagrin. 'Now that we've settled our two main problems, perhaps we should try to solve our immediate problem and extricate ourselves from behind these shrubs.'

She stepped forward, caught her foot on an exposed root and started to fall. He reached out, encircled her small waist and caught hold of her. She looked up at him, her brown eyes staring into his. He had forgotten just how beautiful her eyes were, like a full-bodied cognac and just as intoxicating. His gaze moved down to her full pink lips, slightly parted. One thing he had certainly not forgotten and that was what it was like to kiss those lips—that memory had been etched indelibly on his mind and body.

How he had been able to resist doing more than just kissing her five years ago he would never know. How could he resist her now? The desire to kiss those lips, to hold her tightly and never let her go, was as powerful now as it was then.

His hands moved further round her waist, holding her tighter. Reacting rather than thinking, he pulled her slightly closer to his body. She put up no objection. It felt so good to have her in his arms again. Too good. He continued to gaze at those tempting lips. This was madness. He should never have suggested the ruse that they pretend they were courting. He should be avoiding Charlotte FitzRoy, not spending more time with her. He leant down, his face moving towards hers. He should return to Europe. He should try to forget all about her. She tipped back her head. Those soft, full lips parted further. Her eyes began to close. He moved closer still, slowly lowering his head towards those beautiful lips. She still put up no objection, did not pull away from him. It wouldn't hurt, would it, just one little kiss?

'There you are, Charlotte. I've been looking for you everywhere.' He looked up to see the Dowager Duchess, leaning out of the open window and smiling down at them, the light from the library haloing around her.

Charlotte jumped back as if repelled by a negative magnetic force, and brushed down her skirt, her cheeks bursting into a fiery red.

They hadn't heard the sound of the Dowager's rustling satin as she had entered the library. Nicholas for one had been too distracted by the young woman he was holding in his arms.

And there was no doubting the Dowager had seen exactly what was happening between them. She was beaming with pleasure and doing nothing to conceal her delight. 'I was hoping to introduce Charlotte to the Earl of Grimston. He's just desperate to meet her, but I'm pleased to see you two are becoming reacquainted.'

'As you can see, I've found Charlotte, she was taking a stroll in the garden.' Nicholas hoped the Dowager would not ask them to explain how that stroll took her off the path and into the midst of the thick foliage.

'And we've managed to do more than just get reacquainted. In fact...' He looked over at Charlotte. She sighed slightly, but gave a small, resigned nod. 'We have decided that, with your permission, we'd like to begin courting.'

The Dowager clapped her hands together and leaned so far out the window Nicholas was worried she might tumble forward and join them. 'Oh, yes. Yes. I give my permission. This is delightful.' She smiled at each in turn. 'It should really be my son, Alexander, the Duke, who gives his permission, but I just know that he'll agree with me and say that having you as a son-in-law will be just marvellous.'

Nicholas doubted that very much. Alexander was protective of his younger sister and certainly would not want a man with Nicholas's reputation courting her, never mind marrying her, but as that was never going to happen it hardly mattered.

'We're just courting, Mother,' Charlotte said, her voice strained. 'We have no intention of marrying at this stage. We merely want to see whether we are suitable for each other.'

'Oh, pish posh,' the Dowager said, flicking her hand in Charlotte's direction, while smiling down at Nicholas. 'You couldn't be more suitable. And a winter wedding will be perfect.'

Charlotte drew in a deep breath and released it

slowly. 'No, Mother, we're just courting. That's all. And we need to keep it a secret for now.'

'Secret? Really? Why?' The Dowager looked from Charlotte to Nicholas and back again.

'I have some problems I need to sort out first.' Nicholas adopted his best shamefaced expression.

The Dowager raised one eyebrow and stood up. She was a worldly woman and would know exactly what sort of problems he was referring to. As a wealthy man it was hardly likely to be a financial problem. So that just left one other impediment to an open courtship—there was another woman.

She leaned back out of the window. 'Well, I'm sure you'll be able to sort out any problems quickly, but if being discreet will help, then I can assure you I will remain the soul of discretion.'

Nicholas was certain that the Dowager would be true to her word. She would do anything she could to hasten her daughter's marriage. The only concern Nicholas had was whether he himself would be capable of being discreet when it came to Charlotte FitzRoy.

What had she got herself into? Charlotte had been determined to avoid Nicholas this weekend. Now she was supposedly courting him.

At all other times she prided herself on her common sense, but when she was in Nicholas's company it seemed acting senselessly came naturally to her. She'd proven that once before and there was a definite possibility she was in the process of proving it again.

At least there was one consolation. She would achieve the goal of keeping her mother's matchmaking under control, something Charlotte had been unable to do before. That had to be a good thing, even if it meant spending time with a man who caused her to act out of character and forget that she was a sensible woman who knew her own mind. Charlotte fought to suppress a groan of despair. She just had to hope that achieving her goal didn't come at the price of making a fool of herself once again in front of Nicholas. She would just have to remember at all times that this man had rejected her once before and was perfectly capable of doing it again. Any silly feelings she might harbour needed to be kept firmly under control if she was to avoid history repeating itself.

Charlotte attempted to smile. After all, she was supposedly courting the country's most eligible bachelor. That was surely something to smile about, but her lips refused to curl upward. At least her mother was having no problem smiling. She was beaming down at them like Lewis Carroll's Cheshire Cat, with barely contained excitement.

'This need to be discreet doesn't include the Duchess of Kingsford, does it?' her mother said. 'I'm certain it will be all right to tell her. I know she's been anxious for Nicholas to tie the knot, settle down and have children. It would be cruel not to tell her and put an end to all her worries. I'll fetch her immediately.' She disappeared from the window.

'We didn't say we are going to get married,' Charlotte called out.

Her mother's head appeared once again.

'We said we're courting. So you can temper your matchmaking and stop thinking about wedding plans.'

How many times was Charlotte going to have to re-peat herself?

Her mother's smile quivered and her nostrils flared in that oh-so-familiar look of disapproval. 'You really are a strange girl, Charlotte. This is such happy news, so stop looking so miserable. And you can hardly blame me for being pleased, I've been waiting five Seasons for this.'

Remembering herself, she stopped frowning and smiled at Nicholas. 'But that's all part of Charlotte's unique charm, isn't it? She's not some chit of a girl like those other debutantes. No, she's quite a catch and you're lucky to have her, Nicholas… I mean, Your Grace.'

'Nicholas, please—after all, we're nearly fam-ily.' Nicholas sent Charlotte a quick wink. Charlotte frowned her annoyance. He should not be encourag-ing her mother. The last thing that woman needed was further encouragement.

'And you're right. There's no one else quite like Charlotte.' The look on his smiling face suggested he found this all a jolly good joke.

Charlotte wasn't sure if she was being insulted or complimented by his words and his offhand attitude to this arrangement, but she reminded herself that it hardly mattered. As long as this so-called courtship got her mother off her back and as long as Nicholas played by the rules and realised that it was a courtship in name only, then everyone would be happy. Well, perhaps not happy. What would really make Char-lotte happy would be if everyone left her alone to live the life she wanted to live. She'd be much happier if her mother and the rest of society didn't believe that a woman like Charlotte's only purpose in life was to marry well and breed a future generation of aristocrats. Something she had no intention of doing, ever.

But for now, with her mother's matchmaking temporarily nipped in the bud, she would be able to spend the weekend pursuing her real purpose: raising money for the charity hospital. Eventually her mother would wonder why no progress had been made in the courtship, but that was a problem for another day.

'Anyway, you two young people wait here,' her mother said, that impossibly wide smile once again lighting up her face. 'I'll go and fetch the Duchess of Kingsford so we can tell her the good news.'

Nicholas laughed, although Charlotte could see nothing funny about this situation. 'If you're going to fetch my mother, perhaps we should meet inside the house rather than talk to her through an open window.'

'Oh, yes, of course, you're right, Your Grace. I mean, Nicholas.' Her mother smiled coquettishly. 'You're such a sensible man.'

Charlotte groaned. There was a time when her mother thought Nicholas beneath the Knightsbrooks because he was merely the second son. At that stage she had set her sights on snaring a titled man for her daughter and would not even consider a spare, untitled younger brother. But that was during her first Season. Now any man from an aristocratic family, or with enough money that a lack of pedigree could be overlooked, was suitable for her twenty-three-year-old unwed daughter. And with a title, Nicholas was suddenly someone to be respected and fawned over.

The man himself hadn't changed at all, but now he was respectable, someone to be admired no matter how badly he behaved. That hypocrisy, which was rife throughout society, was something else that never failed to irritate Charlotte.

'We'll meet you both at the hall.' Nicholas held back a branch but continued looking up at her mother. 'But remember, discretion is essential and we're just courting. We don't want any talk of marriage at this stage.'

Or ever, Charlotte wanted to add, but that would perhaps give the game away.

Her mother nodded solemnly. 'Discretion, yes.' That smile that just wouldn't stay away returned. 'I'm so happy for both of you.'

She disappeared from the window and Charlotte wondered whether she should feel guilt at tricking her mother, then decided no. Her mother had backed her into a corner and her desperation was becoming increasingly irritating. Charlotte could not endure a weekend of being pushed in front of every eligible man, no matter how unsuitable he might be. Telling a lie was nothing to feel guilty about, it was merely a survival tactic.

Charlotte climbed under the branch held up by Nicholas, careful this time not to trip on any exposed roots. She couldn't, however, ignore the fact that she had to brush past him in order to escape from her hiding place. Even surrounded by the fresh scent of bushes and the earthy smell of damp soil, she couldn't ignore his own earthy, masculine scent and the hint of sandalwood from his soap. He still used the same soap, the one she wished she didn't remember so well from when he had first kissed her.

She emerged from behind the bushes and shook herself down, while mentally shaking herself free of any inappropriate thoughts and memories.

'You do realise that your mother is now going to be putting all her energy into getting us up the aisle as fast as possible. I think we might have solved one short-term problem, but created a long-term one,' Nicholas said as he also emerged from behind the bushes.

Charlotte shrugged off his concerns. 'Just as we've used your reputation to keep our courtship a secret, we can use that as a reason for not marrying. I can merely tell Mother that I've discovered that you've had countless women in your past and that you can't be trusted to be a faithful husband.'

He flinched as if she had struck him. 'You really do have a low opinion of me, don't you?'

Why was he acting so offended? His reputation as a rake was well known when she had first met him and she had no illusions as to how he had behaved while he was in Europe. 'You're not trying to tell me that you've changed, are you? This so-called courtship is unlikely to make any difference, or have you decided to take a vow of chastity while you are supposedly courting me?'

The pain on his face intensified. This man really was the limit. He was a known reprobate, yet he objected to having that pointed out to him.

'Your mother is right, Charlotte. You are unique,' he said, his voice terse.

He extended his arm for her to take. She hesitated briefly, then placed her hand lightly on his arm. 'So, do you also object to me speaking the truth the way my mother does? Would you rather I sugar-coated everything and tried to act as if the world was full of sweetness and light?' Charlotte could hear the bitterness in her voice, but she couldn't stop herself. 'I'm not like those debutantes who are prepared to ignore everything just so they can get a suitable man up the aisle. I know what sort of man you are, Nicholas, I always have.'

You're the sort of man who can't resist any available woman, but are more than capable of resisting me, even when I offered myself to you with no complications.

Charlotte could feel her cheeks starting to burn brighter and was pleased that the garden path had taken them away from the light of the windows. He would only be able to hear her terse words, not see her embarrassment.

In silence they continued to walk along the path that led around the side of the house and to the front entrance. Charlotte could feel the tension in his body, but had no regrets about what she had said. He was a rake and he should just admit it and not be offended when confronted with the truth.

Maintaining their strained silence, they walked up the front path and he opened the large doors that led to the expansive domed hall. The moment they were through the doors a waiting Duchess of Kingsford rushed towards them, followed by Charlotte's mother.

The Duchess was smiling fit to burst. She grabbed

Charlotte by the shoulders and kissed her on both cheeks. 'I'm so happy, Charlotte.' She kissed a stunned Charlotte again. 'I know you'll make Nicholas the perfect wife and will be a wonderful mother. It's marvellous that two families of such distinguished lineage will be joined together and you'll make a perfect Duchess of Kingsford.'

Guilt once again coursed through Charlotte. It was one thing to trick her mother—after all, she deserved it—but did she have the right to trick the Duchess of Kingsford? Was it right to get this woman's expectations up, only to have them dashed when they announced the courtship was over?

She looked over at Nicholas, sending him a silent question. *Are we doing the right thing?*

He gave a small nod, then turned to his mother and smiled. 'I hope the Dowager Duchess of Knightsbrook told you that it is essential we keep this courtship to ourselves and there will be no talk of marriage.'

The Duchess nodded, but continued to smile, her eyes shining with happiness.

'Mother, this is serious,' Nicholas continued. 'I have a few complications that have to be sorted out before this courtship can be made public, so it is essential you say nothing.'

The Duchess's smile faded and she blinked several times. 'Oh, I see. Oh, that is unfortunate. Well, hopefully you'll sort them out soon, Nicholas.'

Charlotte could see that the Duchess knew exactly what sort of problems a man like Nicholas would have and no further explanation was needed. Just as Charlotte needed no further proof that he was not the type of man any sensible woman would want to marry. And especially a woman like Charlotte, who had no interest in marrying anyone, anyway.

Despite knowing what her son was like, the Duchess of Kingsford was happy to see him married off to Charlotte. Happy for Charlotte to endure a marriage to a man incapable of fidelity, just like Nicholas's father was reputed to be. And a man who was an inveterate gambler, just like Charlotte's father and grandfather. For the Duchess, just like her mother, all that mattered was marriage, not happiness, not compatibility, and certainly not love, if such a thing actually existed. All that mattered was the continuation of the aristocratic lines. Any residual guilt Charlotte felt evaporated. The only person she had to protect was herself, because no one else, not her mother, not the Duchess, was going to do it for her.

'So, it is essential we keep things low-key for now,' Charlotte added. 'Or those complications could get very, very complicated. Couldn't they, Nicholas?'

''Fraid so.' Nicholas gave what looked like a genuine expression of abashed contrition.

'Oh, well, for now we'll keep the happy news a secret,' Charlotte's mother said. 'And it *is* happy news, the happiest news I've ever had. At least one member of the family will be making a sensible marriage.'

Charlotte shook her head and once again groaned inwardly. Her mother had still not completely reconciled herself to her brother's marriage, even though it was obviously a happy one and Rosie was such a delight.

But it was no less than she would expect from her mother. She disapproved of her brother's marriage because Rosie had no background and no money, but she approved of this match with Nicholas because he had both a high position in society and was extremely wealthy, everything her mother wanted in a husband for her daughter. It didn't matter that he was a known rake and that the so-called engagement had to be held up because of his alleged woman troubles. A man like him was still considered a good catch.

'Yes, you do that, Mother,' Charlotte said. 'Keep this a secret between the four of us.'

'And those two debutantes who followed me into the library,' her mother said.

'What?' Nicholas and Charlotte said in unison.

'Yes, that young blonde debutante and her friend, I forget their names. They were obviously listening to our conversation, because when I turned around their eyes were all agog.'

Charlotte looked at Nicholas, who shrugged in answer to her unspoken question. He, too, had no idea what those two young women would do or say. Hopefully they'd just move on to the next man, now that they were under the impression that Nicholas was no longer available.

'Well, even if those two young women now know, we still need to be discreet.' Charlotte gave her mother a pointed look. 'That means, there will be no signs of affection towards each other from either Nicholas or me.' She turned to Nicholas to make sure he understood what she was saying, ignoring the fact that she had been more than willing to give a display of affection when she had thought he was about to kiss her just a few moments ago. She refused to even acknowledge the strange tingling that merely thinking about that almost-kiss had evoked. Instead she'd concentrate on making sure her mother knew the rules of this arrangement.

'We wouldn't want certain parties to get the wrong idea.' Her expression became more solemn to underline the point. 'If certain parties do hear about this arrangement, it might make it even harder for Nicholas to get out of his other commitments, then things could get really complicated and there would be absolutely no chance of us ever getting married.'

Her mother nodded, with equal solemnity. 'We'll have to make sure those young debutantes keep it to themselves. We can take care of that, can't we, Duchess?'

Charlotte suppressed a smile as the Duchess nodded her agreement. With those two on their side there was no way anyone else would ever find out about this false courtship.

'And I'd like you both to do your best to stop any other debutantes from chasing Nicholas,' Charlotte added, causing Nicholas to smile in gratitude. Not that she cared who chased after him, but it was the least she could do to repay him for this clever scheme. 'You know how jealous I can get,' she added for good effect.

'We will,' both mothers said, still nodding.

Finally, Charlotte was able to smile. It looked as though this fake courtship to a notorious rake was going to work out better than she expected. It would get her mother off her back and she had the perfect excuse to avoid Nicholas during this party and then, after the weekend, to never see him again. It was the perfect scheme.

Chapter Five

'Shall we return to the drawing room and *not* tell everyone our good news?' Nicholas said, ushering the two older women down the corridor.

The mothers smiled at him with pure joy, while Charlotte rolled her eyes. Her expression told him loud and clear that the only good news about this arrangement was that it was fake.

But he did feel good about the courtship. While he was more than capable of handling the pursuing debutantes on his own, he liked that he was helping Charlotte out of a difficult situation. He'd hated seeing her being scrutinised by that ageing baron in the drawing room and even though he knew she was perfectly able when it came to looking after herself, he liked the thought that he was making life easier for her.

Hopefully, this time she would appreciate what he was doing for her. He had helped her once before, when he had refused to take her virginity. At the time she had most definitely not appreciated his help and had no hesitation in letting him know all about it in no uncertain terms. Maybe this time it would be different.

Her mother tapped her forefinger to her smiling lips to signal silence. 'Not a word to anyone until we announce the engagement.'

Charlotte threw up her hands in exasperation. 'We will not be announcing an engagement, so stop talking as if—'

He placed his hand on her arm to halt her outburst. Nothing was to be gained by losing her temper. Once the weekend was over, they could inform their mothers that, unfortunately, they had decided to call off the courtship. Life would go back to normal, but at least it would make this weekend almost bearable.

Charlotte exhaled loudly, but followed the two older women, who were now rushing down the corridor towards the drawing room, chatting loudly about wedding gowns and floral arrangements.

Charlotte paused and placed her hands on her hips, watching their rapidly retreating backs. 'They're as impossible as each other. I don't know how we manage to cope with mothers like them.'

'Yes, headstrong women can be very difficult to deal with.' He laughed to himself as she nodded her head in agreement, unaware that he was including her in that description.

The mothers entered the drawing room and disappeared behind the closing door. When they reached it, Charlotte placed her hand on his arm to stop him turning the handle. 'Perhaps we shouldn't enter together. We don't want people to get the wrong idea'

Nicholas looked down at her and raised his eyebrows in mock surprise. 'What? Are you suddenly worried about your reputation? That's not what you said five years ago.'

He cursed himself inwardly as he registered what he had just said. He did not want her to know he remembered exactly what she had said to him, that every cruel word was imprinted on his memory and had been repeated constantly to himself during the time they were apart.

She blushed, but waved her hand as if she had no idea what he was talking about. 'Those two debutantes already know and that's bad enough. I just don't want any other people thinking we're courting, that's all.' Her blush deepened slightly. 'And as you know very well, I don't give a fig about my reputation.' She pulled herself up straighter. 'Although you're right. The last thing anyone would expect *you* to be doing when you've been alone with a woman is making a formal request to court her.'

Nicholas couldn't help but wince, as if she had thrown cold water in his face. Once again she had been able to remind him just how low her opinion of him was. And once again Nicholas was reminded that redeeming himself in her eyes was such an impossible task there was no point even trying.

'In that case you have nothing to worry about, do you?' he all but snarled, opening the door for her. 'Your secret courtship will remain a secret and that reputation you *don't* care so much about will remain intact.'

She scowled back at him as she entered the room.

One thing was certain, no one would ever mistake such a hostile pair for a courting couple.

How wrong he could be.

The moment they passed through the doorway the room fell silent and every head turned in their direction. Some guests were smiling with obvious joy. Some were looking at them with curiosity, while the debutantes and their mothers were glaring at Charlotte with daggers in their eyes.

So much for discretion.

His mother joined them and placed one hand on his arm, the other on Charlotte's, smiling from one to the other. 'Oh, Nicholas, Charlotte, this is all so wonderful,' she gushed.

'I thought we agreed that we were going to keep a low profile,' he said to his mother out of the corner of his mouth.

She shrugged, looked over her shoulder and smiled at the staring guests, then turned back to Nicholas. 'And I had every intention of doing so, but as soon as we entered the drawing room everyone descended on us with questions.' She lowered her voice and tried to stop smiling. 'I suspect those two debutantes didn't keep quiet after all. They must have told their mothers, who probably told the other mothers. It wouldn't have taken long to get around the entire room.' She looked from him to Charlotte and back again, her eyes shining with happiness. 'But it won't matter, will it? You'll just have to sort out that other matter quickly before the wedding day.'

Conversation resumed, but the constant curious looks in their direction did not halt. It seemed that many of the guests were as surprised as Nicholas and Charlotte that they were now an officially courting couple.

Charlotte's mother walked towards them, nodding and smiling at guests as she passed through the crowd, basking in the attention. 'It's not what you wanted, I know,' she said when she reached Charlotte and Nicholas. 'But I'm sure this is all for the best.'

Like his mother, she was smiling with barely contained excitement, causing Nicholas to wonder if this indiscretion was entirely down to the debutantes or whether the two mothers had hatched a plan of their own.

'After all,' the Dowager continued, 'whoever heard of a courtship where the couple don't spend any time together, a couple who keep things quiet and don't show affection for each other? It's ridiculous. This is so much better.' She tapped him on the arm with her fan. 'And you're a resourceful man, Nicholas. You'll be able to sort out your other problem in no time whatsoever and we can move quickly from courtship, to engagement, to marriage.'

'And to having lots of children,' his mother added, causing the Dowager Duchess to increase her nods of agreement. The two women began chatting animatedly about wedding plans, christening robes, and which schools offered the best education for a future duke.

Nicholas sent the obviously annoyed Charlotte an apologetic smile, which she failed to notice.

She was staring at their fellow guests, her eyes wide in shocked disbelief, her lips pursed and her face like thunder. There was no way she could be mistaken for a woman who had captured the heart of the man she wanted to marry. She looked more like a woman who had been captured by marauding bandits and was planning to cause as much damage as possible before she escaped.

He gently removed his mother's hand so he could take Charlotte's arm. It was a gesture of reassurance, but it wouldn't hurt their plan if the room thought it was a gesture of affection. And she looked like a woman desperately in need of some support and affection.

'It's only for this one weekend, Charlotte,' he whispered. 'Then we can have some unfortunate falling out and put an end to this charade.' After all, they had fallen out once before and that had resulted in a complete estrangement. 'Isn't having your mother making wedding plans better than her throwing you in front of every eligible man? All you have to do for the next two days is grin and bear it and then it will all be over.'

She sighed, but her body became no less tense. 'Yes, you're right. It's only for one weekend. I suppose I can stand it for two days.'

'You seem to have come to terms with the bearing part of that arrangement, but not the grinning. Can you at least try to smile, just for appearances' sake? One little smile won't hurt.'

She looked up at him, still frowning. Then slowly the edges of her lips curled into something resembling a smile, while her eyebrows remained tightly drawn together. Nicholas was wrong. It did look like smiling was something that hurt her. He doubted he had ever seen a more pained expression.

'That's much better,' he said with a laugh. Her facial contortions causing him at least to smile with genuine amusement.

Their mothers drifted off, accepting congratulations from the guests with unconcealed glee as they moved around the now loudly chattering room. A stream of people approached Nicholas and Charlotte, shaking Nicholas's hand, slapping him on the back and offering him their hearty congratulations. Several mothers and a few debutantes kissed Charlotte on the cheek and tried to engage her in conversation about the coming wedding, only to be told in no uncertain terms that as yet there were no plans for that particular happy occasion and there wouldn't be for some time. A few eyebrows were raised at her obvious lack of enthusiasm, but no comments were made, at least not to their faces.

The last to approach them was the host, the Marquess of Boswick, wearing a supercilious smile on his face as he swaggered across the room.

He slapped Nicholas on the back with more force than was necessary for a man offering his congratulations. 'I would never have expected this of you, Kingsford. Courting, eh? It certainly is…' he paused, gripped his chin and looked up at the ceiling as if searching for the right word '…interesting news.'

Nicholas shook his head slowly and exhaled loudly. The Marquess was such a buffoon. If Nicholas hadn't taken so much money off him at cards, he would never have consented to attending this weekend party. It was ironic that because the man kept losing to him, Nicholas remained obliged to spend more time in his company, so the Marquess could try to win back his losses. Otherwise Nicholas would do everything he could to avoid ever seeing such a churl.

'Yes, very interesting news indeed.' The Marquess laughed and raised his hand to slap Nicholas on the back once again. Registering Nicholas's expression, he paused and lowered his hand. His smile faltered momentarily, then returned just as smug.

'I always knew you'd take a wife of your own one day, Kingsford. After all, you've taken so many other men's wives over the years.' He looked around at the assembled guests and puffed up his chest, hoping they would laugh at his joke, then at Charlotte and feigned embarrassment. 'Oh, I am sorry, Lady Charlotte, I didn't mean to offend you. I'm sure Nicholas has mended his ways and will be a loyal and faithful husband.'

Nicholas took a step towards him. This really was too much even for Boswick. He didn't care if the man insulted him, but he would not stand for him being rude to Charlotte. His progress was halted when Charlotte firmly gripped his arm.

'Absolutely nothing you could ever do or say would offend me, Lord Boswick,' she said in her haughtiest voice. 'To be offended one would have to care about your opinion.'

Nicholas smiled to himself. There was that acid tongue he remembered so well.

The Marquess raised his eyebrows, suspecting that he had just been insulted, but not sure how. 'Looks as though you might have met your match there, Kingsford. It won't be long before she's got you completely tamed.' He barked out a series of quick laughs. 'Women, they're all the same, every last one of them.' He waved his hands in the air as if including every woman present. 'All they want to do is get married and once they're married all they want to do is geld their poor husband. She'll soon have you signing the temperance pledge. No more carousing for you, Kingsford. You'll soon be sitting at home every night by the fire, taking tea and listening while she reads out sermons.' He looked at the frowning Charlotte and laughed again. 'Oh, yes, I can see it already. This one will get you on that tight leash even before there's a ring on her finger.'

'For your information, I have no intention of keeping Nicholas on a leash, tight or otherwise,' Charlotte shot back before Nicholas could react. 'He will be free to do exactly what he wants.'

Nicholas suspected that what Charlotte was really saying was essentially the same as she had said to Boswick. One had to care to be offended. As she didn't care for Nicholas, nothing he did would offend or upset her.

But that was not how the Marquess had interpreted it. He smiled at Charlotte and turned his back to her, lowering his voice just enough so she could still hear. 'I hope that means you'll still be up for the card game later this evening, Kingsford, and I have arranged some more exciting entertainment of a feminine nature for later on in the weekend.'

He saw Charlotte bristle. Maybe, just maybe she did

care, just a little bit. Was she perhaps just the slightest bit jealous at the thought of him with another woman, or was it anger at the Marquess that had caused her to look so indignant?

'He most certainly can play cards tonight,' she shot back. 'And do anything else he wants to.'

No, she was merely angry at the Marquess. It seemed even the thought of Nicholas indulging in entertainment of a feminine nature was something she did not care about.

'Congratulations,' the Marquess exclaimed, looking back at Charlotte. 'A woman who lets a man do as he pleases. You couldn't have made a better match.'

A woman who couldn't care less what a man did would be more to the point. But Nicholas was not going to inform the Marquess of any of this. Instead he adopted his own false smile. 'I'll certainly still be playing cards tonight, Boswick. Charlotte completely approves of me gambling, as long as I win.' *And I intend to win tonight. I intend to make you pay for everything you've just said, you buffoon.*

'I hope she'll still approve when you lose, because that's what you'll be doing tonight.' The Marquess laughed, pulling a cigar out of his top pocket and rolling it between his fingers. 'But it's good to find a woman who approves of gambling and will let a man be a man, not some tame poodle who has to do as the little woman tells him.'

Charlotte's look of disapproval intensified, but for once, at least she was disapproving of someone other than Nicholas. 'For your information, Nicholas is going to give all his winnings tonight to the East

End Charity Hospital.' She looked at him and to his delight she sent him a small smile. 'So he might be gambling tonight, but it will be for a worthy cause.'

Nicholas almost heard pride in her voice, but knew he must be mistaken. Why would she be proud of anything he did? And he already knew her opinion about gambling. With a notorious gambler for a father she had always made her views very plain on that subject. No, she wasn't proud of him, merely angry with the Marquess and trying to put him in his place. Something Charlotte was more than capable of doing to any man.

The Marquess laughed and put his cigar back in his top pocket. 'A charity hospital, eh? I see she's already started reforming you, old boy, getting you involved in good causes and what not. Could never see the point of them myself. If people haven't got the money to pay for things themselves, like doctors and what not, then they should just work harder and not be such layabouts.'

The Marquess shook his head, as if what he had just said held great wisdom, then barked out a few more laughs. 'But if she's already got you doing her bidding, then you better make the most of tonight's card game because I suspect it will be your last for a while, maybe for ever. A do-gooder like this is not going to be happy married to a gambler.'

His jaw rigid, his fists clenched, Nicholas took a step towards the Marquess. Despite the genteel setting it was time Nicholas let the Marquess know exactly what he thought of his insults. Once again he was halted by Charlotte gripping his arm. 'Let it go, Nicholas,' she hissed at him.

Nicholas continued to glower at the Marquess, whose eyes were now anxiously flicking quickly from Charlotte to Nicholas and back again, like a candle caught in a breeze. He was obviously debating whether throwing insults at them had been a serious misjudgement and if it was time to make a hasty retreat. When Nicholas took a step back, he relaxed and smiled again.

'It's eleven o'clock so if you can free yourself from the ball and chain I'll see you at the card table.' He tipped an invisible hat. 'Goodnight, Lady Charlotte.' That smug smile still on his face, the Marquess turned and headed out of the room.

'I'm sorry about that, Charlotte. The man's a complete ass. He always has been and he always will be. You should have let me teach him a lesson and show him that he was completely out of line.'

Charlotte retained her grip on his arm, still watching the departing Marquess, then looked up at him and smiled conspiratorially. 'Yes, I agree, the man deserves to be taught a lesson and the best way we can do that is to take him for every penny he's got.'

Chapter Six

Charlotte had thought a shooting party was the last place she would expect to find herself. She was wrong. Finding herself, late at night, in the card room at the Marquess of Boswick's country estate was even more unlikely. And even more unlikely than that was to find herself, late at night, seated in the card room at the Marquess of Boswick's estate, next to Nicholas Richmond.

She looked around the room. While the drawing room had been large, light and airy, the card room was a decidedly masculine retreat. Heavy, blood-red velvet curtains hung solemnly at the windows. Wood panelling on the walls gave the room an enclosed feeling, as if the inhabitants were sequestered away from the rest of the house and the rest of the world. Cigar smoke hung in a fog above the tables dotted around the room. While the drawing room had been lit with an abundance of candles and sparkling chandeliers, just a few candelabra sent out their dull light to the card room. It was as if the men's shameful activities had to be done in the shadows, away from prying eyes.

Charlotte wasn't the only woman in the room. Like Charlotte the other women were not playing, but were seated behind their men, showing that their presence in this masculine enclave was only tolerated because their role was purely supportive. Under usual circumstances Charlotte would rebel against being assigned an inferior position, but tonight she would swallow her objections. She did not know how to play cards. Nicholas did and he was raising money for a worthy cause. For that reason, she was happy to take a subordinate position. Well, not exactly happy, but she would accept it. For tonight, anyway.

And at least she did not have to endure the annoying presence of a chaperon. Now that she was courting, her mother no longer seemed to care about such things. Her mother had retired without giving any attention to the fact that Charlotte was to spend the rest of the evening unsupervised in the company of a man. That, it would appear, was another advantage of being in a courtship. It gave her an added level of freedom she rarely got to experience.

The dealer rapidly shuffled the pack, then sent cards flying across the table in the direction of each man, with a practised skill. Charlotte shook her head slowly as she watched the men at play. Perhaps her mother knew what she was doing, leaving her without a chaperon. Her virtue was certainly safe with these men. None had even looked at her since the game began. They were all too focused on their cards. Nor did they appear to have any interest in the fact that

Charlotte and Nicholas were supposedly courting. Unlike the debutantes and their mothers, such things obviously mattered not at all to these men. They had only one interest and that was the hand in front of them. For the moment, nothing else in the world seemed to exist.

Nicholas was seated at a table that included some of the wealthiest men in the land, presumably the table where the highest stakes were played for. Along with the Marquess of Boswick, there were two other dukes, an earl and a shipping magnate who was reputed to be wealthier than most members of the aristocracy. Hopefully, tonight they would all be contributing generously to the East End Charity Hospital, even if they didn't know it.

The Marquess raised the stake and sneered at Nicholas. Like every disparaging look the Marquess had sent Nicholas throughout the evening, he ignored it. Nicholas was like ice. Win or lose, he gave no reaction and it was impossible to read whether he had a good or bad hand. Unlike his fellow players, who reacted with petulant anger when they lost and unbridled joy when they won, Nicholas's expression remained exactly the same. The Marquess, in particular, seemed incapable of keeping his face impassive. Even an inexperienced gambler like Charlotte could tell when he had a good hand. That smug smile and the way he puffed on his cigar with such relish clearly gave it away. As for a bad hand, that was written loud and clear on his face each time he sent Nicholas a look of pure hatred.

The Marquess obviously hated losing, but hated losing to Nicholas most of all.

Unlike Nicholas, Charlotte did not find it easy to

keep her face impassive. As the pile of chips mounted up in front of him, her excitement grew. He was taking a considerable amount of money off all the players and the Marquess of Boswick in particular.

Charlotte couldn't keep that smile of triumph off her face every time the Marquess lost. Not just because the money was going to such a good cause, but because the man was a boorish oaf who had insulted her and Nicholas and also held an appalling attitude to those less fortunate than himself. Charlotte could hardly believe that he had said the people of the East End should work harder; she had never seen people work so hard to feed and clothe themselves and their families. The Marquess was not only a boorish oaf, he was an ignorant boorish oaf.

Another hand went Nicholas's way. Charlotte's excitement bubbled up and she could hardly sit still in her chair. She wanted to clap her hands, dance round the room and hug Nicholas to show her appreciation. Her excitement was all due to the amount of money he was winning for the hospital.

At least that's what she told herself. Her excitement had nothing to do with sitting near Nicholas, to being in partnership with him, united against the Marquess and working together as a couple for the greater good.

Another hand was dealt. Another pile of chips mounted up on the table. This time the cards were not in Nicholas's favour and a bragging marquess pulled the chips towards him, sending boastful sneers at both Charlotte and Nicholas.

Charlotte fought not to react, to either the loss or the Marquess's behaviour. Nicholas was still ahead, the pile of chips in front of him dwarfing those of the other men. He was still the winner at the table.

The next hand went much better. While the other men were groaning their annoyance and throwing in their cards, Nicholas sent her a quick wink and a smile, causing Charlotte's pulse to race.

His face quickly returned to its implacable mask as he piled up the coloured chips. Charlotte found it hard to do the same. As much as she fought her reaction, she couldn't suppress that tingling that had erupted deep inside her. His smile and wink had signalled her role as his co-conspirator. It was as if they really were a couple united in achieving a common goal.

It was just a small smile and wink. That was all. The intensity of her reaction was foolish and Charlotte knew it. But that knowledge did nothing to quash the happiness bubbling inside her.

It seemed she was enjoying herself. Unbelievable. She was sitting in a card room, watching a high-stakes game and actually enjoying herself. That was something else she would have not long ago thought an impossibility. But whether it was the card game, the substantial winnings that were going towards the hospital, or being beside Nicholas, she preferred not to analyse too closely.

Another hand was dealt. Once again the men turned up the corner of the cards to surreptitiously observe their hand. Once again chips were thrown in the middle of the table. And once again those chips ended up in front of Nicholas, adding all the more to his pile.

'You've got the devil's own luck, Kingsford,' one of the Dukes said, throwing in his hand, stretching and announcing he was finished for the evening. 'Lady Charlotte seems to be your lucky charm for tonight.' He bowed to Charlotte and left the room.

Nicholas smiled at Charlotte and gently squeezed her arm. 'Indeed, she is my lady luck tonight,' he murmured before turning back to the game.

Charlotte tried to follow Nicholas's lead and not react, to keep her face impassive. But how do you do that when such a small gesture, a few sweet words, a smile and a light touch on the arm had once again caused warmth to flood through your body? Charlotte breathed slowly and deeply to try to get her rapidly beating heart under control. Hopefully, her slow breathing would also stop her cheeks from burning. And it wasn't just her cheeks. Her whole body seemed to be burning and pulsating. And as for that strange tingling sensation that had consumed her body, Charlotte had no idea what to do about that. It was as if fire was radiating out from the site where he had touched her. She had to stop overreacting. All he had done was touch her arm and smile at her. But each time he acknowledged her presence it became harder and harder to control her foolish body.

Another hand was dealt and the remaining players once again turned up the corner of their cards.

The Marquess looked in Charlotte's direction and smirked at her obvious discomfort. He threw a large number of chips into the pile, misinterpreting her squirming and blushing cheeks as a reaction to the cards in Nicholas's hand. Nicholas met his bet and they showed their hands.

The players groaned their annoyance in unison.

All except the Marquess who threw his cards on to the table, staring at Charlotte as if she was responsible for his loss.

Why the man should be concerned, Charlotte had no idea. He was one of the richest men in England and could afford to lose a few sovereigns.

'Thank you, gentlemen,' Nicholas said, as he pulled the pile of chips in his direction and sent Charlotte another almost imperceptible smile.

The Marquess continued to glower at Charlotte as the dealer shuffled the cards. 'Lady Charlotte appears to be tired, Kingsford. Perhaps she should retire for the night,' the Marquess growled.

Nicholas turned to her, concern etched on his face. 'Charlotte, I'm sorry. As much as I enjoy having you at my side, if you are tired you must retire.'

'I'm not the slightest bit tired.' She glared at the Marquess. 'And if I do get tired, I'm more than capable of looking after myself. I'm not a child. I don't need anyone to tell me when it's time for bed.'

The Marquess sneered at her, but when she refused to look away he looked back down at the new hand that had been dealt to him. The audacity of the man. He was somehow blaming her for Nicholas's winnings. Ridiculous. She looked down as Nicholas lifted the edge of his cards. Two queens and two tens. Charlotte had been observing the game long enough to know that two pairs, especially ones that ranked high, was a very good hand. Once again Nicholas was going to win and put that annoying Marquess in his place.

The Marquess looked up at Charlotte, registered her smile and threw in his cards without raising his bet. Damn. Charlotte was doing exactly what the Marquess did, letting her opponent know how the cards had fallen by the expression on her face.

Nicholas once again won that hand, but without the Marquess increasing his bet the pot was quite paltry.

Charlotte had to take a lesson from Nicholas. Do not show any emotion. The Marquess continued to watch her carefully as the next hand was dealt. When Nicholas flicked up the edge of his cards, she made certain she kept her eyes straight ahead. If she couldn't trust herself not to react, then it was best if she did not know what was in Nicholas's hand. The Marquess sneered, aware of what she was up to.

Charlotte was tempted to smile, but she fought the temptation. Like Nicholas, she would be an unreadable book.

The game continued. Nicholas lost some hands, but won many more. One by one the men left the table as their chips ran out. When only Nicholas and the Marquess were left, the Marquess signalled a tired footman to bring him a new pack of cards, as if this would somehow change his luck.

'How much have you won for the charity hospital?' she whispered in Nicholas's ear as the Marquess unwrapped the new pack and shuffled the cards.

Nicholas looked down at his chips and did a quick calculation. 'About one thousand pounds,' he whispered back.

Charlotte felt her eyes grow wide. One thousand pounds was so much more than she had even dreamed of raising. It would go so far towards converting the abandoned warehouse the Trust had bought into a hospital and buying the necessary equipment. 'That's plenty. You can stop now,' she whispered back.

'No, I can't. I have to give the Marquess a chance to win back his money. If I leave the table before him, he'll be highly offended.' He smiled at her. 'But don't worry. He's good for a lot more than this. By the end of this evening your charity hospital is going to be one of the finest in the land.'

Charlotte smiled back at him. While she did not approve of gambling, this was more than she could have hoped for. Tonight, he really was her champion.

The Marquess dealt a new hand. He had been losing badly all night and surely it was time to stop now, but Charlotte knew from experience that that was not the way inveterate gamblers behaved. Her father could never leave the card table, no matter how much money he had lost.

If her brother could see her now, sitting at a card table and getting excited as she watched the Duke of Kingsford win more and more money, he would be horrified. And rightly so. While it was for a good cause, Charlotte would never approve of gambling, and that was another reason why she and Nicholas were so wrong for each other.

But Nicholas did not seem to react the way the other men at the table had. He did not have that glazed look, as if nothing else mattered except the cards in his hand. He did not react with uncontrolled excitement each time he won, as the other men had. Nor did he display a look of undisguised pain when he lost.

The chips continued to move backwards and forwards and Charlotte wondered whether the game would continue into eternity. She had no idea what the time was. The room contained no clocks. The other tables had also cleared, leaving the two men and Charlotte alone in the otherwise empty room.

After a few more hands a servant quietly entered, opened the heavy curtains and snuffed out the candles. Charlotte could hardly believe what she was seeing. It was light outside, the early morning sun reflecting on the trees bearing their colourful autumnal foliage. She had spent the entire night watching a card game.

The servant bowed to the Marquess. 'Will you be requiring anything, my lord?'

The Marquess waved him away, but looked up at the windows and registered that it was now daytime. The servant bowed once more and departed.

Another hand was dealt. The Marquess looked at his cards, sneered at Nicholas, then pushed his remaining chips into the centre of the table.

'If you're any sort of gentleman, you'll do the same,' the Marquess snarled.

'That's hardly fair,' Charlotte cried out, unable to abide by her self-imposed rule to remain impassive. 'You can't expect Nicholas to bet everything on one hand after he's been beating you all night.'

Nicholas placed his hand gently on hers, then pushed the large piles of chips into the centre of the table.

Charlotte could hardly believe it. What was the point of such a move? They'd played all night and now it all came down to this one hand. Why had they even bothered with all the previous games? Charlotte would never understand gamblers and never wanted to.

The two men looked at each other, Nicholas revealing nothing of the hand he held, the Marquess glaring at him as if wanting to commit an act of violence. Charlotte held her breath, not daring to draw any air out of the room in case it affected the outcome.

Nicholas showed his hand, two aces and two twos. The Marquess stared at them intently as if trying to change the outcome, then threw his own hand into the centre of the table face down.

Nicholas turned to Charlotte and smiled. 'The charity hospital is certainly tonight's winner.'

Slowly she exhaled her held breath, all the pent-up tension releasing from her body, to be replaced by ripples of pleasure. He had won. She looked down at the enormous pile of chips. This was better than she had expected. She looked up at Nicholas and smiled. He had won and he had done it all for her.

Before she knew what she was doing she wrapped her arms around him and in her excitement she kissed his lips, wanting to share her happiness with him.

As soon as her lips touched his she knew she should stop. Happiness was one thing. This was something completely different. The way her body reacted to the touch of his lips on hers was undeniable desire. Demanding, desperate, hopeless desire. Despite the long night, every part of her body was suddenly awake, alive and wanting more.

This was madness. She needed to break from him. Now. She was only kissing him in congratulations for his winning. A quick peck was all that was required.

Instead her lips were still on his, her arms had un-accountably wrapped themselves around his strong shoulders, her head had somehow tilted itself back-wards, and worst of all, her lips had parted, as if ask-ing him to kiss her back.

And he did. His arms enveloped her. He pulled her up, out of her seat. Standing close to her, he held her tightly against his chest. His strong, muscular chest. Her mind was telling her to stop this now, but that command was drowned out by the throbbing that had consumed her. A throbbing that had erupted in the most intimate part of her body. A throbbing that was now pounding throughout her entire body. A body that was aching for him, demanding more than just his kiss.

She should not be reacting like this. But how could she condemn herself for doing what felt so right? How could she not want to feel those hard muscles up against her breasts? How could she not want to feel his lips on hers? How could she not urge him to do more than just kiss her? She parted her lips wider and moaned lightly as he ran his tongue along her lips and entered her, tasting her, claiming her.

This might be wrong for so many reasons, but it felt so right. Kissing him again was something she had thought about constantly during the time they had been apart. Dreamt about. And now it was happening. She ran her hand up the back of his head, threading her fingers through his thick hair, holding him closer.

Her lips parted even wider and her tongue entered into the erotic encounter, loving the masculine taste of him, relishing the musky smell of him, and the feeling of the rough skin of his now unshaven cheeks on her own.

'If you're finished I'd like to settle this debt and get some much-needed sleep.' Charlotte heard a voice as if from a distance.

'I said, I want my bed,' the voice said louder and Charlotte remembered they were not alone. The Marquess of Boswick was witnessing the encounter. Charlotte broke from Nicholas, her already burning cheeks erupting with further fiery intensity. She had been such a fool to expose her need to Nicholas so blatantly. There was no way he could not have registered just how intensely she wanted his kisses. She had wanted him desperately five years and one month ago and nothing had changed. She had learnt nothing. And, yes, he had kissed her back, but he would, wouldn't he? That didn't mean this kiss meant any more to him than their first kiss had.

Charlotte brushed down her gown. 'Congratulations…' Her voice came out as an absurd squeak. She coughed to clear her throat. 'Congratulations, Your Grace,' she said, as if her kiss had never happened.

He smiled at her. 'Thank you, Charlotte,' he murmured. Charlotte chose not to think about what she was being thanked for, her words or that kiss.

The Marquess was standing with his chequebook already in his hand. 'So, are you finished?'

Charlotte immediately turned her attention to the Marquess as he leant down to write the cheque.

'If you would be so kind, please write out the cheque to the East End Charity Hospital Trust and give it to Charlotte,' Nicholas said, smiling once again at Charlotte and causing her already pounding heart to increase its furious tempo.

The Marquess looked at Charlotte, raised his eyebrows in question, but did as requested and with a grim smile handed it to Charlotte. She looked down at the sum and almost swooned. One thousand five hundred pounds had been raised in one night. Her hand shot to her mouth and she laughed. 'I think we're going to have to name a wing after you, my lord,' she said to the Marquess. 'After a generous contribution like this.'

She smiled at Nicholas who was smiling back at her. Only the scowling Marquess was not amused.

'I take it you'll let me win it back off you tonight, Kingsford.'

'I shall. And hopefully my lucky charm will be by my side once again.'

Of that, Charlotte was unsure. She was grateful to Nicholas for raising such a substantial amount of money, but after that kiss, after exposing the depth of her need for him in such an embarrassing way, an intelligent woman would be careful to ensure she never again put herself in a situation where she acted with such foolish abandon. And Charlotte liked to think she was a very intelligent woman.

Chapter Seven

Nicholas couldn't remember the last time he had enjoyed himself so much. He certainly couldn't remember the last time he had taken so much pleasure from gambling. In fact, in all the years he'd spent at the card table, he had never really enjoyed himself. But this evening had been different and that was due to two reasons: the charity hospital and Charlotte.

He could see why Charlotte gave so much of her time to helping others. There was something rather noble about doing something that would benefit the less fortunate. Plus, if he was being completely honest, he'd also got a lot of pleasure from doing something that would get him into Charlotte's good graces. He'd been so determined to win money for her and the hospital that he had almost slipped from maintaining his notoriously emotionless demeanour. For once he had actually cared about winning and was devastated every time he lost. All because the money was going to a worthy cause. He'd had a purpose for gambling. It hadn't just been a way to pass time and while away idle hours in further idleness. Perhaps that was some-thing he should do more often, particularly when it also made Charlotte so happy.

He smiled in her direction. She was staring at the cheque as if she couldn't believe what she was hold-ing in her hands. With her eyes sparkling, her cheeks still flushed, and her lips plumped up with that sen-sual just-kissed look, he had never seen a woman look more beautiful.

He'd had to work hard all night to not let her pres-ence affect him. He had not wanted to drop his guard and let the other players know that he was anything other than completely calm. Under normal circum-stances he did not even try to maintain a guarded ap-pearance, it was just the outcome of not really caring. But tonight he had cared—he had cared about win-ning for Charlotte. Occasionally he had slipped and had let her know how pleased he had been to have her at his side. That pleasure had increased with every winning hand and he had been proud to have won so much money for her.

Throughout the long night he had been aware that she was following every move with rapt attention, something he would not have expected from a woman who had previously objected to gambling with such vehemence. Was the change in attitude because the money was going to a worthy cause or was it because of him?

That kiss would suggest that he played at least some part in the change that had come over her. When she had thrown her arms around him it was obvious that her kiss was motivated by more than just excitement at the amount of money he had won for her charity. There was real, burning desire behind that kiss.

It was just as he remembered her kisses. He smiled to himself as he watched her fold up the cheque and place it in her reticule. Her lips tasted exactly as he remembered them, the feminine scent that had filled his senses was just the same. And her reaction to his touch was just as passionate, just as fervid.

That kiss had been the perfect end to a perfect night, even if it should never have happened. As much as he had enjoyed it, kissing a respectable, unmarried woman, even one he was courting, was enough to get tongues wagging. If he was to keep Charlotte's good name untarnished, he was going to have to keep a tight rein on his own passions in future. She might be a beautiful, intelligent, captivating woman, but she wasn't for him. He had no interest in marriage and she had to save herself for the man she did marry. No one must know about their kiss.

At least they had one thing to be grateful for. No one had seen them when they had first kissed and the only person to witness tonight's kiss was the Marquess. He was not a man to care about such lapses in propriety and, even if he was, his angry expression clearly showed that he was much more concerned about last night's losses, and how he could win them back tonight than anything that had happened between Nicholas and Charlotte.

'Well, gentlemen, I think I should retire for the evening.' Charlotte looked out the window, where the weak autumn sun was shining in a blue sky. The day had already started, it was long past evening.

'Goodnight, Charlotte,' he said. 'And thank you again for being my lucky charm.'

She patted her reticule, which held the substantial cheque, and smiled with a surprising coyness. 'No, thank you.'

She turned to the Marquess. 'And thank you, my lord, for this generous donation.'

The Marquess merely huffed a response as he stowed his chequebook away in the sideboard.

She bobbed a quick curtsy to them both, hesitated, then left the room. Nicholas remained staring at the door through which she'd parted, then turned back to the Marquess. 'I'll bid you goodnight as well, Boswick.'

'I'll see you back here tonight, Kingsford,' he growled in response. 'I want my money back.'

Nicholas nodded, sure that the coming night he would be collecting even more money for Charlotte's charity.

After such a game Nicholas knew he would not be able to sleep, so instead of heading upstairs to his bedroom he walked through the silent house towards the front doors. His fellow guests were still asleep. Only the servants were about at this early hour, quickly but quietly putting the house to rights before anyone else rose from their beds.

He walked through the front doors and breathed in the fresh scent of the outdoors, a stark contrast to the enclosed, smoky card room. The morning air contained a damp chill and dew still lay on the grass. Red, yellow and orange leaves, caught in the light breeze, were falling from the trees like multicoloured snowflakes, and scattering across the gravel path. It was still too early for the gardeners to be about their work, otherwise the fallen leaves would have been quickly whisked away, so the garden could maintain its pristine appearance.

He walked along the path, the gravel and dry leaves crunching under his feet. This weekend had not been what he had expected. He had expected to be bored, to spend the weekend fighting off that familiar, dispiriting sense of ennui that always descended on him. He had expected to be doing what he usually did, trying to fight off his boredom by indulging in every vice that came his way. But bored was the one thing he had not been since he found Charlotte caught up in the bushes outside the Marquess's library.

And as for that rush of emotion that had coursed through his body when they had kissed, that was as far removed from boredom as it was possible to get. When had he last felt such intensity when he had a woman in his arms? The answer to that question was easy— five years ago when he first kissed Charlotte FitzRoy.

He stopped walking and drew in a deep breath. Charlotte might be the perfect antidote to boredom, but she could not be used to stave off that jaded malaise that so often consumed him. She deserved more from a man than to be a convenient diversion.

He looked down at his feet and scraped his boot backwards and forwards across the gravel pathway. Was that why he had suggested this fake courtship? Because he needed to be entertained, diverted from his constant state of boredom? He had convinced himself that he was doing it to help Charlotte, to save her from her mother's relentless pursuit of a husband and from the horror of being inspected by men like Baron Itchly and the Earl of Uglow. But was it really because he wanted to spend time with her? Was it because he was bored with the life he led and Charlotte at least could hold his interest?

He resumed walking down the path. He knew the answer to that question as well. That was exactly what he had done. He hadn't been thinking of Charlotte, or at least not entirely. He had been thinking primarily of himself and his own pleasure. And now they had kissed again, something he should never have allowed to happen. Something that should not happen again. She did not deserve to be used in such a cavalier manner. She was a respectable, unmarried woman, for goodness' sake. She had to be treated with the respect she deserved.

He drew in a deep breath to strengthen his resolve. He had one day and one evening to get through. Then he would leave. One day and one evening of pretending to be courting Charlotte. One day and one evening of keeping his feelings for her under control. One day and one night of making sure he did not, under any circumstances, do anything that might diminish her chances of one day marrying a man who deserved her.

He could do this. Of course he could. It was his own selfish desire to find a diversion for his boredom that had got him into this predicament in the first place. He should never have made that now-regrettable suggestion that they pretend to be courting. Now it was up to him to get them through it without compromising Charlotte any further.

It was not much to ask, but it was going to be a difficult thing to achieve, particularly as what he really wanted to do was to compromise the hell out of her. He kicked at a stone and sent it skidding down the path.

It had been hard enough to resist the first time and the passing years had certainly not made it any easier.

Who knew what might have happened if the Marquess hadn't been present when they kissed? If they'd been alone?

He kicked another stone up the path, harder and further. If he couldn't trust himself when he was alone with Charlotte, then there was only one answer—they must never be alone.

That was one thing he was going to have to ensure for the rest of this weekend. Hopefully either the Dowager or Charlotte would have the good sense to provide a chaperon at all times. If not, he would make sure they were always in company and not just the company of a man like the Marquess. That man couldn't care less about any woman's reputation, or what they got up to in his presence. He continued walking, wandering off the gravel path and on to the dew-soaked grass. But they should be careful, even in the Marquess's company. His lack of concern for a lady's reputation meant there was a danger that he could gossip and that would never do. Nicholas and Charlotte had been caught out once before by gossiping tongues, when the debutantes had revealed their courtship to the entire party. It would not do if the Marquess let knowledge of their kiss slip.

There was only one thing for it. No matter whose

company they were in, respectable or otherwise, he must refrain from kissing Charlotte ever again.

He stopped walking. There was only one problem and it was a big one.

Both times he had kissed her, it had been Charlotte who had instigated it. How could he stop himself from kissing her if she was already in his arms, had already pressed her lips against his?

He couldn't. That was the simple answer to that question. Expecting Nicholas to show self-restraint when presented with such an irresistible temptation was asking far too much.

He turned and walked back to the house, aware that wandering off the path had meant the edges of his boots were now coated with mud.

The euphoric mood that had possessed him when he had taken money off the Marquess had now well and truly evaporated, to be replaced with complete bafflement over what he should and should not do. Life would be so much easier if he was indeed the amoral rake Charlotte took him for. Then he could have his way with Charlotte FitzRoy, get her out of his system and move on. But unfortunately for him, he did have a small lingering sense of morality and that meant he had to keep his distance from her.

He approached the entrance to the house, where the beaters, a circling pack of dogs, their handlers and the gun loaders were now congregating. Servants were loading hampers of food, piles of linen, chairs and tables on to waiting carts, all in preparation for the day's shoot.

While the rest of the guests were out killing as

many small birds as they could, he would try to get some much-needed sleep. He mounted the stairs, his mind no more settled than it had been when he began his walk. Would sleep be possible? He didn't know. But one thing he did know, and he repeated it again and again as he used the scraper beside the door to remove the mud from his boots, respectable women like Charlotte FitzRoy were not for him.

Charlotte paced backwards and forwards, across the Persian rug on her bedroom floor. Despite the late, or was that early, hour she was far too agitated to sleep.

Damn, damn and damn it again.

She was supposed to be keeping her feelings to herself. She was supposed to avoid making a fool of herself again in front of Nicholas. She most definitely was not supposed to kiss him. And she had failed on all three counts. Charlotte paused at the gilt-edged looking glass and gently touched her lips. Lips that were still tingling. She slowly drew in a deep breath. Her lips weren't the only part of her body that was still tingling. Every inch of her body was alive and excited by what she had just experienced. She continued pacing, trying to exercise away the whirling thoughts rushing through her mind and the agitation that was possessing her body.

Why, oh, why had she had to go and kiss him? Yes, she'd been excited that he had won so much money for the charity hospital, but she should have used some restraint. She looked towards her bag containing the cheque, discarded on the edge of her four-poster bed. Yes, she was pleased by what he had achieved, but a polite thank-you would have sufficed. She had not needed to kiss him. Now he knew exactly how much she wanted him.

She paused in her pacing and once again stared at the looking glass. 'Yes, you should be blushing after the way you humiliated yourself, yet again,' she told her reflection.

She returned to her pacing, her face still burning. Although, at least this time Nicholas had not rejected her. He had kissed her back. She stopped and gently stroked her lips again. He had kissed her back with such intensity, as if he wanted to devour her, unleashing a passion in her that she did not know she possessed.

She closed her eyes, her finger still tracing a line along her bottom lip, remembering the touch of his lips on hers. It was just as wonderful as she remembered, better than she remembered, because this time he had not removed her hands from around his neck and told her no. She inhaled deeply, as if trying to recapture his scent, that manly, musky scent, with that hint of sandalwood from his shaving soap. Her body shivered at the memory of his firm, hard, muscular body pressed against hers. Her toes curling up in her shoes, she remembered the feeling of his arms around her, his hands moving down her back as he pulled her in closer.

She resumed walking. How could she resist such a man, when he was irresistible? How could she resist his kisses when they were like laudanum, opium or some other powerful narcotic that took hold of you and left you desperate for more? Much more.

As foolish as it was, that was exactly what she wanted. Despite the passing years, she still wanted him, and only him, to be the one to show her all about the pleasures of physical love between a man and a woman. And if that kiss was a preview to what it could be like then it was going to be spectacular.

What had that foolish debutante said? That he was a sinner and she was looking forward to experiencing some of that sinning. Swaying slightly, Charlotte gripped the bedpost to steady herself. She wanted a bit of that sinning as well, more than just a bit, and she wanted it more than she had wanted anything else in her life.

Her eyes flew open. She stood up straight, her mind suddenly clear. That was what she wanted and that was what she would get.

She *would* experience what it was like to be made love to by Nicholas. He hadn't rejected her kisses this time. There was no reason why he would reject her if she once again asked him to make love to her.

Mademoiselle LeBlanc had been right. There was no reason why an unmarried woman should be expected to deny herself sensual pleasure, just because that was what society demanded. And she would deny herself no longer.

Her mind made up, Charlotte began undressing. She would not call her lady's maid. It was too late in the evening, or to be more precise, too early in the morning. Instead she struggled out of her dress and corset, pulled on her nightdress and climbed into bed, suddenly aware of just how tired she was.

All those years ago she had asked Nicholas to show

her about physical love between a man and a woman. But that had been her first Season and Nicholas was still convinced that she would want to marry eventually and should remain chaste until that time. It was such an offensive social convention. Her cheeks burned hotter, from anger this time, not embarrassment. Mademoiselle had been right. Why should a woman have to be a virgin on her wedding night when a man was almost expected to have had many women in his bed before he married? And continue to have other women after he married, if he chose to. It was outrageous.

And why should a woman like Charlotte, who had vowed to never conform to the dictates of society and marry, not get to experience physical intimacy? It was unfair and it was ridiculous. And surely Nicholas would see that.

She pulled up the covers to her neck and gripped them tightly, her heart fluttering with anticipation. It was a reasoned argument and Nicholas would see that. After all, he was an intelligent man. And that kiss showed that he was certainly interested in her. She might not know much about men, but she wasn't stupid. There was passion behind that kiss. He wanted her as much as she wanted him. He had rejected her in the past, but he wanted her now. He would not reject her again.

With that exciting thought in her mind, Charlotte attempted to get some much-needed sleep.

Chapter Eight

With a new sense of resolve, Charlotte woke later that day, stretched in the bed and rolled over to press the bell to summon her lady's maid. She had a big day ahead of her. Today was the day she was going to seduce a notorious rake. Charlotte bit her bottom lip to suppress a small giggle. This had most certainly not been her plan when she had arrived at the Boswick estate. And it most certainly had not been her plan when she had first seen Nicholas standing in the drawing room. Her goal had been to acquire a donation for the charity hospital and then leave, while at the same time completely avoiding Nicholas. Thanks to him she now had a sizeable cheque to present to the charity hospital trust. And now, also thanks to Nicholas, she would finally lose her virginity. Last night's kiss had shown her that he would not be rejecting her for a second time. She could remain an unmarried woman but still experience the sensual pleasure that was denied all unmarried women of her class. It was a perfect plan.

Charlotte climbed out of bed, pulled back the heavy damask curtains at the large sash windows and looked out at the parklands stretching to the horizon. The weak autumn sun was already heading towards the horizon. It seemed Charlotte had slept late in the day, something she had never done before. But then she had never spent the night at a card table, surrounded by inveterate gamblers, seated at the side of a notorious rake. Nor had she ever ended the evening with a passionate kiss in the arms of a man whose reputation as a ladies' man was legendary.

She ran her tongue along her lips and looked out at the garden and the woodlands beyond, at the trees festooned with their splendid autumn colours of red, yellow and gold. No one else was about, except a few gardeners clearing away the fallen leaves from the paths and garden in front of the house.

Unlike her, most of the guests would have risen at a more respectable time and would now be out in the fields indulging in healthy outdoor pursuits.

She smiled and a small shiver rippled through her body. Thanks to Nicholas she had joined the ranks of the less respectable guests who stayed up all night and laid in bed all day. And thanks to Nicholas she was about to become even less respectable. She was about to do something society as a whole frowned on. She was about to break one of their ridiculous rules that put stringent restrictions on women while giving men complete freedom.

Her mother disapproved of her mixing with the people of the East End and the medical staff who selflessly gave their time to help them, but one advantage that mixing with such people had given her was that she had learnt how women avoided pregnancy. That was better advice than was usually given to young women of her class, far better than all those embroidery and singing lessons she had received.

A man like Nicholas was unlikely to need instruction in such things, but if he did, it would be one thing that Charlotte would be able to teach him. Another delicious shiver ran through her body at the thought of all the sensual things Nicholas would be able to teach her.

She rubbed her hands together and turned from the window, anxious to begin her task. She had read enough scientific journals to know exactly how one attracted a mate. It all came down to having the correct plumage and performing the right mating rituals. Peacocks showed off their brightly coloured tails and lions displayed their striking manes. Well, tonight she, too, would display herself to her potential mate in all her finery.

A quiet knock on the door signalled her maid's arrival and Charlotte called out for her to enter. After bobbing a quick curtsy, Betsy crossed the room and removed a grey skirt and cream blouse from the wardrobe.

'Instead of dressing, I think I'll have breakfast in my room. And can you please prepare a bath for me?'

Betsy sent her mistress a wary look. In all the years Betsy had been in her service, Charlotte had never once had breakfast in bed, but she returned the skirt and blouse to their hangers.

'And I think I'd like to wear the blue gown to dinner this evening,' Charlotte added, causing Betsy to raise her eyebrows and give a cautious smile.

'Oh, yes, m'lady, an excellent choice.'

Charlotte usually chose to wear a sensible skirt and blouse to all occasions, much to her mother's chagrin. Despite this, each Season her mother ordered a wardrobe of elegant gowns to be made for Charlotte in the hope that one day she would start to adopt the more frivolous styles chosen by the other young women. Normally Charlotte eschewed such foolish, vain behaviour, but tonight was different. Tonight, she was on a mission. Tonight, she would be performing a courtship ritual and seducing a rake.

'And perhaps you could dress my hair in one of those French styles you've been so keen to try.'

Betsy's smile grew bigger. 'Oh, yes, I'd love to, m'lady. I'll arrange for your breakfast now.' Her gaze flicked to the window. Betsy was probably thinking that it was a little late for breakfast, but was too polite to say so. 'And then I'll run your bath and get your gown ready for this evening.'

She smiled once more at her mistress, then rushed out, obviously excited that for once she would be able to do her job properly and prove to the other lady's maids that she was just as skilled as them at making her mistress look as attractive as possible.

After dining on a light breakfast of cheese and cold meats, Charlotte undressed and climbed into the bath Betsy had prepared in the adjoining room. She luxuriated in the warm water, lathered up the sponge with the rose-scented soap and rubbed it slowly over her body. The thought that she was preparing herself for Nicholas made the experience of bathing so sensual it sent ripples of delight coursing through her body. She laughed to herself. It reminded her of those exotic tales she had read of concubines being prepared for the emperor's bed.

Charlotte dried herself in the warm towel Betsy had left draped over a wooden chair, wrapped herself in her silk robe and went through to her bedroom so Betsy could help her dress. But Betsy had other plans. She was taking her job of making Charlotte look as attractive as possible very seriously and had a range of beauty preparations ready to be applied. Under normal circumstances Charlotte would not countenance such frivolity, but tonight she would leave herself in Betsy's expert hands.

First, Betsy insisted that Charlotte rub lemon juice over her face to lighten the skin and remove the freckles that dotted her nose so she could achieve the necessary pale white complexion of a fashionable lady. Charlotte was loath to tell her that after twenty-three years of not caring about how she looked and spending endless hours out in the sunshine without a hat or parasol, Betsy was fighting a losing battle. But Betsy was enjoying herself and Charlotte would not ruin her fun. And if she was being entirely honest, she, too, was enjoying this pampering as well.

Betsy then prepared and applied a face mask of almond oil and oatmeal, which she insisted would soften Charlotte's skin and give it a healthy glow. Charlotte was then instructed to sit still while Betsy used the silver-backed brush to give her hair the requisite one hundred strokes to make it shine.

That done, Betsy sponged off the face mask and applied rose water to Charlotte's face to further soften her skin and began styling her hair. Charlotte could see happiness on her maid's face reflected in the gilt looking glass. Smiling, and humming to herself, Betsy divided the hair into sections, backcombed it, teased it out, curled it, plaited it, and generally did an assortment of tricks to pile Charlotte's hair on to the top of her head in a voluminous, ornate concoction.

She teased out a few curls around Charlotte's face and draped one curling lock down her neck on to her shoulder. Charlotte assumed that she was finished. But no. Betsy went into Charlotte's jewellery box, which contained a wealth of jewels Charlotte never wore, removed several jewel-encrusted combs and placed them strategically in Charlotte's hair.

Finally, Betsy stood back and admired her workmanship and smiled. Then she frowned in concentration.

'I think you could do with a touch of powder, m'lady,' Betsy said, picking up a pot and a small puff. 'It's not make-up, mind, so you don't need to concern yourself,' she insisted. 'Just something to take the shine off and even out your skin tone.'

Charlotte had no idea whether she should concern herself or not, never having previously worried about such things as make-up, shining faces or skin tone, so she let Betsy do what she thought best.

'Right, m'lady, let's get you dressed.' Betsy rushed over to the wardrobe and removed the blue gown. Despite the Knightsbrooks no longer being a wealthy family, Charlotte's mother always demanded that money should not be skimped when it came to fashion, insisting that appearances needed to be maintained. The fact that Charlotte chose not to wear these expensive concoctions of silk, satin and lace if she could avoid it was no deterrent to her mother. Charlotte always preferred plain, sensible clothes that did not impede one's movements, but tonight was not about being sensible. Tonight was about being beautiful, feminine and irresistible.

Charlotte ran her hand along the embroidered silk fabric. She had to admit the dress was gorgeous and showed the superb skills of the dressmaker and the women who had woven the lace and created the intricate gold and silver embroidery that adorned the full skirt and train.

She removed her robe, pulled on her chemise and Betsy attached the corset around her waist. She tugged tightly, causing Charlotte to almost lose her balance.

'Perhaps you should hold on to the bed post, so I can get better leverage,' Betsy said, giving the laces another firm tug.

Charlotte did as she was asked, still trusting Betsy to know what she was doing, although it was starting to seem a bit excessive. Betsy gave another even firmer pull and Charlotte felt something on her back. Looking over her shoulder, Charlotte gasped at what she was seeing. Her lady's maid had placed her foot in the small of Charlotte's back and was leaning back so she could pull the laces as tight as was humanly possible.

'I believe that will do, Betsy,' Charlotte said. 'After all, I'd like to be able to breathe this evening.'

Betsy gave a disappointed moue, but lowered her foot and tied off the laces. 'As you wish, m'lady, but a small waist will give you the fashionable silhouette to match the dress.'

'Well, I won't be very fashionable if I pass out on the floor through lack of oxygen.'

'No, m' lady.' Betsy gently lifted the dress off the bed. She helped Charlotte step into the skirt, lifted up the lacy bodice so she could put her arms through the sleeves, then secured the row of mother-of-pearl buttons up the back. Charlotte slipped her feet into a matching pair of embroidered silk evening slippers, then turned to the looking glass to see the finished effect.

She could hardly believe what she was seeing. Was that really her, that fashionable young lady staring back at her with wide eyes and an open mouth? She closed her mouth and tried to adopt a more composed look.

She really did look like a peacock, showing off her beautiful plumage to attract a mate. Perfect. She moved her head slowly from side to side and watched as the light caught the coloured jewels in her hair. She could now see why women wore such ornamentations. The jewels not only caught the light, but their sparkling caught the eye. Exactly what she wanted. She wanted to catch Nicholas's eye. She took a few steps towards the looking glass and watched as the soft flowing fabric of her silk skirt and train swirled around her, reminding Charlotte of a peacock's rustling tail.

'You look beautiful, m'lady,' Betsy said, standing beside her and admiring her work. 'I always knew you could be.' The maid blushed and began brushing down the long train. 'I mean, you always was an attractive young woman, but I think this look really suits you.'

'Thank you, Betsy, you really have worked wonders.' Charlotte turned her head from side to side to once again admire the hairstyle and watch those twinkling jewels.

'All we need now is a bit more powder, a necklace, some earrings and you'll be done.'

Charlotte sat back at the embroidered bench in front of the looking glass as Betsy picked up the powder. But instead of putting more on her face, Betsy patted the powder puff across her décolletage visible above the low-cut gown.

'I expect a few men are going to be wanting to look at them tonight,' Betsy said with a giggle. 'So we want them to look their best.'

Charlotte smiled at her reflection. There was one man in particular she was wanting to look at *them* tonight and hopefully do much more than just look.

Betsy clipped a diamanté necklace around her neck, the family's real diamonds having been sold many years ago to pay her father's debts, and Charlotte attached the matching earrings.

'Right, I'm ready.' Charlotte stood up and Betsy handed her a fan and her gloves. Charlotte looked at the fan. She never carried one and she certainly never used it to flirt the way other young women did. That was something she was going to have to master. After all, she had the plumage, all she needed was the correct mating ritual.

She opened the fan, flicked it in front of her face and tried to do that coquettish look the other women were able to achieve as if instinctively.

Betsy grimaced, causing Charlotte to slam shut the fan and dump it on the dressing table—it was obviously too late for her to learn that particular skill.

'If you want to know how to use the fan, there are a few simple rules, m' lady,' Betsy said, picking up the fan. 'If you want to let some gent know you want to get to know him better, then hold it in your left hand.' Betsy handed the fan to Charlotte, who took it with her left hand.

'Now, if you want to get rid of that gentleman, then just twirl it in your left hand and he'll hopefully get the message.'

Charlotte did as Betsy instructed, although once she had Nicholas's attention she could think of no reason why she'd want to get rid of him.

'If you want him to follow you, put the fan in your right hand.'

Charlotte flicked the fan to her other hand. This was more like it. These were the sort of things she needed to know.

'If he asks you something and the answer is yes, let it rest on your right cheek.'

Charlotte moved the fan to her right cheek.

'If it's no, then let it rest on your left cheek.'

The fan stayed on Charlotte's right cheek.

'The left cheek, m' lady.'

'Yes, I've got that, Betsy. What else?'

Betsy gave a small giggle. 'In that case, if you really want to be bold and you want the gentleman to kiss you, then you put the handle of the fan up to your lips.'

Charlotte instantly tapped her lips with the handle of the fan.

'A bit more gently, I think, m' lady,' Betsy said. 'And if you want to tell him you love him, then twirl the fan in your right hand.'

Charlotte did not bother to follow that instruction. She would not be telling Nicholas any such thing. She was tempted to ask if there was any way a fan could be used to tell a man you wanted him to make love to you, but she suspected there would be no such fan gesture and she wanted to spare Betsy's blushes.

'Thank you, Betsy, you've been most helpful.' Charlotte practised the fan gestures one more time in front of the looking glass to make sure she didn't get her signals mixed up, watched on by the smiling Betsy.

'Right, I think I'm ready,' she said, pulling on her elbow-length white gloves.

'You look a real stunner, m'lady,' Betsy said. 'Now you go and stun them all with your new look.'

Charlotte thanked her smiling lady's maid one more time and headed down the corridor, determined that tonight one guest was about to be completely stunned.

Chapter Nine

Nicholas's head wasn't the only one that turned in Charlotte's direction when she entered the drawing room. She had been transformed from a duckling to a swan, although he had always thought her a beautiful duckling. But something had happened overnight to make her dress in this new manner and this transformation was intriguing, to say the least.

She stood at the door, her head lifted, a slight smile on her lips, while every man in the room continued to gawp at her. What was her game? Was she suddenly joining the ranks of the husband-hunters? Had she decided that if this Season was to be her last, she was going to make a final push to secure her future as a married woman after all? Nicholas looked around the room at the other men admiring her appearance and his irritation intensified. He had seen her beauty when she was dressed in plain clothing with her hair pulled back in a tight bun. What gave them the right to suddenly start admiring her beauty just because she was wearing a fancy gown and had her hair all piled up in curls and clips on top of her head?

She looked towards him and her smile grew wider. With studied elegance she walked slowly towards him, her progress followed by several men, along with the disapproving looks of a number of the debutantes.

Nicholas fought to suppress his irritation. Charlotte had the right to dress however she wanted. She had had to endure the disapproval of society when she refused to dress conventionally, she should not have to endure his disapproval just because she was now conforming and dressing to impress. He had no right to be irritated. Nor did he have any right to be jealous, if that's what that gnawing in the pit of his stomach was. It did not matter if she now had the attention of most of the men in the room. He wanted Charlotte to marry, to be happy. That was why he had used such restraint, so she would still be marriageable. If she had decided now was the time to find a husband, then who was he to begrudge her the admiration of other men?

She stood in front of him, lowered her head and gave a small curtsy. Such formality was also unlike her, but if that was the role she wanted to play, then he would follow suit.

'Good evening, Charlotte,' he said with a formal bow. At least she was still bold enough to approach a man at a social gathering without being accompanied. It was good to see that one thing about her hadn't changed overnight. Although given his resolve to keep his distance from her, perhaps it would be better if that part of her personality had also undergone a transformation.

'Good evening, Nicholas.' She took out her fan and gave it a small flutter in front of her face while she batted her eyelashes. Nicholas's heart sunk. What on earth was going on? Was his feisty, independent Charlotte trying to be coy? Please, no, not that.

'Are you feeling warm?' He gestured towards the fan, causing its movement to immediately cease. Her smile faltered and her eyelashes stopped fluttering. She frowned briefly before resuming smiling.

Nicholas cringed. He had insulted her. That had not been his intention. He had no right to criticise her behaviour. If she wanted to behave like every other young woman, then so be it. It was no concern of his.

'You're right, the room is a little warm,' he said, trying to undo the damage.

She gave a little laugh, although he could not see the humour in his comment on the room's temperature. She lifted up her closed fan in front of his face, as if showing him how tightly she could clasp it.

Nicholas's confusion was mounting with every passing second. What on earth was she doing now? He needed an explanation. 'Are you having a problem with your fan, Charlotte?' he asked as tactfully as possible, hoping he was not insulting her.

She frowned at him and he sighed with relief. Thank goodness for that. A critical Charlotte was someone he was used to. But the familiar did not last long. She quickly resumed batting her eyelashes in a frantic manner. This was absurd. What on earth was wrong with the woman?

'Are you all right, Charlotte?' he asked, trying to

keep the confusion out of his voice. 'Is there a problem with your eyes?'

The blinking stopped and she gave a small laugh, even though what he had said once again contained no humour. She bit the edge of her lip and appeared to be thinking, then smiled and raised the fan to her lips. 'I'm not having a problem with my eyes or my fan, Nicholas,' she whispered. 'But I do have a problem you can help me with.'

It might not be the fan, but something was definitely a problem. She was now tapping the fan on her lips. Very odd. Perhaps she was unwell. Perhaps her corset laces were pulled too tight.

'Charlotte, you're acting in a very peculiar manner tonight.' He spoke slowly, as if to someone slightly deranged. 'What exactly is the problem?'

She tapped her lips again, slightly harder. If she didn't stop this bizarre behaviour she was in danger of causing herself an injury. He shook his head slowly, trying to work her out.

'Oh, for goodness' sake, Nicholas, can't you see what I'm trying to say to you?' she said in a terse voice.

Thank goodness. That irritated response proved the real Charlotte was in there somewhere, buried beneath this strange coquette she had somehow metamorphosed into overnight.

But what was it she claimed she was trying to say to him?

Nicholas knew he wasn't an intellectual genius—hadn't Charlotte once informed him that he was dim-witted?—but as she had hardly said a word to him since she had entered the room, he could hardly be blamed for not understanding what she was trying to say to him.

'I think you'll have to repeat yourself. I seem to have missed something.'

'Oh, for goodness' sake, every woman in this room knows what I'm saying—why can't you understand?'

He looked around the room and saw several woman staring in their direction, smiling and laughing behind their own fans.

Before he could ask her once again to explain herself, the Earl of Danfield joined them. The smile on his face clearly showed that, unlike Nicholas, he was not in the slightest bit confused by this transformed Charlotte.

'I don't believe we've had the pleasure,' he said, taking Charlotte's hand and kissing the back while staring up into her eyes. Nicholas shook his head and swallowed a groan of annoyance. The Earl had met Charlotte last night at the gaming table. Either he didn't remember or was playing a disingenuous game. Nicholas introduced them and they were joined by several other male guests, all eager to supposedly make Charlotte's acquaintance for the first time.

Nicholas debated with himself whether he should mention to these unmarried men that he and Charlotte were supposed to be courting. But that was not part of the arrangement. They were pretending to court so the debutantes would leave him alone and Charlotte's mother would stop trying to pair her off with unsuitable potential husbands. There had been nothing in their arrangement about stopping Charlotte from finding a husband who was, in fact, suitable. Each of the men now surrounding her had substantial fortunes, most had a title and several would make acceptable husbands. He should be encouraging their attentions, not silently cursing them with a range of unfortunate fates that would diminish their chances of becoming a husband and end the possibility of them ever becoming a father.

'Will you be gracing the card table with your presence again tonight?' the Earl of Danfield asked, not caring that he was now exposing himself as a liar who had already met Charlotte. 'You certainly brought Nicholas luck last night. I've never seen a man have such a winning streak. I'm afraid I lost terribly.' He frowned at Charlotte in mock sorrow. 'Perhaps tonight you can share that luck around a bit more.'

'No, she won't be,' Nicholas stated with more annoyance than he intended. 'Last night Charlotte was seated beside me because all my winnings were going to the charity hospital for which she is raising funds and tonight I plan to win even more money for the hospital.'

Charlotte turned her attention to him and smiled, an enchanting, genuine smile that lit up her face. 'Oh, that will be wonderful. Thank you, Nicholas.'

Nicholas could feel himself puff up with pride as he was bathed in that smile. He turned to the Earl of Danfield in triumph. 'So that means Charlotte will be my lady luck tonight, exclusively.'

He knew he should not be behaving like this. If Charlotte wanted to attract the attentions of a man like Danfield, then she should be allowed to do so.

He should do nothing to interfere with her chance of making a suitable marriage. After all, he didn't want to marry her. He didn't want to marry anyone. And even though Charlotte had said she also did not want to marry, what woman really wanted to remain on the shelf, to live the life of a spinster?

Lord Danfield shrugged. 'Well, as long as you take money off the Marquess of Boswick and not me I don't mind in the slightest and I wish you good luck with your fundraising, my dear.'

His face took on a calculated demeanour. 'And you can trust Kingsford will be able to oblige.' He turned to Nicholas. 'It seems the time you spent in Europe has paid off and an expertise at card playing is one of the many skills you acquired over there that the rest of us can only marvel at.'

He gave what could only be described as a ribald laugh, then stopped and looked at Charlotte, adopting a fake apologetic air. 'Oh, my apologies, my lady. The rumours are bound to be exaggerated. I'm sure Nicholas actually spent his time in Europe in art galleries and pursuing his studies in ancient Greek and Latin, not in anything less reputable.' He sent Nicholas an undisguised wink. 'Didn't you, Kingsford?'

Several men in their group guffawed, and a few ladies standing nearby tittered behind their fans.

Any advantage Nicholas had earned by winning money for Charlotte's hospital had been undone with that reminder of how he achieved his skill at gambling and how he spent most of his time. Damn Danfield. Nicholas scowled at the man, even though he had said nothing that wasn't the truth.

Charlotte was the only one in the group not smiling. Instead she, too, was frowning at Danfield. 'I have no delusions about how the Duke of Kingsford spent his time in Europe,' she said in that familiar haughty manner. 'And you're right, his ability at the card table has served a good purpose. An expertise in Latin and ancient Greek would not help the poor of the East End who are in desperate need of free medical services. It would not stop people dying from treatable diseases. It would not save the life of one single child. And as for anything else he got up to in Europe, I'm sure it is no better or worse than many other men in this room. The only difference is its public knowledge. I wonder how many other men here tonight frequent brothels or keep mistresses? But that's acceptable, isn't it, as everyone turns a blind eye.'

The guffawing and tittering came to an abrupt halt. Silence descended on everyone within hearing distance of Charlotte's raised voice. Smug smiles were replaced by looks of shock and horror. Nicholas alone was now smiling. That was the outspoken Charlotte he admired so much.

'Looks as though you've caught yourself a lady with a sharp tongue, Kingsford,' the Earl mumbled, before making a hasty retreat, while the nearby ladies turned their backs and began talking rapidly and quietly.

Nicholas continued smiling as the gathered men all took their leave.

Yes, I've got myself a sharp-tongued lady, and isn't she just perfect?

* * *

Charlotte could not believe her first attempt at flirting could go so badly. She had learnt a lot about the mating habits of animals through reading scientific journals, but it seemed the one animal she knew nothing about was the human male.

The journals had talked about attracting a mate through plumage and courtship rituals, but her new look and her fancy hairstyle hadn't worked. And as for her rituals with the fan, she would rather not even think about that debacle. When it came to men, she had always chosen to ignore her mother's advice and the only advice Mademoiselle LeBlanc had given her was to just be herself. Well, that was easy for Mademoiselle. She was a free-spirited woman who lit up every room with her vivacious personality. Being herself tended to get Charlotte ignored at best.

So what was she supposed to do now?

Another lesson she had learnt from the scientific journals was that when an experiment repeatedly failed, it meant the premise was incorrect.

Did that mean her premise in this instance was incorrect? Was she wrong in thinking that Nicholas had even the slightest interest in her? Had she put too much importance on last night's kiss and that almost-kiss in the garden?

And yet he hadn't departed like the other men. He was still standing beside her. He was still smiling at her—that had to be a good sign, didn't it? She just wished he was smiling because he was entranced by her new look. She wished he was smiling because he was dazzled by her beauty, not amused by the way she had just insulted the Earl of Danfield.

Unsure how to continue, she looked down at the fan clenched in her hand. That had been nothing more than a joke. Nicholas had no idea what her coded messages had meant, although they had not been lost on several of the debutantes. They had been twittering and laughing behind their gloved hands as she had twirled and tapped her fan. Instead of being a seduction technique, her behaviour had been a source of cruel amusement for the other women.

She placed the fan on the table and sighed.

'So, will you be joining me at the card table later this evening?' Nicholas said. 'Looking the way you do tonight, you're sure to put those men off their game.'

Charlotte's heart jumped at the sound of the compliment. He *had* noticed her appearance. Perhaps all was not lost after all.

'What exactly do you mean?' she asked, aiming for a flirtatious tone.

He swept a look up and down her body, causing her breath to catch in her throat and her skin to tingle as if it was being gently stroked by his gaze. Her reaction was both exciting and frightening in equal measures. All she knew was that, despite her body's disturbing reaction, she loved having him look at her that way.

His gaze returned to her eyes. 'I mean, you look beautiful tonight, Charlotte, and your beauty is likely to distract the other men at the table, which has to be to our advantage.'

Was that a compliment? He said she looked beautiful. That had to be a compliment. But why did he have to say she would distract other men? There was only one man she wanted to distract and it was him.

She swallowed to relieve her suddenly dry throat. 'But not you, Nicholas?' she asked quietly.

'Your beauty has always distracted me,' he replied, his voice taking on a husky tone, causing her heart to beat so hard and fast she could feel it pounding throughout her body.

She drew in a few shaky breaths. He had said she looked beautiful. Now was the perfect time to act like the seductive, free-spirited woman she wanted to be.

But no flirtatious words came. Instead she continued to look up at him. All she could do was gaze into his deep blue eyes. She had always thought his eyes the most attractive feature in his handsome face. She still loved the contrast between the ocean-blue eyes and the thick black eyelashes. Although she'd also always adored his lips as well. Her gaze moved to his full, sensual lips. Perhaps they were his best feature.

But thinking about his face was getting her nowhere. She needed to say something suggestive, something that would let him know what she wanted. She should not just be staring up at his lovely lips. She *had* to say something flirtatious.

She opened her mouth, willing something suitably seductive to emerge, but still no words came. Instead she stood in front of him like a fool, her mouth open, her mind blank.

She was never lost for words, but right now, when it mattered so much, she appeared to have completely lost the ability to speak.

A gong resounded round the room, signalling that

it was time for dinner. As if emerging from a trance Charlotte looked around at the men and women pairing up in preparation for entering the dining room.

She had ruined a perfect opportunity. Nicholas had said her beauty distracted him—what better opening for her to flirt her heart out could she possibly be presented with? And she had missed it.

Nicholas extended his arm to her. She looked down at it, suddenly nervous about touching him. This was ridiculous. Touching him was exactly what she wanted to do. And even more than that, she wanted him to touch her. What on earth was wrong with her?

With half-formed thoughts whirling through her mind, she took his arm and they joined the line of guests and walked into the expansive dining room. To calm herself down, Charlotte forced herself to focus on the sumptuously decorated oval table laid out for the forty guests attending the weekend party. She concentrated on the highly polished silverware, the cut-glass crystal glittering in the candlelight and the forty place settings arranged with military precision, all the while trying hard to ignore the fluttering feeling in her stomach that standing so close to Nicholas was causing.

They stopped at the place settings bearing their names and waited with the other guests for the host to give the signal for them to sit.

As Charlotte stared at the ornate silver candelabra in the middle of the table, she gave herself a serious talking to. She had to ignore the way her body was reacting and focus on the task at hand. She had managed to secure his attention. That was good. He had said he was distracted by her beauty. Even better. He'd certainly given her an enticing look. Better still.

Now she just had to stop acting like the naive, inexperienced woman she was and try to behave more like the sophisticated, seductive woman she wanted to be. She looked up at him and gave what she hoped was an alluring smile, although the trembling of her lips suggested her smile contained more agitation than allure.

The host raised his arm and the footmen moved forward like a line of well-disciplined soldiers and pulled out the seats for the ladies. They sat down, to the accompaniment of rustling silk and satin, followed by the gentlemen.

Charlotte drew in a deep breath and looked along the table. Every woman, young and old, was dressed as elegantly as Charlotte. Unlike Charlotte, that was something they did every evening. The women were all smiling, their jewels glittering in the candlelight, their polite laughter gently tinkling, their voices taking on a polite, sing-song quality. It was all so easy for them, yet so hard for her.

She caught her mother's eye and saw her tilt her head in Nicholas's direction, encouraging her in her pursuit of the most eligible man in the room. Charlotte sighed to herself. For once she had the same goal as her mother. But how was she supposed to go about pursuing Nicholas? Her fan work showed a decided lack of finesse, batting her eyelashes had resulted in him thinking there was something in her eye and, when she'd tried to act the coquette, he had looked at her as if she had lost her mind. The only time he had looked impressed was when she had put that annoying Earl of Danfield in his place. But being rude to the other guests was hardly a seduction technique.

Perhaps Mademoiselle LeBlanc was right, she should just be herself, speak her mind clearly and precisely, and let him know what she wanted.

Charlotte took a sip of white wine to fortify herself, then lowered the glass in despair.

No, that wouldn't work either. She had tried speaking her mind clearly and precisely in the past. She had let him know in no uncertain terms what she wanted and it had resulted in her complete rejection. And hadn't her mother told her repeatedly that men don't like women who spoke their mind, that they don't like opinionated women?

Well, it seemed Nicholas was happy for her to be outspoken and to have a sharp tongue when she was speaking up in defence of him, but would he like it when she disagreed with him? That was most unlikely.

Charlotte sighed and slumped slightly in her chair. At least she tried to slump. Due to Betsy's firm hand with the corset laces, and her even firmer foot, slumping was a complete impossibility. She was held upright, as rigid as a plank of wood.

She saw her mother once again making that head-tilting gesture, urging her on. Charlotte drew in a deep breath, remembering her mother's instruction on how to flirt. Smile a lot, laugh at his jokes and ask him about himself. She rarely, if ever, took her mother's advice, but as she had no ideas of her own, she might as well do what her mother suggested.

She turned to Nicholas, ignored the butterflies in

her stomach and gave him what she hoped was her sunniest and most seductive smile.

'The Earl of Danfield mentioned your time in Europe. Travelling around Italy and France must have been fascinating.'

Her smile became strained as he looked back at her, his dark eyebrows drawn together in question. 'Do you really want to hear what I got up to in Europe?'

Charlotte swallowed and forced herself to keep smiling, an action that required some dexterity. He was right. She most emphatically did not want to hear about his time in Europe. The last thing she wanted to hear about, or even think about, was all those women he had had in his bed. Women he hadn't rejected. Women that weren't her. She continued smiling, wishing she had asked him about something else, anything else.

Her smile quivered before she gritted her teeth together and forced it to remain fixed to her face. If asking about himself had failed, she needed to try another tactic. What else had her mother said? That's right. Laugh a lot.

She gave a small laugh, attempting to give it the tinkling quality other women managed so easily. 'Oh, are you saying that tales of what you got up to are unfit for a lady's ears?'

He shook his head slowly from side to side, his face still bearing that incredulous look he had worn in the drawing room. 'Are you all right, Charlotte? You're acting very strangely tonight.'

Dejected, she attempted to slump, but was once

again thwarted by her corset. Instead she sighed, loudly.

'What's wrong, Charlotte?' he asked quietly as the footman served the oxtail soup. 'You don't appear to be yourself tonight.'

She forced herself to smile once more, determined to give flirting another try. 'Nothing's wrong, but I did go to a lot of trouble with my dress and hair tonight.' She resisted the temptation to try a bit more eyelash batting, remembering that had been a complete disaster last time she had tried it. Instead she waited for him to respond with the compliment for which she had so blatantly been fishing.

He smiled. 'I've already told you I noticed the change, as has just about every man in the room, including Baron Itchly and the Earl of Uglow. They were both looking at you with renewed interest in the drawing room and have been sending you very obvious looks since we sat down. Have you decided to relent on your decision to not find a husband before the end of the Season?'

'I have not,' Charlotte said loudly before she had time to think, drawing the attention of the guests seated across the table and causing them to angle their heads to look around the large display of out-of-season spring flowers in the middle of the table to see what the disturbance was.

'I haven't,' she repeated more quietly. 'I still have no intention of marrying. Ever.'

He took a sip of his soup. 'Well, you're going to have to fight off the offers looking like that.'

Charlotte registered the compliment and decided

to focus on that and not on his reference to the possibility that she might be trying to attract a potential husband. 'So do you like my new look?' She patted the side of her head.

He lowered his spoon and turned and faced her. 'You told me once before, in no uncertain terms, that a woman should be allowed to dress however she wants and should not be expected to dress just to please a man. So, I assume that tonight you have dressed in a manner that pleases you and for that I applaud you.'

I dressed to please you, Charlotte wanted to scream at him, but she was sure screaming at a man would not be considered flirtatious behaviour. Instead she gave what she hoped was a polite smile. Desperately trying to think of something else to say she ate her soup, hardly tasting a thing as she ran through a list of non-controversial conversation topics. Oh, why hadn't she paid more attention to her mother's lessons on suitable conversation openers?

The soup bowls were removed. She was forced to follow the rules of etiquette and turn to her other neighbour and make conversation with him during the entrée of duck pâté. This time her mother's advice worked splendidly. Charlotte didn't hear a word the man said, but he seemed quite content that all she did was smile and nod her head while waiting for the course to end.

When it finished and the steamed salmon was served, Charlotte turned her attention back to Nicholas. She had to give this flirting thing one more try. After all, it worked for so many other women, surely it could work for Charlotte as well. She was an intelligent woman and it was hardly a complicated mathematical problem. She must be able to master something so simple.

She tilted her head and smiled in what she hoped was a suitably feminine manner. 'I'm so glad to be talking to you once again, Nicholas. Unlike you, my other dinner companion is such a bore.' That was one lesson gleaned from her mother's constant nagging—men loved flattery and being told they were superior to all other men.

Once again Nicholas shook his head and frowned. 'What on earth is wrong with you tonight? I'm sorry you find your other dinner companion a bore, but I would have thought good manners and a basic sense of decency would mean you'd keep that opinion to yourself. I would have expected better from you, Charlotte.'

Charlotte's smile froze on her face. She could not believe how he had just spoken to her. How dare he? How dare he criticise her when all she was trying to do was to draw his attention the way all the other debutantes had done? He hadn't chastised them when they had fluttered their eyelashes at him. He hadn't told them they were peculiar, or that he expected better from them. So what gave him the right to talk to her like that?

'For your information I am not acting in a peculiar manner, unless you think flirting is peculiar.'

His knife and fork hit his plate with a clatter. He stared at her, shaking his head, his eyes wide. 'What? Why?'

'Oh, for goodness' sake. Surely a man like you must

know exactly what I'm after. It's what I've always wanted from you. I want you to make lo—'

'Charlotte, keep your voice down.' His shocked eyes grew even wider and he looked around the table. 'Speaking like that will ruin your reputation,' he added in a hissed whisper.

She stood and threw her napkin on the table. 'I don't give a fig about my reputation. I told you that five years ago and nothing has changed.'

To her mortification she could see a smile was quirking at the edges of his lips. He was laughing at her. How dare he laugh at her. He found her outburst funny. He found her desire for him to make love to her something to laugh at. She had been so determined not to humiliate herself in front of Nicholas and now she had done exactly that. She had exposed her vulnerability to him, and he was laughing at her. How much more humiliation could she possibly take? Well, she would not remain at this table and be mocked. Turning her back on him, she strode out of the dining room with as much dignity as she could muster.

Chapter Ten

Nicholas stood up and followed Charlotte out of the room. He nodded his apologies to the Marquess as he passed the head of the table. The Marquess's mocking smile made it obvious he was enjoying the drama and no doubt thinking that it was the first sign that Nicholas was indeed now under the thumb.

He reached the door, stopped and looked back at the Dowager Duchess to see if she wanted to accompany him as a chaperon. She shook her head slightly and gave an almost imperceptible flick of her hand to tell him that he should go to her daughter and sort out whatever problem there was and she would not be accompanying them.

The footman opened the door and, before it had even closed behind him, the previously silent room erupted into loud chatter. Nicholas had no illusions about what the topic of conversation would be. He could only hope Charlotte was telling the truth when she said she didn't give a fig about what society thought of her, because her dramatic departure from the table in the middle of a meal was certainly going to keep the gossips entertained for some time to come.

He looked down the corridor. There was no sign of Charlotte. He asked a passing maid if she had seen where she had gone and was told a young lady had been seen walking out the front of the house and into the garden.

Nicholas walked quickly through the front doors and saw her halfway down the path, beside a statue, pacing up and down and mumbling and gesticulating to herself as if in an argument with an invisible opponent.

When he arrived at her side, he raised both hands, palms upward to indicate he deserved an explanation for her outburst. She said nothing, her eyes sparkling with anger.

'Well, what was that all about?'

'What was all that about?' she shouted, stumbling over her words. 'You have the audacity to ask me what that was all about?'

'Yes, I do have the audacity to ask you about your bizarre behaviour tonight. You have to admit it has been out of character and, as for that outburst at the table…yes, I do expect an answer.'

The angry fire in her eyes grew more intense. 'Do you want me to spell it out so you can laugh at me again, so you can continue to humiliate me?'

Even in the moonlight he could see tears in her eyes. He had never known Charlotte to cry. He took hold of her hands. 'I am not laughing at you, Charlotte. I would never laugh at you. Nor would I do anything to humiliate you,' he spoke softly. 'I just want to understand. Let's go for a walk so we can discuss this.'

The fire in her eyes didn't die, but at least she followed his lead and allowed him to slowly walk her around the garden.

They went down the path, away from the light streaming out from the well-lit house. The garden, gently bathed in the light of a full moon, provided a sense of intimacy, one in which he hoped Charlotte would feel comfortable revealing to him what was troubling her.

The night air was also having a cooling effect on her temper because he could feel the tension in her arm start to relax. Now was the time to broach the subject. 'So, Charlotte, are you going to tell me what is wrong?'

'There's nothing wrong with me. Absolutely nothing.'

He waited for her to continue. She said nothing, forcing him to suppress his irritation. Getting annoyed with her would solve nothing. 'There is something wrong,' he said gently and slowly as if talking to a child. 'If there was nothing wrong, you wouldn't have stormed away from the dinner table.' To Nicholas that seemed self-evident, but it was apparent that it needed explaining to Charlotte.

'I said there was nothing wrong with *me*. I didn't say there was nothing wrong.'

Nicholas shook his head slowly. 'Are you saying there's something wrong with *me*? That I've done something wrong?' He thought for a minute. For once Nicholas had acted the perfect gentleman all night. He could think of nothing he had done that would cause offence. He went back over what he had been doing just before her outburst. 'This isn't because of what I said when you insulted your dinner companion, is it? Or was it when I asked you what you were up to with your fan?'

Charlotte couldn't be that sensitive, could she? She was never sensitive in the past. She might have changed. But to change that much seemed unlikely.

'No, I am not upset over them. I would have thought it was patently obvious what everything that has happened tonight was about.'

'It's not obvious to me, so you are going to have to explain it in simple terms that even someone as dim-witted as me can understand.'

She huffed out a sigh of exasperation. 'Surely you knew what I was doing. I was trying to flirt with you. That was why I dressed like this tonight.' She released his arm and flicked her hands towards her skirt to indicate her dress and pointed at her ornate hairstyle.

'Oh,' was all Nicholas could think to say.

'Yes, oh. And as for that fan work, I was trying to tell you I wanted you to kiss me again. That's why I was tapping my lips, apparently that's what it means.'

'It does, but I believe you're supposed to lightly stroke your lips, not hit them hard with your fan while frowning at the man you're trying to attract,' Nicholas said, unable to stop himself from smiling despite his promise not to laugh.

'Well, as you weren't listening to me, I had to shout it at you,' she said, her voice rising as if to prove her

point. 'It was the only way I could make you understand what I wanted.'

'Oh, I suppose I was being dim-witted.'

She frowned at him. 'Well, yes, you could say that.'

'It's what you called me five years ago,' he said quietly, smarting at the remembered insult.

She shook her head. 'I said what?'

'If I remember correctly, you said I was dim-witted, lacked intelligent conversation and was only useful for one thing.'

She stopped walking and looked up at him as if
unsure what he was talking about, then realisation
dawned on her, and her hand shot to her mouth. 'Oh,
Nicholas, I said that because I was so hurt. I had just
kissed you, asked you to make love to me and you
had rejected me. I lashed out in anger.' Even in the
subdued evening light he could see that her cheeks
were burning fiercely. She shook her head, looking
up at him with pleading eyes. 'I've never thought you
dim-witted, Nicholas, far from it. I was just angry at
being rejected.'

It was Nicholas's turn to feel uncomfortable. 'I
didn't reject you, Charlotte. I told you at the time that
I would not make love to you because I would not ruin
you. I didn't want to destroy your chances of making
a suitable marriage.'

Her face quickly moved from contrite back to annoyed. 'And I told you I didn't want to marry anyone,
that I was just like you, with no interest in marriage.'

'You were eighteen. How can anyone know what
they really want at eighteen? You said you didn't want
to marry then, but how were you to know whether in

a few years you would meet the man you did want to marry? And I didn't want to risk ruining your chances at happiness.'

'But I didn't marry, did I?' she said quietly. She resumed walking slowly down the path. 'Despite not being ruined, I'm still not married and still have no intention of doing so.'

'This is not an appropriate conversation for an un-married young woman to have with a man.' Nicholas knew he was sounding pompous, but the last thing he wanted to think about or talk about was Charlotte's virginity.

She drew in a deep, strained breath, but contin-ued to look him steadily in the eye. 'Inappropriate or not, I think you know what I'm saying to you. When I wanted you to make love to me, I didn't want to just experience what it was like to make love to a man— well, I wanted that as well—but I only wanted it with you, no one else.'

Nicholas's heart beat harder in his chest at her ad-mission. 'But why me? Was it because of what you said, that the bedroom was the only place where I was of any use, that I lacked wit, intelligence, any conver-sation skills?'

She shook her head, gripped his arm and looked up at him, her eyes imploring. 'Oh, Nicholas. I was angry, hurt, embarrassed. You had turned me down. I'd all but thrown myself at you, asked you in no uncertain terms to make love to me and you had said no. How would you expect an eighteen-year-old girl to react? To just accept it with a shrug of her shoulders and forget about it? I was so hurt I thought I'd never recover. And I don't believe I *have* ever recovered.'

'Oh, Charlotte. I'm so sorry. I never intended to hurt you.'

Her lips quirked into a teasing smile. 'Well, don't be sorry. Make up for it by kissing me. Now.'

He smiled back at her. There was the forthright Charlotte he remembered, but kissing her was still wrong. 'Charlotte, we can't. It's wrong.'

'Well, it shouldn't be. And it's just a kiss. No one will know. Don't you want to kiss me?'

'Of course I do.' He looked back at the brightly lit house at the end of the gravel path. 'But not here.' He moved her to behind the nearest statue, bent down and lightly kissed her waiting lips, reminding himself to keep his passions firmly in check. Despite what she said, this was still unacceptable behaviour.

She pulled back from him and looked up into his eyes. 'I said kiss me, Nicholas, don't treat me like a porcelain doll who might break. Really kiss me.'

'My pleasure,' he murmured, staring at those lovely pink lips, his resistance dissolving. He pulled her firmly towards him and his mouth came down on hers. He ran his hand down her back, reacquainting himself with the touch of her curves, that feminine taste of her and her lovely, fresh, inviting scent.

She moaned lightly as she moulded her body into his, her hands sliding up the back of his neck and curling through his hair. Her need for this kiss was palpable as she opened her mouth wider and tilted back her head. When her tongue entered his mouth, first tentatively and then with more confidence, he released his own moan of satisfaction. He was no longer just kissing her. She was kissing him back with a ferocity that was intoxicating.

She pulled back from him, tried to speak, but found she couldn't. Her breath was coming in fast gasps, those lovely mounds of her breasts, visible to him above her dress, moving up and down enticingly. Her eyes were sparkling in the moonlight and her lips were swollen with desire.

'Come with me,' she finally gasped, taking him by the hand.

Unable to think clearly, he allowed her to lead him from behind the statuary, further down the path to the enclosed garden which contained the maze and an array of exotic plants. Leaning back against the garden wall, she looked up at him. 'We're away from any prying eyes now,' she murmured. 'No one will ever know, Nicholas, so make love to me, now.'

Her arms wrapped around him, pulled him towards her and she found his lips again. During those long years they had been apart, Nicholas had been fantasising about making love to Charlotte. He had imagined what she would look like naked, how her soft skin would feel under his touch, what it would be like to be deep inside her, joining with her, becoming one with her.

Having the woman he had dreamt about constantly finally back in his arms was like being caught in a torrential downpour after a long period of drought. With her lips on his, her body hard up against his, her breasts pressed against his chest, he could no longer think straight.

She pulled back from him again, looked up at him, her eyes pleading. 'I want more, Nicholas.' Her words were little more than a whisper, but her body was shouting at him loud and clear. Her red lips were plump, her eyes hooded, and her breasts were rising and falling rapidly with each gasping breath.

He had rejected her once. It had been the right thing to do at the time and he had been pleased with his decision, yet had regretted it for the entire time they had been apart. Charlotte did not believe he had done the right thing, and she had not forgiven him for rejecting her. Could he do that to her again, reject her? Or could he go against one of the few rules in his moral code and make love to an unmarried woman, ruining her prospects of ever marrying?

He closed his eyes and drew in a series of deep steadying breaths.

No, he would not do what she asked. He would not make love to her. Despite her protestations that she cared nothing for the rules of society, he would not ruin her.

Nicholas could not believe his restraint. The throbbing pain in his trousers wanted him to do as she was commanding, but the small part of his brain that was still capable of reasoning was telling him that this was wrong, so very wrong. He could not take her virginity. She was an unmarried woman. She was off limits.

'Please,' she gasped. He registered the desperation in her voice as she pulled him towards her and kissed him again.

No, no, no, he commanded his body, as he kissed a line down her neck, causing her gasps of desperation to become gasps of pleasure. She tilted back her head, exposing her silky soft neck to him, and almost purred with contentment. As his kisses moved lower, the purring turned to low moans, getting louder and louder as he kissed a line across the soft, round mounds of her breasts.

He would not make love to her. She would remain a virgin, but that did not mean she would not experience the sensual pleasure her body was crying out for.

With a firm tug he pulled down the front of her gown and smiled as her breasts emerged, pushed up high above her corset, the tight nipples pointing up at him.

He took a moment to admire the beauty displayed before him. Her breasts were just as he had imagined, full, round and enticing. He looked up into her eyes to see if there was any sign of protest, any look of alarm. She had said this was what she wanted, but was it really?

All he saw were her eyes twinkling in the moonlight, her lips parted as she drew in shallow, rapid breaths.

Still watching her, he cupped her breasts gently, loving the feeling of their fullness in his hands. Her eyes closed, she leant in towards him. Slowly he rubbed his thumbs across the tight buds, watching her beautiful face as he did so. Her head was now leaning back, her eyes closed, her mouth open, her lips damp. With each stroke she moaned a little louder. Still cupping her breasts, he leant down and took one nipple in his mouth, running his tongue along the hard, erect nub, causing the moans to become gasps.

'Oh, Nicholas,' she cried out as he sucked and nibbled, while still tormenting her other breast with his hand. Her hands moved to behind his head, holding him to her breast, letting him know how much she wanted his caresses. He moved to her lovely twin, sucking and gently nibbling on the sensitive bead, until her moans became loud cries. Her fingers dug into his scalp. She was losing control, completely surrendering herself to the experience.

Reaching down, he pulled up the soft material of her gown, bunching it around her waist, and ran his hand up the inside of her thigh. Releasing her breast, he once again looked into her eyes, assessing her reaction to what he was doing, what he was about to do. Was she ready for this?

Her eyes were still closed, her breath panting out through her open lips. It was the look of a woman caught up in the ecstasy of expectation, but he still knew he had to take things slowly. Had to remember she was an inexperienced virgin. He moved his hand up, higher and higher, inching towards his destination, until it was above her stockings, and he was caressing the silky skin of her inner thigh. He watched her face for any sign of objection. None came. Instead her breath was coming faster and faster. She opened her eyes, looked at him, nodded her head and swallowed, before closing her eyes again.

His hand moved up to the parting in her drawers and he said a silent thank you to the maker of women's underwear who conveniently left a parting between the two legs. His hand entered and he ran his palm gently across her mound, all the while watching her beautiful face. Her breath came faster, her lips parted wider. He slid his hand between her legs and slowly traced his fingers along the folds. She gasped and, to his delight, placed her hand on top of his, urging him on. He entered her gently and slowly with one finger, then two, feeling her wet arousal on his hand. Rubbing slowly and firmly, he entered her deeper, the sheath clasping tightly around his fingers. The temptation to finish this off by ripping open his trousers, entering her and feeling his own release within her was all but overwhelming, but he would not do that.

She had said she wanted to know what physical pleasure between a man and a woman could be like. He reminded himself of his promise. He would let her experience what it was like to have a man pleasure her, without ruining her virginal state.

And the look on her face, the gasps she was emitting, showed she was indeed being pleasured. Louder and louder came her cries as his hand moved faster and faster. Kissing her again, he momentarily stifled those cries then moved down to her beautiful waiting breasts, sucking each one in time to his stroking, urged on by her cries.

She gave a loud gasp as a shudder rippled around his finger, telling him that she had experienced the pinnacle of pleasure. She all but collapsed against his shoulder and he wrapped his arms around her small waist to stop her from falling, holding on to her and loving that he had given her such sensual satisfaction.

Her breath slowly returning to normal, she looked up at him. 'Thank you, Nicholas,' she said, smiling at him. 'That was wonderful, but you promised to make love to me.'

Nicholas could remember making no such promise.

She looked down at the tell-tale sign in his trousers. 'And I think you are more than ready for that,' she said with a sigh.

Nicholas drew in a deep breath and fought off every inclination that was coursing through his mind and body. 'I said I wouldn't ruin you and I meant what I said.'

'But I said I don't care about that.'

He took hold of her hand, brought it up to his lips and kissed it. 'And I said it was something you should save for your wedding night.'

'And I said there won't be a wedding night. So make love to me, now.'

Nicholas couldn't help but smile. What woman other than Charlotte FitzRoy would make such a command? It was an order he was having to fight hard not to follow.

A loud rustling noise from the edge of the maze drew their attention. Was there someone there? Watching them? He quickly lowered Charlotte's skirt and pulled up the front of her gown, hiding those beautiful mounds from his gaze.

Two cats emerged from the maze and Charlotte gave a small laugh. 'It seems we're not the only ones indulging tonight.'

Nicholas released his held breath at the sight of the two animals. It would have been a disaster if they had been spotted. The tomcat looked up at him and Nicholas was sure he had a self-satisfied smirk on his face. A look Nicholas unfortunately couldn't share.

'I think we should return to the house,' he said, further straightening up her gown. 'People are going to be wondering why we've been away for so long so we're going to have to act as if none of this has happened and pretend we've just had a small argument of no consequence and everything is now all right.'

He was expecting some resistance, but she nodded her agreement. Was that relief that he was experiencing or an increased level of frustration? He didn't know. All he knew was they were going to have to return to the house and pretend that nothing untoward had happened between them. Something that was going to demand a level of acting skill Nicholas was unsure he possessed.

Chapter Eleven

Act as if nothing had happened? Had he really suggested she should act as if nothing had happened? When you had just experienced something so wonderful you felt as though the earth had moved off its axis, how could you possibly act as if nothing had happened? She looked up at the night sky. She hadn't noticed before that radiant full moon smiling down at them, or the velvet black sky full of twinkling silver stars. Were they shining even brighter tonight than they usually did? She was sure they were.

Charlotte took Nicholas's arm and almost skipped up the path as they made their way back towards the house. She couldn't keep an insane smile off her face. She wanted to dance, to sing, to shout out to the world that she had just reached a level of ecstasy she had not imagined possible. Her body was certainly singing. She felt like a different woman, more alive than she had ever felt before, and every inch of her skin was still tingling from Nicholas's touch. Instead of returning to the house she wanted to drag him back behind the trees, to beg him to caress her again, to do what he had just done, to give her that exquisite thrill one more time.

But he had insisted they return to the house and act as if they had merely had a small tiff which they had now settled. She clung on to his arm more tightly and put her head on his shoulder, wanting to absorb as much of his touch as she could, to be as close to this magnificent man as it was possible to be.

The only small niggling doubt that was clouding her otherwise sunny disposition was the thought that that might be it. Nicholas had given her a taste of what intimate pleasure between a man and a woman could be like, but he had been adamant that there would be no more. There would be no consummation. He would not ruin her chances of marriage, despite her protestations. It was almost worth marrying Nicholas herself to get what she wanted.

She stumbled slightly as they walked up the steps, causing Nicholas to look down at her with concern. 'Are you all right, Charlotte?'

She nodded, no longer smiling like a demented fool. Where had that thought come from? She did not want to marry anyone and she certainly did not want to marry Nicholas. Yes, what she had experienced was earth shattering. And, yes, she would like to experience it again and again, and again, but was it something she would sacrifice her freedom for? She looked up at Nicholas, who smiled down at her in reassurance.

It was tempting. Oh, so tempting. To spend every night in this man's arms had to be the very definition of temptation. But he was a rake. She had always known that. That was one of the reasons she had been so attracted to him in the first place, because she thought he would have no objections to seducing an eighteen-year-old virgin. After all, wasn't that what rakes did? But she had chosen the wrong rake, one who had an annoying sense of honour. Despite that honourable side to him, he was still a rake. If he did marry, he'd never be faithful to his wife. He'd been a ladies' man when she'd first met him and the years hadn't changed him, if the rumours of what he'd got up to in Europe were to be believed.

She would sacrifice her freedom for the sake of fleeting physical pleasure, only to be stuck with a man who would soon move on to another woman. And that would be something she could not bear. Once she had him, she knew she would never be able to share him. No, she needed to put all thoughts of marriage where they belonged, firmly out of her mind.

Not that she really had much choice in the matter anyway. He had made it clear that he did not want to marry either and as a wealthy man with a title he could have his choice of virtually any woman he wanted. He didn't want to marry anyone and that included Charlotte.

It was time to put what had just happened in perspective. It had been beyond wonderful for her, but for Nicholas it would have been just like that first kiss they had shared. It would have meant nothing to him. He had merely done a spinster a favour.

Charlotte's sweet happiness suddenly had a bitter edge to it.

They walked into the house, still arm in arm, although Charlotte no longer had the same sense of deep connection to Nicholas she had felt just a few moments ago. Nothing had really changed as a result of their time together in the garden. Well, a lot had changed for her, but nothing had changed *between* her and Nicholas.

They paused in the house's hall to compose themselves before they joined the other guests. Nicholas smiled as he tucked a strand of hair behind her ear. Despite her determination to try to act as if nothing had happened, she couldn't stop herself from leaning her head in towards his hand. He gently ran his finger along her cheek.

She looked up at him, willing him to kiss her again.

'We need to go in, Charlotte,' he whispered, his voice husky. 'Someone might see us and we have been gone far too long.'

Reluctantly she nodded. Dinner would now be over. The women would all be gathered in the drawing room taking coffee while the men remained in the dining room for port and cigars. They would have to part company, even if it was only briefly. Charlotte did not want to leave his side, but she had no choice. Women and men always retired to separate rooms after dinner. That was another ridiculous convention that would cause a scandal if it was flouted.

Nicholas lifted her hand and gently kissed the back of it. 'Will you be joining me at cards this evening? Hopefully I'll win some more money for the hospital.'

Charlotte nodded her head rapidly. 'Oh, yes.' She was horrified to hear her words come out in a girlish gasp. 'Yes, I will,' she repeated in a less gushing manner. 'And hopefully you'll get lucky again tonight.' The fire on Charlotte's already burning cheeks increased, and she bit her bottom lip, thinking of other ways in which she would like him to get lucky.

He smiled at her unintended joke. 'Until then,' he said and kissed her hand one more time.

They remained standing in the hallway, her hand still in his. Charlotte did not want to leave him. She wanted to spend the rest of the evening with him and him alone. Damn propriety, damn what society expected. He tilted his head towards the doorman standing outside the drawing room, waiting to open the door for her. They were no longer alone. He released her hand and reluctantly, she turned and walked down the hallway to the drawing room.

The footman opened the door for her. She paused to take one more look at Nicholas before she entered. Contentment coursed through her. He was still standing at the entrance, watching her.

That had to mean something, didn't it? He hadn't just walked away without a backwards glance. Or was she clasping at straws, wanting to see something that wasn't there?

They exchanged one last smile and she entered the room.

The murmur of polite conversation died. Every head turned in her direction. Charlotte froze. Did they know what had just happened while they were outside? She felt different—did that mean she looked different as well?

Her mother rose from the seat by the fire and made her way across the room towards Charlotte. Conversation resumed, but she was still receiving many furtive, and not so furtive, glances. There could be no doubting that she was the one and only topic of conversation among the ladies.

'Well, you look like the cat that got the cream,' her mother said. 'I take it whatever it was that upset you at dinner time has now been settled.'

Charlotte released her held breath. That's right. After everything that had happened, she had forgotten that the last time these ladies had seen her she had been making a scene in the dining room and storming off in a fit of pique. They had no idea about what had since happened between her and Nicholas; they were merely outraged by her earlier scene.

Charlotte smiled at her naughty little secret. If they knew what had happened after she had stormed out, they'd be more than outraged. It would be smelling salts all round.

'Yes, Mother. I'm fine now. I'm sorry I behaved so badly at dinner time.'

Her mother looked at her sideways, as if assessing the change that had come over her. 'Good, and I take it all is now right between you and the Duke of Kingsford.'

'Mmm, yes, it is.' Charlotte fought hard to stop herself from smiling again.

'Good.' Her mother looked her up and down. 'And I must say you look wonderful tonight, Charlotte. I always knew you could look beautiful if only you'd try. And I assume from that silly grin you had on your face when you entered the room that Nicholas appreciated the effort you had gone to for him.'

It seemed Charlotte had failed in her battle to act as if nothing had happened. She needed to try harder. 'I didn't make an effort for Nicholas,' she said, feigning as much umbrage as she could. 'It was just a waste packing this gown if I wasn't going to wear it.'

Her mother raised her eyebrows.

'Oh, all right, Mother. Yes, I did dress this way to impress Nicholas. But I don't think Nicholas cares how I dress.'

'I'm not too sure about that. After all, something has put that colour in your cheeks and that sparkle in your eye, and if I was a gambling woman I'd put my money on it being due to the Duke of Kingsford showing his appreciation for the effort you have made.'

Her mother tilted her head sideways and raised her eyebrows again. 'Is that what he was doing while you were away from the party for so long, showing you just how much he appreciates the way you look tonight?'

Charlotte's hands shot to her hot cheeks, still burning despite having come in from the cool autumn evening. She looked at her mother and was horrified to feel her cheeks grow even hotter under her scrutiny.

Her mother gave a small laugh and clapped her hands lightly together. 'I knew leaving you two alone without a chaperon was a good idea. I believe we'll be announcing your engagement soon and wedding bells will be chiming once again at Knightsbrook.'

Charlotte grabbed her mother's arm. 'Nothing happened between us, Mother,' she hissed.

Her mother reached up and pulled a leaf out of Charlotte's hair, inspected it with pretend interest as if trying to work out how it got there, then smiled.

'Nicholas has compromised you, my dear. He knows the consequences of such actions. He will have to do the decent thing and marry you. There's no other way and you know it.'

Charlotte grabbed the leaf out of her mother's hand and crushed it. 'Nothing happened, Mother.'

'A leaf in your hair, a flush on your cheek, neck and…' her mother indicated Charlotte's décolletage '…and elsewhere. Oh, something happened all right. Something Nicholas will have to make amends for.'

'No, Nicholas did not do what you're accusing him of,' she said, louder than she intended. Her heart pounded frantically in her chest, her mouth suddenly dry, a painful tightness gripping her chest. She leant in towards her mother. 'I'm still a virgin, Mother. On that you have my word,' she whispered through clenched teeth.

Her mother's triumphant smile did not waver. 'Your dishevelled appearance would say differently. Nicholas knows society's rules and for once you're going to have to follow them as well. A winter wedding will be perfect. I'll start making the preparations immediately.' With that her mother walked back across the drawing room and took a seat next to Nicholas's mother. In horror, Charlotte watched the two women talking with increasing animation.

This was a disaster. On shaking legs, she made her way to the nearest chair and all but collapsed into the plush upholstery. What had she done? She had been so selfish. She had wanted Nicholas to make love to her, telling herself that she did not care about her reputation. Never for a moment had she consid-

ered that she would be putting Nicholas in a compromising situation. If her mother got her way, Nicholas
would be forced into a marriage he did not want and
it was all her fault.

Nicholas had been right to reject her when they
first kissed and he had been right again tonight. She
should have listened to him. She should not have put
him in this untenable position. Now he was going to
have to marry her because they thought he had taken
her virginity, when he had in fact been honourable,
and done no such thing. But who was going to believe
that? It suited her mother to believe that Nicholas had
taken her innocence. She wanted her daughter married and, as far as her mother was concerned, having
the Duke of Kingsford ruin her daughter was a dream
come true. Unfortunately, Nicholas was an honourable man, albeit an honourable rake, and she knew
that he would marry her to save her reputation, even
if its tarnished state was only in her mother's mind.

The older woman smiled in her direction. Marrying her daughter off to the Duke of Kingsford would
be the pinnacle of her mother's husband-hunting ambitions. No wonder she looked so self-satisfied. She
had won a decisive victory.

Nicholas tried to ignore the banter from the other
men as he nursed his glass of port. After the scene
Charlotte had made in the dining room and their long
absence it was inevitable that he would be in for some
serious ribbing. Particularly as Charlotte had been
spotted by one of the men entering the drawing room
in a somewhat dishevelled state, her hair no longer a

perfect coiffeur and her cheeks blushing. He had attempted to dismiss it as the effect of the night-time breeze, which had elicited howls of disbelief from his fellow guests.

But it all signalled one thing. Even though Charlotte was technically still a virgin, he had taken an enormous risk with her reputation. He had made a big mistake. He should never have followed her outside without a chaperon. He should never have taken her in his arms, kissed her or caressed her. The only thing he had done right was to not make love to her and that had required a level of self-control he didn't previously know he possessed.

But damage had still been done and he had to put things to right. He had to ensure that Charlotte was still marriageable and that no man would see her as a ruined woman.

He took a sip of his port and contemplated how he was going to do this. He could make a ribald joke about trying to have his way with Charlotte, but being firmly rebuffed. That would not do. He did not want her to be the subject of these men's bawdy conversation. But, somehow, he was going to have to ensure that her good name was fully restored, otherwise she would be off the marriage market. He could, of course, marry her himself.

He spluttered on his port. Where on earth had that thought come from? He would never marry. It was something he had never even considered before. He did not want to be like his parents, or so many other married couples he knew, only able to bear their spouse if they saw as little of each other as possible.

No, he enjoyed the life of a bachelor too much to give it up. Didn't he?

He looked at the men around the table. While he did not envy the married men, was there much to envy in the bachelors' lifestyle? Cards and other forms of gambling had long ceased to hold an appeal for him. He'd had many willing women in his bed over the years and no doubt would have many more in the years to come, but even that pleasure had a certain emptiness to it. An emptiness he had not felt when Charlotte was in his arms. That had been different. He didn't know how, but it was. He had felt something deep, something intangible, something that was just right.

He drained his port and poured himself another. All this introspection was not like him and was a pointless activity. They would not be marrying, if for no other reason than they were completely unsuited. She needed a man who was learned and who cared as much for all those social causes as she did. She didn't need a man like him, a man who was, as she had said, only good for one thing. A man who was known as a rake and a gambler.

Charlotte needed a respectable, well-educated man and to secure such a marriage she would need to have an unsullied reputation. Something that wasn't going to happen if he couldn't keep his hands to himself.

That was the big question, wasn't it? Would he be able to keep his hands to himself if she offered herself to him again? He smiled, remembering how forthright she was when she commanded him to kiss her. Then he remembered how she looked when she reached the pinnacle of sexual pleasure. That was something he most certainly did want to see again, even though he knew he shouldn't. He had given her some of what she had asked for, but they would go no further. He would not even allow himself to think about what it would be like to have her in his bed, to run his hands over her naked body, to caress her breasts, to stroke and enter her most intimate parts, to have her writhing underneath him.

He moved uncomfortably on his chair. No, he most certainly must not think of that. He needed to distract his mind, immediately.

'So, whose money am I going to take tonight?' Nicholas said to the assembled men, eliciting loud calls of refute from most and a look of disdain from the Marquess of Boswick.

The conversation changed from women to cards, much to Nicholas's gratitude, and there was much posturing and posing over who would win tonight, who would get their comeuppance and who would be going home with less money in their pocket.

Once the men had drunk the port decanter dry and finished their cigars, they rose from the table to join the women in the drawing room, although many gave the appearance of needing to get that formality out of the way as quickly as possible so they could get down to the serious business of gambling.

Spending another evening at cards would have not long ago filled Nicholas with that familiar sense of weariness, but tonight he would once again be gambling to raise money for the charity hospital. Having a purpose changed everything. He could see why Charlotte dedicated so much of her time to worthy causes. It certainly gave a point to one's existence.

He could, he supposed, just offer to make a generous donation. After what they had just shared one would think she would now be willing to accept a donation from him.

Damn it. He had told himself he was not going to think about what happened between them. He downed the last of the port in his glass, telling himself once again to think of something else, anything else. He pushed back his chair and strode out of the room, joining the men heading towards the ladies' drawing room.

As he walked down the hallway, he reminded himself that nothing had changed. Everything was exactly the same between himself and Charlotte. They were still pretending to be a courting couple, that was all. And that courtship would terminate at the end of this weekend party, just as they planned. He would be saved from the pursuing debutantes and Charlotte would be saved from her matchmaking mother. Nothing had changed.

He entered the drawing room. His mother and the Dowager Duchess both stood up and raced towards him, matching smiles on their faces. Nicholas looked in Charlotte's direction. She was sitting on a chair staring into space, her shoulders slumped, her face pale.

He was wrong. Something had definitely changed.

Chapter Twelve

He looked over the heads of the twittering mothers, across the room to where Charlotte was sitting by herself. Only a few minutes ago she had looked happy, radiant even, her skin glowing, her eyes shining. Now her face was set in a stern mask, her body slumped in dejection. She looked even more miserable than she had when he had first seen her in this very drawing room, two days ago.

Yes, something had definitely happened.

The mothers' chattering broke through his thoughts. They were saying something about the local church, flowers and wedding gowns.

Wedding gowns. Did they really say wedding gowns?

He looked down at the two women. The mothers had got it into their heads that he and Charlotte were about to marry. No wonder Charlotte looked so shocked. Marriage was the last thing she wanted, to anyone, especially him.

Something had happened to make the mothers

think they were no longer merely courting, but were now engaged, with an imminent wedding already in the planning stages.

Nicholas might not be a genius, but it didn't take one to work out what had changed, what had made the mothers think a marriage was now inevitable. They had jumped to conclusions about what had taken place while he and Charlotte were alone together.

The mothers should be outraged by what they assumed had happened. They should be condemning his behaviour, not chirping away like contented birds. It seemed when it came down to it, getting their children into so-called successful marriages trumped morality every time.

This was a disaster.

He excused himself and crossed the room, watched by several smirking men, and a raft of disapproving debutantes and their mothers. The Dowager and his mother weren't the only ones who had jumped to conclusions. Yes, this was a complete disaster. Charlotte's good name was in tatters and now she was going to be forced into a marriage she did not want. He was going to have to do something, anything, to make this right.

He sat down beside her and smiled in an attempt to console her, although it would take a lot more than smiles and kind words to make her feel better.

She looked back at him, then lowered her eyes and shook her head slowly. 'I'm so sorry, Nicholas. My mother has got it into her head that we actually made love while in the garden and now she's insisting that we marry. I've told her that nothing happened, but she refuses to believe me. This is just impossible. I'm so, so sorry.'

Well, something *did* actually happen, in case she had forgotten, but pointing out that detail to this sorrowful woman would not be helpful.

Instead he tried to take her hands. She pulled them out of his reach as if touching him was now a dangerous activity.

'You have absolutely nothing to be sorry about,' he said in his most reassuring voice. 'Your mother's behaviour is not your fault and don't worry, she won't make you do anything you don't want to. I promise.'

Nicholas was unsure that he could keep that promise, but he knew he had to try.

Charlotte raised her eyebrows in disbelief. 'You have met my mother, haven't you? If she wants something, she will move heaven and earth to achieve it. And there's nothing she wants more than to see me married to anyone and a wealthy, titled man is her dream.'

Nicholas shrugged. 'She's not invincible. She tried to force your brother to marry an American heiress, didn't she?'

Charlotte nodded. 'Yes, I suppose she did.'

'And she failed, didn't she?'

Charlotte nodded again, her stern expression starting to soften.

'Well, this time her plans will also fail. Rest assured we won't be getting married. Your mother might be a seemingly unstoppable force, but with the two of us combined, we're definitely an immovable object. She won't get the better of us.'

Her lips quirked in a slight smile. 'I hope you're right, Nicholas.' She looked down and her small smile died. 'But she thinks that you took my virtue and now you must do what's right. I've tried to tell her she's wrong, but she won't believe it. Or, at least, she didn't want to believe it. The woman is insufferable.'

Once again, Nicholas decided not to mention that what they'd actually got up to was certainly enough to ruin a woman's virtue as far as society was concerned. There was no point arguing technicalities at this point. What he had to do was save Charlotte from being forced to marry him while still ensuring that her reputation remained as pure as the driven snow.

An idea occurred to Nicholas. For once, his reputation might be an advantage. It might actually *save* a woman's virtue and ensure her reputation remained unsullied.

'Trust me, Charlotte. I have a plan that might work. But can I ask you to turn your back on me and put your nose in the air as if I've gravely offended you?'

'What?' Her eyebrows knitted together and she tilted her head in question.

'Just do it, Charlotte, quickly, before your mother reaches us.'

They both looked across the drawing room. The Dowager was cutting a path through the crowded room, walking swiftly towards them, her arms swinging, her silk skirt swishing, her face beaming with happiness. She was the epitome of a woman celebrating a decisive victory.

'And remember, you despise me.'

Charlotte gave him another confused look, but did

as he asked, turning her back to him just as the Dowager arrived.

Nicholas stood, made a formal bow and gestured towards his seat on the sofa.

The Dowager fluttered her fan rapidly as if unable to contain the excitement bubbling inside her and sat down. 'I should be angry with you, my boy, but I'm a forgiving woman and, as you're soon going to be part of the family, I think we should try to start off without any bad feeling between us.'

'He is most definitely not going to be family,' Charlotte said through clenched teeth, looking over her shoulder with narrowed eyes.

'Oh, yes, he is.' The Dowager Duchess attempted to pull her face into a serious expression as she admonished Charlotte, failed and continued smiling. 'He knows what he's done and he knows the consequences. Now, sit down next to me, Nicholas, so we can discuss how we can remedy this situation and make right the wrong you have done.' She patted the seat beside her.

Nicholas joined the Dowager Duchess on the sofa and looked at her with feigned confusion. 'What situation, Duchess? I'm afraid I don't understand. What have I done? What wrong needs to be put right?'

The Dowager's beaming smile died an instant death. Her nostrils flared as she leant towards Nicholas. 'You know exactly what you've done to my daughter. What happened when you were unchaperoned,' she said in an aggrieved whisper. 'There's no point denying it. And you will be doing the decent thing or, believe me, you will pay for this.'

Charlotte started to turn, her face equally angry.

He shook his head slightly and quickly to let her know he would handle this.

'I'm afraid, Duchess, you have me at a loss. I can only assume you misunderstood what happened between Charlotte and me when we were alone together. Perhaps Charlotte was too upset to tell you the truth.'

The Dowager's smile of triumph returned. 'Oh, yes, you're right, my Charlotte was far too upset and embarrassed to tell me the truth. After all, she is, or was, an innocent young woman. But I'm not, Nicholas. I'm aware of the ways of the world and know exactly what happened. And I know exactly what you are going to have to do to restore my daughter's good name.'

She turned towards Charlotte and gently touched her slightly dishevelled hairstyle, causing Charlotte to flick her head away in irritation.

'It's obvious what happened,' the Dowager said, unable to keep the glee out of her voice.

'Yes, it is. If Charlotte was too embarrassed to tell you what happened between us, then I suppose it's up to me to tell you.'

The Dowager lowered her hand. Her nostrils once again flared as if she could smell something unpleasant. 'Believe me, I do not need to hear the sordid details.'

'No, of course not. All you need to know is that we were outside arguing and we've both agreed that it would be best if we called off the courtship.'

The Dowager narrowed her eyes, her chin lifted in defiance. 'Argument? You did not have an argument.' Slowly she looked from Nicholas to Charlotte, whose head remained turned away, then back to Nicholas.

'I'm afraid we did, Duchess.' Nicholas shook his head as if in regret.

The Dowager tapped Charlotte's hand. She turned slowly and Nicholas briefly saw a smile on her face before she looked suitably outraged. 'Yes, Mother, we had an argument. Why else do you think we were away for so long? And as you pointed out, I came back with pink cheeks and messy hair. How else would I have got in that state if it wasn't because I was giving Nic—giving that man a piece of my mind? I was furious. So, yes, the courtship is now off.' She held her mother's gaze in an unwavering stare.

The Dowager turned back to face him. Charlotte sent him a quick wink and he had to fight hard to keep from smiling. He was right. They made a great pair and the Dowager was no match for them.

'But Charlotte was smiling when she came into the drawing room. You don't smile after an argument.' The Dowager's eyes flicked from Nicholas to Charlotte and back again, that triumphant smile returning.

'You do if you're Charlotte and you've won the argument. Nothing makes Charlotte smile more brightly, I'm afraid, than when she's put someone in their place.'

The Dowager nodded slowly and frowned. 'Yes, that's true, I suppose.'

Charlotte's brow furrowed and her lips pursed. He could see she didn't agree with this description, but thankfully was keeping quiet and realised now was not the time to raise any objections.

'What was the argument about?' the Dowager asked. 'I'm sure whatever it was it is something that can be solved. After all, young people do have misunderstandings on occasions. That doesn't mean they have to call off their courtship. Tell me what the argument was about so I can help you solve whatever problem you're having.' Nicholas could hear the desperation slipping into her voice. He was well on his way to victory.

Instead of looking pleased with himself, he attempted to look shamefaced. 'As you already know, we had decided to postpone announcing our engagement because I have certain problems that need to be set right before we could do so.'

The Dowager went back to fluttering her fan, this time in agitation, not elation. 'Oh, yes, that. Well, I'm sure you'll sort that out as soon as possible and it shouldn't be a hindrance to the two of you marrying—it's no reason for you to argue.'

Nicholas looked around the room as if making sure no one else could hear what he was about to say and leant in towards the Dowager. 'That's what I had assumed as well, but I'm afraid it won't be that easy to sort out, after all, as Charlotte is not happy with the arrangement I have proposed.'

The Dowager Duchess raised her eyebrows.

He leant in closer to confide in her. 'During dinner I asked Charlotte whether she would mind terribly marrying a man who already had a mistress.'

The Dowager's already stiff posture grew more rigid. 'I see. Was that why Charlotte made that unsightly scene and stormed out of the room?'

Was that all the Dowager cared about? It seemed even being told the man you were courting, the man you were planning to marry, had a mistress wasn't considered sufficient reason to break with protocol and draw attention to yourself.

'Yes, I'm afraid it was,' Nicholas continued, looking disapprovingly at Charlotte as if he, too, could not understand her inappropriate behaviour. 'That's why I followed her. I wanted to try to explain the situation.'

'That's right, Mother,' Charlotte said, turning at last to face them. 'He told me all about his mistress and I told him that under no circumstances would I share him with another woman. If he wasn't prepared to stay completely faithful to me, then I would never consider marrying him. As he's not capable of doing that, then there is no point in continuing the courtship.'

Nicholas had to admire Charlotte's acting skills. The vehemence with which she had made that statement certainly sounded convincing. He looked at the Dowager to see if she had believed it.

'Charlotte, really,' the older woman gasped out. 'Remember where you are and keep your voice down.' Her gaze quickly darted round the room, then she leant in closer to Charlotte. 'Men are different from us,' she whispered. 'I'll explain all about that later when we are alone, but now is not the time. And sometimes a married woman has to be prepared to make some concessions.'

She smiled at Nicholas and his sympathies for Charlotte and every other unmarried society lady increased. They really were in an untenable position, expected to put up with just about anything from a husband, particularly if that husband had money and a title.

'Please excuse my daughter, Nicholas,' she said,

as if he had done nothing wrong and the fault all lay with Charlotte. 'As you know Charlotte can be a bit provocative at times. It's all part of her charm. Once you're married, she will come to see that in a successful marriage a woman is expected to give her husband a certain amount of freedom.'

Nicholas swallowed down the bile that had risen up his throat. He should not be shocked that the Duchess would put marriage ahead of her daughter's happiness, but he was. Charlotte was right when she condemned society's hypocrisy that gave men complete freedom while expecting woman to not only accept it, but to remain chaste themselves.

'Mother, I've already told you, I will not share Nicholas,' Charlotte hissed in her convincing manner. 'He said he won't give up his mistress so that's that. We will not be marrying. The courtship is over.'

'Let's not be too hasty, Charlotte,' the Dowager said with increasing desperation.

'I don't want to marry him and you can't make me. You tried to force me to marry Nicholas and you failed. What you had imagined, even hoped, had happened between us didn't. We were arguing. We were not—'

'All right, Charlotte.' Her mother cut her off. 'You've made your point, stop being so provocative.'

'I thought you said being provocative was part of my charm?'

The Dowager opened her mouth and closed it, lost for words.

'So, Mother, unfortunately for you, I'm still a virgin. My virtue is safe and Nicholas…the Duke of

Kingsford does not have to marry me, and I'm not going to marry a man who can't be faithful to me. We are no longer courting, so let that be an end to it.'

'Please, Charlotte, all right, just keep your voice down, please.' The Dowager fanned herself rapidly as she looked around the room.

It looked as though they had won. They had achieved exactly what they had set out to achieve. Their fake courtship had served its purpose. It had saved him from the marauding debutantes and Charlotte from a weekend of having to endure her mother's matchmaking. Now they had also used Nicholas's bad reputation as a means of conveniently ending it. It had all worked perfectly.

Unfortunately, now that they were no longer courting, Charlotte would not be able to join him at the card table tonight. Nicholas had been looking forward to once again having her at his side, but he would still do his best to raise as much money for her charity as he possibly could. Then tomorrow they would go their separate ways.

Separate ways.

His pride at coming up with a plan to save them from an unwanted marriage was suddenly wiped away. A pain gripped his chest, as if an iron fist had punched its way in and was clenching his heart.

If this was what success felt like, Nicholas would hate to experience failure.

Chapter Thirteen

Nicholas had been true to his word. He had saved them from an unwanted marriage and got the better of her mother. Charlotte should be feeling happy, but that hard knot in the pit of her stomach and pain in her heart did not feel like happiness.

What on earth was wrong with her? She did not want to marry Nicholas, the mere thought of it was ridiculous. And he did not want to marry her. It was highly unlikely that her mother would give up in her quest to get Charlotte up the aisle, but for now she was safe and Nicholas would not have to marry her.

That was a victory, not a defeat. She needed to cheer up and savour the moment.

The courtship had served its purpose and now it was over. Charlotte had achieved everything she had wanted over the weekend. Her mother had been kept at bay. She had raised money for the charity hospital and had been given a sensual experience she would never forget. And Nicholas had not been forced into marriage by her scheming mother because he had supposedly compromised a young woman.

She couldn't have hoped for a better outcome. And yet…

Nicholas excused himself so he could inform his mother that she, too, had got it wrong and he would not be marrying after all. Charlotte watched him cross the room and the pain in her chest intensified with every step he took away from her.

Would this be the last time she saw him? Tomorrow morning they would be leaving Boswick, going back to their own lives. He would be returning to a life that contained other women and she would have to content herself with the memory of what she had experienced this weekend.

But it was all for the best, she reminded herself as she watched him talking quietly to his mother. Charlotte would have hated herself if she had put Nicholas in the untenable position of having to marry her when he had done nothing wrong. Well, he had caused her to scream with ecstasy, to writhe under his touch, and society would definitely deem that unacceptable behaviour for an unmarried couple. But society was wrong. No one should have to marry against their will.

She drew in a deep breath and exhaled slowly, trying hard to feel pleased with the way things had worked out. The weekend could have gone quite differently. She could have spent it being thrust in the direction of men like Baron Itchly or the Earl of Uglow. She could have come away empty handed, having been turned down by the Marquess of Boswick. Instead of presenting the charity hospital's board with an enormous cheque, she would have had to tell them of her failure. And she could still be a woman who knew absolutely nothing about physical love between a man and a woman. Nicholas had not gone as far as to take her virginity, which had been her ultimate goal, but what he had shown her had been even more wonderful than she had imagined. So wonderful that she wondered how she'd ever be able to live without his touch.

But that was exactly what she was going to have to do. Nicholas was now out of her life. She would not be sitting beside him at cards tonight as she had planned. She exhaled another deep sigh. Despite her objections to gambling she had been looking forward to being at his side as he won more money for the hospital. Even if he had lost, she was looking forward to being with him. And if he had won, perhaps he would have given her another victory kiss. She touched her lips lightly. Now she would never be kissed by him again. She would never be caressed by him again. Her body clenched at the memory of where his fingers had stroked. Her breath caught in her throat and she closed her eyes. She would never again experience that rapture under his touch.

Would it have been better if she had never experienced such ecstasy? Now that she knew such exquisite delirium was possible, how was she going to cope with knowing she would never experience it again? Nicholas would never touch her again, caress her again. She would never again feel the touch of his lips on hers, never again feel his hands caressing her body, stroking her intimately, his hands and lips taking her to a peak of pleasure and causing her to let go into a free-fall of glorious release. How was she going to continue, knowing that such rapture existed?

A few tears sprung to the corners of her eyes.

'Oh, my dear, brush away those unsightly tears. You made your choice, now you're going to have to live with it. I think you made the wrong choice, but so be it. You could have been perfectly happy with the Duke of Kingsford, even if he did have other interests that didn't involve you.' Her mother patted her hand. 'Your father was just the same. I didn't always approve of his card playing, but I tolerated it and we had a perfectly happy marriage.'

That certainly dried up Charlotte's tears. *A perfectly happy marriage.* Her father's endless gambling parties had made life all but unbearable for his wife and children. If that was her mother's definition of a perfectly happy marriage, goodness knew what a miserable one looked like. But as it was a marriage to a titled man, perhaps that's all it took for her mother to consider a marriage to be a happy one.

Her mother looked around the room, ignoring Charlotte's look of disapproval. 'But the good thing is, no damage has been done and I'm sure Baron Itchly and the Earl of Uglow will still be interested. Perhaps even more so now that the Duke of Kingsford has seen you as an attractive prospect.'

She turned to Charlotte. 'So wipe away your tears and try to fix your hair. It's getting late and the weekend is almost over. We must make the most of the time we've got left.'

Charlotte stared at her in disbelief. But why should she be surprised? Her mother had been willing to consent to a courtship with Nicholas when she thought he had problems with another woman that needed to be sorted out. She had even thought he was a suitable match when he had refused to give up his mistress. Charlotte shuddered to think just how badly a titled man would have to behave before her mother deemed him unacceptable as a husband.

'I'm afraid, after everything that has already happened this evening, I would like to retire early,' Charlotte said.

She stood up to take her leave and her mother grabbed her arm. 'But Lady Redcliffe said Baron Itchly has been showing interest in her daughter. If we don't make a move tonight you might lose your last chance.'

Thank goodness for that.

Charlotte fought to keep her voice even. 'I'm sorry, but I really don't feel that I can pursue Baron Itchly tonight.' *Or any other night.*

Her mother pursed her lips together in disapproval. 'This isn't like you. You're usually made of sterner stuff than this.' They both looked over at Nicholas, still chatting quietly with his sorrowful-looking mother and once again being eyed by a roomful of unmarried women. 'Don't let your experience with the Duke put you off men, Charlotte. They're not all like him.'

That was something Charlotte was well aware of. Not all men were like the Duke of Kingsford. No other man would be capable of making her body react the way he did. Releasing a deep sigh, she turned back to her mother. 'Yes, Mother, you're right, but as I said, I'm very tired and want to retire for the night.'

She left the drawing room, forcing herself to not look in Nicholas's direction. He was now a free man. It wouldn't take long before word got around that they were no longer courting and she did not need to stay in the room and watch the circling debutantes move in on their prey.

The clock struck eleven and Nicholas excused himself from the drawing room. When he entered the card room that familiar sense of ennui descended on him, although tonight it was combined with a level of emptiness and loss he had never experienced before. The other men had already taken their places at the tables, eager to get the night's gambling underway. He took his seat across from the Marquess of Boswick. Once again, the man was eyeing Nicholas as if he was a bitter rival. Even before the first hand had been dealt, the Marquess had let his emotions get the better of him and once again that would be his downfall.

This rivalry was becoming increasingly tedious. The Marquess should just admit defeat instead of insisting that Nicholas give him another chance, again and again, to win back his money. But Nicholas knew that would never happen. It wasn't about the money. It was about the Marquess's pride and his pride was even bigger than his enormous fortune.

Nicholas reminded himself that tonight he would again be raising money for Charlotte's charity and it would be the last thing he would be doing for her before they parted ways. That knowledge should stop him from being overwhelmed by the tedium of a life that was an endless round of trivial activities. Charlotte's passion and commitment was something he had always admired about her. Her life had purpose. She was committed to helping those less fortunate than herself, not whiling away the hours in pointless, self-indulgent pursuits like himself and the other men at this card table.

The first hand was dealt. Nicholas turned the edge of his cards and saw they were of little value. With well-practised skill he kept his face impassive, so no one would know whether he had a winning or losing hand.

Chips were thrown into the centre of the table and, as predicted, the Marquess wavered, letting Nicholas know that he, too, had been dealt a losing hand.

Nicholas swallowed the yawn that was threatening to destroy his impassivity and waited for the men to make their predictable moves.

The night wore on with this same repetitive tedium. The chips piled up in front of him. That at least should be giving Nicholas some satisfaction. If the game continued this way, he would be raising another sizeable sum for Charlotte's hospital. In fact, many things about this weekend should be making him feel satisfied, not despondent. He had survived most of the weekend without being harangued and harassed by the debutantes and their mothers. And he had reconciled, if that was the right word, with Charlotte FitzRoy.

Five years ago, they had parted in animosity. Tonight, they parted as co-conspirators. They had worked as a team to stop their mothers from trying to marry them off to other people, or to marry them off to each other. Plus, he no longer held any grievance towards her over the insults she had flung at him. She had lashed out because she had been angry at him for what she took to be a rejection.

He turned up the edge of his cards and threw a few extra chips into the growing pile in the centre.

He smiled to himself at the memory of her telling him to kiss her five years ago and then doing exactly the same again tonight. The Marquess instantly threw in his hand, misinterpreting his expression. Five years ago, Charlotte had wanted to do more than just kiss and she had made the same request again tonight. In all that time she had not made that request to anyone else. Did that mean anything? It must.

Nicholas reminded himself that now was neither the time nor the place to be thinking about Charlotte Fitz-Roy. He had to stop the image of how her face looked when he had stroked her intimate folds from entering his mind. He should not be remembering the way her head was tilted back, her mouth open as she panted in ecstasy, her red lips swollen, her firm breasts rising and falling, her nipples...

'Are you going to show us your hand, Kingsford, or not?' The Marquess's voice snapped him out of his inappropriate thoughts.

Nicholas turned over his hand, which evoked a round of groans from the other players.

'Looks as though luck is on your side again tonight, Kingsford,' one player said, throwing in his hand with disgust. Then he sent Nicholas a malicious smile. 'Although apparently your luck with the ladies was out tonight. Lady Charlotte put up some resistance, I hear.'

Nicholas gritted his teeth tightly together. He was loath to discuss Charlotte with these men. They didn't need much encouragement to descend into coarse talk that no woman should be subjected to.

'Lady Charlotte and I are no longer courting, that's all you need to know,' he snarled at the smirking player. 'And if you know what's good for you, you'll drop the subject.'

'Wouldn't let you keep your little bit on the side, is what I heard. Some women, eh, don't know their place.'

Nicholas put his cards slowly and deliberately down on the table, all the while glaring at the man across the table. One more word from that imbecile and Nicholas's reputation for calm under pressure would come to an end and he would let this man know the full force of his wrath.

The man's smile faded. 'I don't mean any offence by it, though.' He quickly looked away from Nicholas and back at the cards, now trembling in his hand.

Tension around the table became almost palpable, with the other men sat staring at their cards as if making eye contact with anyone else at the table was now forbidden. The whipcord tension in Nicholas's body uncurled, knowing that no man at this table would dare to mention Charlotte FitzRoy's name again in his company.

The card game continued and Nicholas forced himself to regain his cool demeanour, something he had never before lost during a card game. He suffered a few losses, which were more than made up for by his many wins and, as the night wore on, several players drifted away.

Once again they had got to the early hours of the morning with only Nicholas and the Marquess of Boswick at the table.

As the Marquess's losses had mounted up, he had got angrier and angrier, making more and more mistakes, getting more desperate and reckless.

When a servant entered the room to extinguish the candles and open the curtains, both men knew they would have to end this match soon. Once again, the Marquess chose to gamble everything he had left on his last hand. He sent Nicholas a smile as if he had a line-up of winning cards, but the furtive movements of his eyes suggested he was bluffing.

In response Nicholas met his bid so he could see the Marquess's hand. He was grateful to see his pair of queens was enough to beat the Marquess. Not because he wanted to win, but because it meant the Marquess was now out of chips and would hopefully call it a night, or early morning as was the case.

The Marquess threw down his cards. 'I'll get you back for this, Kingsford. I'll make you pay and I'll get back everything you've taken from me, and much more.'

Nicholas nodded to the irate Marquess. It seemed he would have to endure yet another interminable rematch. The tedium was reaching such an unbearable level. Should Nicholas escape back to Europe? This time to flee from gambling and his dreary life, not just to try to escape the memory of Charlotte FitzRoy.

He had tried to flee from her memory once before and had failed. How could he possibly succeed now? He knew the memory of what had happened between them tonight would never leave him. He would never be able to forget how she looked tonight, her face a vision of ecstasy. He would never be able to forget the touch of her silky skin, the taste of her lips, or that feminine scent that still lingered on him. He would be tormented by those memories no matter how far away he ran.

'I suppose a cheque will suffice,' the Marquess barked, breaking into Nicholas's tortuous thoughts.

He nodded. 'Yes, and would you kindly make the cheque out to the East End Charity Hospital Trust.'

The Marquess strode across to his desk, pulled out the drawer with more force than was necessary and threw his chequebook on to the desktop. 'This is not the last you'll hear of this, Kingsford,' he said as he scrawled his signature on the cheque. He all but threw it at Nicholas, then stormed out of the room.

Nicholas exhaled loudly with impatience. The man really was a sore loser and it wasn't as if he couldn't afford his losses, plus the money was going to a worthy cause, not into Nicholas's pocket.

He looked down at the cheque in his hand and smiled. He had to admit it felt good to know you were helping others and Charlotte would be so happy that he had won another thousand pounds for her hospital.

He wished he would be able to see the expression on her face when she saw this new cheque, but if he

was to ensure everyone still believed that he had mis-
behaved inexcusably and the courtship was off, then
he could not see her again this weekend. Especially
as he could not guarantee how he would behave if he
did see her again. He might be able to keep an impassive face at the card table, but he could not guarantee
he would be able to do so in front of Charlotte.

It had been a long night, but he would not be retiring to his bed. Instead, he summoned his valet to arrange his immediate return to his London town house.

Chapter Fourteen

The envelope was sitting on her breakfast tray, addressed to Lady Charlotte FitzRoy in Nicholas's strong hand. As soon as the maid had left Charlotte clutched it to her chest and smiled.

She had been so distraught when they had parted last night, thinking that was the end, that they would never see each other again. But he had written her a letter. All night she had tossed and turned, unable to sleep, unable to shake off the despair that was consuming her. It had been bad enough to lose him last time, but now it was infinitely worse. She looked down at the envelope, but she'd had no need to fret, he hadn't forgotten her. He had sent her a letter.

She was tempted to rip open the envelope to get to the contents, but she was determined to savour the experience. It was not over. He had written her a letter. Would it be a jesting letter? Would he make sport of what had happened in the drawing room, of how they had got the better of her mother? Or would he mention the experience they had shared? Had he written about kissing her, caressing her? Would he even have become poetical in his descriptions of the intimacy they had shared? She smiled at the absurdity of that image. Nicholas was not one for poetry. She had never heard him wax lyrical, but, then again, he was a man full of surprises. Still, he had written her a secret note, that was romantic enough.

She opened the letter, bursting with anticipation and happiness.

It contained a cheque. She pulled open the envelope and looked inside to see if a note was somehow secreted within its folds. There was no note. She looked at the cheque more closely. It was for one thousand pounds, from the Marquess of Boswick to the East End Charity Hospital Trust. Nicholas had won again last night. Even more money would go to the hospital.

That was good news, wasn't it? Yes, it was excellent news and Charlotte had no right to feel so deflated. But a note, even a short one that let her know he was thinking about her, would have been nice. After all, thinking about him was the only thing she had done since she'd left the drawing room last night. She pushed aside her breakfast tray, the food uneaten.

Of course there would be no note. The mere idea of it was ridiculous. She was ridiculous. What on earth was she doing? Pining after a man like Nicholas, like some lovesick fool. It was ludicrous. He had promised her nothing. She had got from him what she wanted, more than she thought was possible, and she had no right to expect more.

She climbed out of bed and began pacing the room, her bare feet moving across the soft woollen rug to the hard, wooden floorboards and back again. The problem was, she did expect more. She certainly wanted more. Not marriage. No, she never wanted marriage, not with Nicholas and not with anyone, but she wanted more of him.

She looked at the empty envelope, screwed up and cast aside on the breakfast tray. After what they had shared last night, this couldn't possibly be the end. Could it? She sank down on to the edge of the bed.

Yes, it could be. Nicholas owed her nothing, had promised her nothing. She was fooling herself to think otherwise. The man was a rake, a rake with principles and honour, but a rake all the same. She picked up the envelope, screwed it into a tighter ball and threw it across the room, casting it away as she knew she had to cast away all thoughts of Nicholas.

It was time to put him firmly out of her head and get on with her life. She reached for the bell pull to call her lady's maid. Her hand stalled in mid-air, then dropped to her side.

Perhaps Nicholas hadn't sent her a note because he intended to talk to her in person today and whatever he had to say he didn't want to commit to paper. She began pacing again. Perhaps, just maybe, he now realised she was serious about not wanting to marry, that she really did not care about maintaining her virginal state and saving herself for marriage. Maybe he wanted her to become his mistress.

She stopped walking as a delicious thrill coursed through her body. Even Nicholas must be able to see that as long as they were discreet no one would ever know that they were seeing each other. Her mother would never be able to force them into marriage if she didn't know that Charlotte had become his mistress. And she was a sensible woman. She was more than capable of being discreet.

This was beginning to make sense. She started pacing again, biting at her thumbnail as she thought this through. Nicholas would know not to send her a note. He would know that it would be too risky to leave any written evidence of what was happening between them. Yes, that was it. He was being careful.

A secret liaison, how exciting, how romantic. They could continue what they had started last night in secret.

Charlotte rushed across the room to pull the bell cord to summon her lady's maid, eager to start the day, although there was no real urgency. Nicholas would have been at the card table until the small hours of the morning and would be late at rising.

That would give her plenty of time to go to as much trouble dressing this morning as she had last night. She could take her time with her hair and in making herself look as irresistible as possible, irresistible enough to tempt a rake.

A secret liaison would be even better than their fake courtship.

'You're in a good mood this morning, m'lady,' Betsy said when she opened the door to her.

Betsy was right, she was in a good mood. She almost felt like singing. Her life was about to take a wonderful new direction. Being Nicholas's mistress was worth singing about. Living the life of a Bohemian woman was worth singing about. She would be a free woman, just as Mademoiselle LeBlanc had been.

She took off her nightdress and put on her chemise. Betsy helped her into her corset and when she pulled in the laces as tight as she could, Charlotte put up no protest. Who cared whether she would be starved of oxygen? She wanted curves, lots of curves that Nicholas would be tempted to touch.

Unfortunately, the only day clothes she had packed were skirts in dull colours, but she combined her grey skirt with a pretty cream blouse with a high lacy collar.

Betsy styled her hair, not as ornately as last night, but the back combing and curling meant it was just as voluminous, and the curls draped around her neck looked just as feminine.

Charlotte searched through her jewellery box and chose a pearl necklace and earrings. Standing back, she carefully inspected her appearance in the full-length looking glass. That was something she had never done before this weekend. Her appearance had never mattered to her. In fact, she had always been scornful of women who took many hours primping and preening in front of the looking glass, judging them harshly for having nothing better to do with their time.

She did a small twirl to see how she looked from behind and hesitated. Could her corset be a bit tighter? Was the grey skirt a bit too dull?

'You look lovely, m' lady,' Betsy said.

She smiled her thanks to her lady's maid, hoped she was right and headed for the door. Anticipation coursed through her, making her very fingertips tingle with excitement as she headed down the stairs. Hopefully Nicholas would soon be awake and their secret liaison could begin.

'What do you mean, he's left?' Charlotte demanded of the Marquess's head footman. The man looked slightly embarrassed, although Charlotte suspected that was for her sake, not because of anything the footman had done. After all, he was just the messenger. She was the one standing in front of him, her hands on her hips, her voice raised above what convention demanded of a polite young woman.

'I believe the Duke left early this morning, my lady,' he repeated.

He had left without saying goodbye, without arranging a further meeting. He didn't want to see her again. That was it. He was gone, out of her life.

She turned and walked off down the hallway, unsure where she was going.

Well, so be it. If that was what he wanted, then why should she care? She turned and began walking back, still not sure where she was going, only aware she needed to keep moving to try to burn up the angry energy pulsing through her.

If he didn't want to see her again, then she would just get on with her life, put this whole incident behind her. She didn't need him. She didn't need any man. And she certainly didn't need a man who didn't even have the decency to say goodbye to her either by note or in person. She most definitely did not need a man like him in her life.

She had plenty to occupy her time. She was not some silly, simpering woman who sat around waiting for a man to pay her attention. She would just have to get even busier, devote even more time and energy to organisations like the charity hospital. She stopped walking, remembering the substantial cheques in her room that she had acquired courtesy of Nicholas's skills at the card tables.

She started walking again. She most certainly did not need to tell the charity hospital's board how the money had been acquired. If they weren't told, they would just think it was just a generous donation from the Marquess. She wouldn't want anyone to think the Trust or Charlotte herself was beholden to that man, a man who didn't even have the decency to say goodbye.

'Will there be anything else, my lady?' the footman asked, watching her pointless activity.

'No, sorry, that will be all,' Charlotte said, absent-mindedly as she turned and walked up the hallway she had just walked down. The weekend party would end today. Charlotte and her mother would be returning to their home in Devon and that would be that. Nicholas would get on with his life and Charlotte would get on with hers. Good. After all, she had a lot to do. She was still on the organising committee for the charity hospital and she had recently joined a newly formed group advocating for women to get the vote. They were important activities that demanded her attention and would occupy all her time and thoughts.

She had far too much to do and think about than to waste her time over a man. Charlotte stopped. Her mindless walking had taken her out through the front entrance. She looked down the gravel path, then on to the enclosed garden and the maze. Tears sprang to her eyes at the memory of what had happened between them in that very place.

She turned abruptly and walked back through the door. She must not think of what had happened. She would not think of the intensity of that experience. She had to put this entire weekend into perspective. Even though she thought she deserved some sort of gesture from Nicholas, presumably he saw things differently. Just like the last time they kissed, what had happened between them had obviously meant much more to her than it had to him. For Nicholas she was just one more woman in a long line. When she had first kissed him it had meant so much to her that she had been thinking about it ever since. Now she was in danger of letting history repeat itself. She was in danger of making a fool of herself over a man, all over again. She was in danger of still acting like a foolish eighteen-year-old debutante who swooned just because a man had shown her some interest.

Well, this time he had done a bit more than just show some interest and what had happened between them had been more intense than just a kiss, but still, for Nicholas, a man who'd had countless women, it would be of no account. She turned swiftly and commenced walking again. And that's exactly what it would be for Charlotte. Of absolutely no account.

She would return home and never ever think about Nicholas Richmond, the Duke of Kingsford, again.

Chapter Fifteen

Nicholas was wrong. He had thought it would get easier as time passed. But it had been a month since he had last seen Charlotte FitzRoy and he was still as raw as he had been on the day he departed from the Boswick estate.

He'd thought the pain when he'd left Charlotte and fled to Europe had been intense, but it was nothing compared to what he was feeling now. Some days the temptation to throw caution to the wind and contact her was all but overwhelming, but that would benefit neither of them. He had to stay strong. He had to remain resolute.

He looked out the window of his London town house, at the carriages travelling past, the uniformed nannies walking by, pushing large black perambulators, and his well-dressed neighbours out for a stroll down the street lined with trees still bearing the last of their autumn foliage.

He had hardly left his house since he'd returned from Boswick. Where would he go? What would he do? Every idea on how to pass the time that occurred to him instantly filled him with a crushing sense of tedium.

So what was he to do now? Become a monk? Well, he was getting plenty of practice at that. For the last month he had been living an almost monastic lifestyle. He'd hardly crossed his doorstep in all that time. He'd stopped going to his clubs and had no interest in seeing any of the other carousing bachelors he had once spent time with, and he definitely had no interest in contacting any of the women with whom he had once idled away his hours.

It wasn't just because he had no interest in such things. It wasn't just because he knew that lifestyle would not blunt the pain. It seemed Charlotte FitzRoy and her do-gooder approach to life had ruined him for all that. She had made him see that the way he lived his life was trivial and self-indulgent. She had taught him the value of caring for others. He smiled morosely. Was that what was going to happen? He was now about to become a crusading do-gooder, out to change the world? Although the danger in that was he could cross paths with the very woman he was trying to avoid.

He turned away from the window, crossed to the sideboard, picked up the crystal decanter to pour himself a brandy, then replaced it on the tray. Even the usually comforting effects of alcohol no longer held any appeal.

There was only one thing he wanted, only one thing that would numb this pain. He wanted to see Charlotte again, but that was out of the question. Neither of them was the marrying kind so they had to remain apart. Things had gone too far for them to be merely friends—whoever heard of an unmarried woman and an unmarried man being just friends anyway? It was one of the many things that society deemed unacceptable.

He walked back to the window and aimlessly stared out. Once again he had made the right decision. Just as he had five years ago. Under the circumstances the only thing to do was to have no further contact. The outcome was all for the best. As far as the rest of society was concerned, he had behaved like a rake and she had quite sensibly rejected him. It was a highly plausible story, one which would only continue to be plausible if they never saw each other again.

He just wished he didn't miss her so damn much. Life would be so much easier if he wasn't forever thinking of her, if that image of her beautiful face wasn't constantly appearing in his mind's eye, if he wasn't remembering her when she was happy, when she was angry, when she was embarrassed and when she was laughing.

A knock on the door drew his attention away from the window. The footman entered the drawing room, bowed and extended a silver tray towards Nicholas, bearing a white card. He read the gold embossed lettering and groaned.

'Thank you, Charles, please show him in.' Why on earth was the Marquess visiting him? He never made social calls to Nicholas's house. They were not friends, merely rivals at the card table. Nicholas might be desperate for a diversion to take his mind off Charlotte, but doubted he could ever be so desperate for a diversion that he'd want to see the Marquess and particularly not now. He was possibly the last person Nicholas felt like seeing, but manners dictated he could not turn the man away. He'd promised the Marquess a rematch, yet another chance for him to try to get his money back. Nicholas hoped that was not why he was here. He simply could not face that level of tedium at present, or perhaps ever.

If Boswick was here for another attempt to recoup his losses, then Nicholas would have to let him know in no uncertain terms that they would not be playing cards, today or anytime soon.

The footman opened the door and the Marquess entered.

'Boswick, what brings you here?' Nicholas asked, adopting a level of sociability he did not feel.

'Yes, I'd love a drink, Kingsford,' the Marquess said, looking over at the sideboard bearing the decanters, surrounded by a circle of crystal glasses.

Nicholas raised his eyebrows at the presumption, but poured two glasses of brandy and handed one to Boswick.

The Marquess took a drink, sat down and smiled at Nicholas. Not a friendly smile, more a self-righteous smile that suggested the Marquess was feeling very pleased with himself.

Nicholas sat in the wing chair opposite and waited while the Marquess continued to sip his brandy. Hopefully the man would quickly get to the point of his unexpected visit and leave Nicholas alone with his thoughts.

'So, what brings you out during daylight hours?'

Nicholas finally prompted when it became apparent the Marquess was in no hurry. After late nights at his club and other places of entertainment, the Marquess rarely rose before late afternoon, so it was a surprise to see him out and about at this time. That was a lifestyle Nicholas also usually adopted, but one he had ceased indulging in since his return from the Marquess's country estate.

The Marquess swirled his drink round in his glass. 'I was hoping to see you at the club, but you've been conspicuous by your absence over the last few weeks. You left me no choice but to track you down at your home.'

Nicholas stifled a groan of irritation. Was the man really that desperate to lose more money to Nicholas that he had to follow him to his home? 'I'm afraid you've had a wasted visit, Boswick. If it's a card game you're after, I have no interest in gambling and I have no intention of returning to my club in the foreseeable future.'

The Marquess took a long drink, then waved his empty glass in the air. Nicholas took it from his outstretched hand, refilled the glass, and returned to his own seat, hoping the Marquess would not ask for another drink, but would realise he had made a wasted trip to Nicholas's home and that he should leave, the sooner the better.

'So you're not going to give a chap a chance to get even with you and recoup his losses. Not very sporting of you, is it, Kingsford?' The Marquess took another long quaff of his brandy.

Nicholas exhaled loudly. This time he didn't bother

to stifle his irritation. 'Boswick, every time we've played, I've beaten you. Isn't it time you just admitted defeat?'

The Marquess placed his glass on the side table, his smug smile now a cruel sneer. 'I said it's not very sporting of you, but then I suppose it's just what I should expect from a man with your character.'

Nicholas stood up and indicated the door. 'You've said what you've come to say, now you can leave.'

The Marquess remained in his seat, took another long quaff and replaced the now empty glass on the side table. 'I'm not leaving until I get an assurance from you that you will be placing an announcement in the newspapers that you cheated when playing cards at my estate.'

Nicholas glared down at him, not sure whether he should laugh or call for the doctors so the man could be taken away to an asylum. It seemed the Marquess had gone completely insane. That could be the only explanation for his outrageous suggestion. 'And why would I do something so absurd? Why would I tell such a lie and destroy my reputation into the bargain?'

The Marquess held up his empty glass again to indicate that he wanted a refill. A request that Nicholas ignored.

The Marquess shrugged, placed the empty glass back on the side table and sent Nicholas another smug smile. 'Because if you don't, then I will make it known that one Lady Charlotte FitzRoy is nothing more than an unpaid harlot who allowed you to perform a lewd act on her in the garden of my own estate. Once that gets out the lady, if that's what you can call her, will never be able to hold up her head in society again and neither will her mother.'

Nicholas took a step towards the Marquess, his raised fists clenched tightly. The Marquess cringed back in his seat, his hands up, his previously self-righteous face now ashen white.

'Hit me, Kingsford, and I'll make it even worse for her,' he said, his voice trembling. 'Do as I say and she will be safe.'

Nicholas froze, then slowly lowered his fists to his sides. The temptation to let the Marquess feel the magnitude of his anger was so intense Nicholas could barely contain it, but that would not do. It was essential that he keep his boiling temper firmly under control if he was to get the better of the Marquess and avoid causing any harm to Charlotte.

'You are beneath contempt,' he uttered through clenched teeth.

The Marquess picked up his glass again, his hand visibly shaking, realised it was empty and replaced it on the table. 'That's as may be, Kingsford, but you will do as I demand or that little chit will be disgraced in the eyes of society, as will her entire family.' He looked up at Nicholas, a smirk distorting his lips. 'The choice is yours, Kingsford. Ruin yourself or ruin that little strumpet.'

There was still a third choice, one that his clenched muscles and boiling blood was desperate to unleash. He could beat the Marquess within an inch of his life, then toss him out on the street. But that was a choice that would not help Charlotte and had to be reluctantly dismissed.

He drew in a series of long, deep breaths to try to calm the fury that was raging within him and threatening to explode. 'You'd destroy a woman's reputation just because you can't bear the thought of having lost money at the gaming tables,' he stated, slowly and precisely. 'Money you can easily afford to lose. Money that I might remind you has gone to a very worthy cause. What sort of man are you? Certainly you're no gentleman. You despicable churl.'

The Marquess remained unmoved by Nicholas's disdain, instead puffed himself up in self-righteous indignation. 'You accuse me of not being a gentleman. You're the one who was unable to show the restraint demanded of a gentleman. Do I need to remind you that it was you who was making an unmarried lady moan and cry out like some cheap bawd? My valet was taking the air and couldn't help but hear what you were up to, said the wench was screaming out—'

He had gone too far. Nicholas was across the room before the Marquess had time to react. He pulled him out of his chair by his collar and crushed him against the wall.

'Hit me, Kingsford, and the lady will be ruined,' he coughed out through a constricted throat. 'I'll tell the world what you did, what she did. That she's nothing but a cheap hussy.'

Nicholas paused, his face an inch from the Marquess's, his fist drawn back, ready to silence the Marquess's foul words.

'She'll be humiliated, the dishonour will be unbearable,' the Marquess choked out.

He was right. The temptation to beat this low life

had to be resisted. It might go some way towards quenching Nicholas's fury, but it would only make the situation worse for Charlotte. And the Marquess was also right about Nicholas. He should have shown more restraint. He should have acted like a gentleman. He only had himself to blame and only he could make this situation right. He released the Marquess, who slumped down on to the floor.

He nodded his agreement. 'All right. I'll contact the newspapers.'

The Marquess stood up, coughed several times, then adjusted his collar, which had become dislodged during the fracas.

'But not without a guarantee that Lady Charlotte's reputation is safe.'

'You have my word as a gentleman,' the Marquess said, attempting to puff himself up, but coughing again instead.

Nicholas released a mirthless laugh. 'Obviously that will not be enough. What I demand from you is a signed note on stationery bearing your crest stating that you have blackmailed me into making the claim of cheating at cards in exchange for preserving a young lady's reputation. Once I have that letter I will write to the newspapers. If you go back on your word and say anything about Charlotte, I will release your letter and your reputation will be destroyed. Agreed?'

The Marquess thought for a second, then nodded. 'And when your reputation is in tatters, I assume you'll be returning to Europe.'

Nicholas shrugged. He had no idea what the future would hold, but he knew his position in society would now be untenable. Society could tolerate a lot from a man of his position. He could fail to pay his bills, cheat on his wife, take countless mistresses, treat his servants and tenants with any level of cruelty he cared to, and it would all be forgiven and forgotten. But cheating at cards was one sin they would never forgive.

'I'll show myself out, shall I?' The Marquess waited, as if expecting Nicholas to say goodbye, then slunk off towards the door.

Nicholas sat at his desk and released a resigned sigh. He pulled out a pile of papers and unscrewed the lid of his ink pot. It was lucky he no longer had any interest in gambling because after he wrote these letters no one would consider playing cards with him again. Nor would anyone invite him into their homes, the membership at all his clubs would be terminated and society as a whole would turn its back on him.

He dipped his pen in the ink and wrote a series of announcements, declaring himself to be a card cheat who had taken money off the Marquess of Boswick by deception. The letters completed, the envelopes addressed, all he had to do now was wait till he received the Marquess's letter and he would post them to all the major newspapers read by members of society.

That completed, he stood up and once again looked out the window, this time seeing nothing of the scene outside. He had believed himself tired of the life that he lived. Well, once his letters were published that life would change for ever. What his future now held he had no idea.

Chapter Sixteen

'You had a lucky escape, that's for certain.' Charlotte's mother looked up at her from behind the newspaper, folded it up and continued eating her breakfast. 'I always knew that the Duke of Kingsford was no good.'

Charlotte fought to stifle any reaction. She did not want her mother to know how the mere mention of Nicholas's name caused her heart to jump within her chest and a painful agitation to erupt in her stomach.

She pushed away her plate. Despite hardly eating for more than a month, she had no appetite and couldn't face the food in front of her. It was five weeks and one day since she'd last seen him and it had been five weeks and one day of torture. She had tried hard not to think about him, but it seemed the harder she tried the more difficult it got. He was constantly in her thoughts throughout the day and even invaded her night-time dreams, giving her no escape from the relentless misery that gripped her.

'Yes, Mother, perhaps you're right,' she chose to respond, rather than pointing out that not long ago her mother hadn't cared one little bit whether the Duke was *no good* or not. She hadn't cared if he had a mistress, hadn't cared that he was a rake. All she had cared about was how quickly she could get him up the aisle and married off to her daughter.

Her mother tapped the folded newspaper. 'And that just proves it. The man is a complete scoundrel. It's just fortunate your brother is not here to see this. He'd be outraged, and quite rightly. too. You should read this.' She pushed the newspaper across the table in Charlotte's direction.

Charlotte did not want to read about what Nicholas had been up to. She did not need to know what scandal he had been involved in. She knew he moved in the same set as the Prince of Wales, the so-called fast set. The papers loved reporting the more disreputable activities the Prince and that crowd of aristocrats got up to, and she knew that Nicholas's behaviour was even more disreputable than most. The last thing she needed to hear about was that he had been seen about town with a married woman or had been caught in one of London's less reputable establishments.

Despite that, she reached out and pulled the newspaper towards her. It was as if her mind and curiosity were refusing to protect her shattered heart. They were determined to see just what level of torture she could endure.

'Read the public notices,' her mother commanded.

Charlotte scanned down the birth and death notices, advertisements for skin lightening tonics and pills guaranteed to cure every ailment known to man, and lists of people who had been forced to declare bankruptcy and were now facing time in the debtors' prison. Not surprisingly, those notices contained no mention of Nicholas. Then she saw it. Nicholas Richmond, the Seventh Duke of Kingsford, admitting that at a recent party hosted at the Boswick estate in Somerset he had cheated at cards on two consecutive nights and unlawfully taken money off the Marquess of Boswick.

She dropped the paper as if it was scorching her fingers. 'It's not true,' she gasped out. 'He did not cheat. I was there on the first night. I was seated right beside him. I know he didn't cheat. This...' She pounded her fist on the paper. 'This is a complete lie.'

Her mother shook her head and signalled to the footman to pour her another cup of tea. 'It must be true, Charlotte. It's there in black and white. The man has admitted it himself. He's a cheat. It's appalling. He'll be shunned now and quite rightly, too. We should only be grateful that he's not dragging our good name down with his.'

'But I was there, Mother. I know he did not cheat.' Charlotte's voice was rising, causing her mother to frown.

'Settle down, Charlotte, there's no need to raise your voice. You're hardly an expert when it comes to cards. It was the first time you'd ever watched men playing, so you couldn't possibly know what he was up to. If he's been able to fool other card players for all these years, then you can be certain he would fool you as well. No, my dear, you're better off without that man.' She took a sip of her tea and reclaimed the newspaper.

Charlotte continued to shake her head. 'It's not true,' she said quietly. 'It's simply not true.'

'Well, whether it's true or not it's in the newspaper. Everyone will have read it. You just need to be grateful that you're no longer associated with the rascal.'

She looked across the table at Charlotte, her brows knitting together, and slowly lowered her china cup to its saucer. 'Although we might be able to use this to get you some sympathy. It will certainly be a good talking point at the next social event we attend.' Her mother nodded and smiled. 'Yes, this might just work to our advantage.'

Charlotte stared back at her mother, too shocked to speak. Was that all she could think about, how this could improve her daughter's marriage prospects? A good man's reputation had been destroyed. How could she possibly be thinking about how it would work to their advantage?

But why should she be surprised? Wasn't that the only thing her mother ever thought about? Charlotte had only one Season left, maybe two at the most, until she was officially on the shelf. Getting her only daughter married off was her mother's constant obsession, nothing else mattered.

'I think there are more important things to consider, such as clearing the Duke's good name, or at the very least finding out why he put that lie in the paper,' she shot back at her mother.

'Don't be ridiculous. You need to forget all about that man and move on.'

Under normal circumstances Charlotte would agree with her mother. She did indeed need to *forget all about that man and move on*, but these were no longer normal circumstances.

She looked across the table at the newspaper. His declaration made no sense. Why on earth would he make a false claim? Something must have happened since she last saw him to cause him to tell such a lie and somehow Charlotte had to find out the truth.

Her mother had told her she was being foolish. She had even tried to forbid it from happening, had argued that it was now more essential than ever to put distance between herself and the Duke of Kingsford, but Charlotte had refused to listen. She was adamant. She would travel down to London immediately to talk to Nicholas in person and find out the truth. Eventually she wore down her exasperated mother and the only concession Charlotte was prepared to make to her was that she would take Betsy as her chaperon and do everything she could to make sure no one saw what she was doing.

The coach was quickly organised and the two women headed off to the local train station to make the journey up to London. As she paced up and down the small station, Charlotte also began to wonder if her mother hadn't been right and this was a very bad idea. Seeing Nicholas again was going to cause further hurt to her already damaged heart. But what choice did she have? She had to find out the truth. A letter would not suffice. She had to look Nicholas straight in the eye and find out why he had made that false claim in the newspaper.

The steam train hissed into the station, sending smoke billowing around their legs. Charlotte was so grateful that the train would get her to London and back in the same day, although she was unsure whether her impatience would be able to tolerate even such a fast journey. She wanted to see Nicholas immediately.

They took their seats in the first-class compartment. Charlotte tried to remain seated and watch the countryside go by outside the window, but it was impossible. She needed to be moving or her desperation to be in London, to see Nicholas and sort out this bizarre situation, would cause her to burst.

Throughout the journey she repeatedly stood up and sat down. She even walked up and down the narrow corridor several times, causing the groups of men chatting together and smoking pipes and cigars to raise their eyebrows and give each other sideways looks. If Charlotte had the energy, she would have got angry at these men who expected a woman to sit in docile stillness while they were free to wander at will. She would have given them a piece of her mind. But luckily for them she did not have the energy right now.

Arriving at London's busy Paddington Station, she pushed through the jostling crowds and hailed a hansom cab to Nicholas's town house. The driver was highly entertained to pick up two ladies travelling alone, but his amusement died when Charlotte used her sternest voice to give him strict instructions to take them directly to the Mayfair address and promised him an additional fee to ensure he did so with as much haste as possible. The busy London streets, packed with horses, carts, omnibuses, pedestrians and men on bicycles did nothing to settle Charlotte's mounting impatience, but finally, after what seemed like an interminable journey, they arrived at Nicholas's town house.

She quickly paid the driver, rushed up the steps and pounded on the front door. A footman opened it, looked both ways along the street, as if expecting to see the gentleman who was accompanying these two young ladies. Charlotte huffed her disapproval at his assumption and told the footman she wanted to see Nicholas immediately.

'I'm afraid the Duke is unavailable to see visitors at present,' the footman said in dismissal.

'Then I'll wait.' She pushed past the astonished man, followed by a blushing Betsy.

The footman rushed down the hallway, managing to get in front of her just before she entered the drawing room.

He blocked her way and indicated towards the reception room. 'If you'll wait a moment, madam, I'll see if the Duke is available to take visitors.'

Charlotte hesitated, her hand reaching out for the doorknob. Would it be wise to just burst in on Nicholas? The footman was obviously trying to protect his master. But from what? Perhaps Nicholas was with another woman. With a sinking heart she realised that was a definite possibility. She knew he did not cheat at cards. While that claim was a lie, she knew his reputation as a rake was grounded in fact. He'd had many women before their first kiss, no doubt had had count-less others during the years they were apart, and that was a habit he was unlikely to have broken.

She stepped back from the door and lowered her extended arm. As much as she wanted to talk to Nich-olas, seeing him with another woman was something she did not want to witness, something which she was sure would completely destroy her. But it was essen-tial that she see him to find out why he had made that outlandish claim in the papers.

She drew in a deep breath and fought to ignore the pain in her chest. 'Tell him Lady Charlotte FitzRoy wants to talk to him and that it is extremely impor-tant and urgent.'

The footman opened the door a fraction as if wor-ried that Charlotte was going to cast him aside and force her way in. He slid around the door, never tak-ing his eyes off Charlotte, then shut it behind him.

Charlotte paced a circle around the entrance hall, from the front door to the ornate stairway. Her impa-tience to get this situation sorted out and to discover the truth was building up inside her, overriding the pain and sorrow that had been gripping her so in-tensely for the last five weeks.

She was sure she would explode if she didn't soon find out why Nicholas had made that preposterous ad-mission in the newspapers. And it *was* preposterous. Nicholas was not a cheat. He had many faults, but deep down she knew he was an honest, honourable man.

The footman reopened the door and bowed to her. 'The Duke will see you now, my lady.'

Charlotte pushed past him, hurried into the room,

then stopped. He was standing at the window, the light behind him. How had she forgotten just how breath-takingly handsome he was? It seemed she had and right now she was indeed finding it hard to breathe. No wonder she had fallen so hard for this man. What woman in her right mind wouldn't? His blond hair was longer than it had been when she had last seen it and the dark rings under his eyes suggested that, like herself, he had not been sleeping. But he still looked magnificent.

He, too, seemed to be assessing her appearance and for a moment Charlotte wished she had taken more time with the way she had dressed. She wished she hadn't rushed off to London, but had first styled her hair and changed out of her plain skirt and blouse, but she had been so desperate to see him again, to find out why he had lied, that the thought of changing her clothes hadn't occurred to her. Until now.

'Charlotte, this is unexpected,' Nicholas said, indicating a chair. 'So, what is so urgent that you had to upset my footman?'

His question about her arriving at his home without an invitation caused the seriousness of the situation to crash back down on her. How could she have been distracted, even for just a few seconds, by something as trivial as her clothes and her hair?

'What on earth is this about?' She slammed a news-paper down on the table, the page open to the public notices, his admission circled in ink.

They both looked down at the paper and Charlotte noticed the splodges of ink dotting the entire page, showing how her frantic circling had been done with a furiously wielded pen. He looked back up.

'Well?' she demanded, thumping the page with her forefinger.

He raised his hands, palms upward, and shrugged. 'What can I say? I was caught. I had no option but to admit my fault.'

Charlotte shook her head furiously. She could not believe what she was hearing. She would not accept it. Why was he saying that? He was no cheat. 'But I was seated beside you the entire time. If you had been cheating, I would have seen. This is wrong, so why did you put this notice in the paper? Why? It makes no sense.'

To her annoyance he shrugged again. 'It was your first time, Charlotte. You were inexperienced. If you had played cards as often as I have, you would have been able to spot when a man was cheating. Just accept it for what it is and leave it alone. I'm an immoral cad. I'm everything you ever thought I was.'

Her heart raced, her muscles tensed. 'No. I can't believe it. I won't believe it. It can't be true.' Charlotte could hear the pleading in her voice. Somehow he had to make this right. If he had cheated at cards then, she had to question everything she had ever believed about Nicholas Richmond. She had always known him to be a rake, but she also knew him to have a sense of honour, to be essentially a good man, and she would not, could not, believe otherwise.

'Then why else would I put such an announcement in the paper?' He looked back down at the ink-splattered newspaper. 'Why would I say it if it wasn't true? I was caught out and I had to make amends.'

'But...' Charlotte moved over to the nearest seat, her legs suddenly weak. 'That's what I want to know. That's why I came to London so you could explain it to me, to tell me why you did it, why you made an admission that wasn't true.'

'I'm sorry, Charlotte.' His voice was not much more than a whisper.

She looked up at him, shaking her head, wanting him to say more.

He continued to stare down at her, saying nothing.

Could it be true? Could he really be a cheat? Was the money he raised for the charity hospital all gained under false pretences? She still could hardly believe it was true, but he had looked her straight in the eye and admitted it to her. He was a cheat.

He drew in a deep breath and rang the small brass bell on the table. Charlotte saw the footman appear in the room.

'Lady Charlotte is leaving now. Can you please order a hansom cab and ensure she and her lady's maid get safely on the next train back to Devon.'

Was that it? She continued looking at him, her eyes beseeching him to explain, to make this right. 'Nicholas?' she pleaded, desperate for him to say something, anything.

'I'm sorry, Charlotte,' he repeated, turning his back on her and looking out of the window.

She remained standing in the middle of the room, unable to move. As if in a dream she felt Betsy's hand on her arm. On legs that felt like lead she allowed

Betsy to guide her out of the room. Without saying goodbye to Nicholas, she left his house, her last illusion about him completely shattered.

Chapter Seventeen

Charlotte was a fool, a complete fool. Nicholas had stated it clearly and unambiguously to her face that he was indeed a cheat. He had cheated in front of her, had obtained money for her charity through cheating. And yet she still could not accept that it was the truth.

A sensible woman would just forget all about him and move on with her life. Charlotte had always believed herself to be sensible, but it seemed she was wrong about that as well. The strong feelings she still harboured for Nicholas showed just how much of a deluded fool she actually was.

As difficult as it was to believe, she just had to accept that he was not the man she thought he was. She had been trusting and naive, but he had opened up her eyes to the truth. Nicholas was not as honourable as she had assumed. The sooner she accepted that, the sooner she could shake off the crushing weight she was carrying around with her.

And that was exactly what it did feel like, as if she was carrying a heavy burden that was draining her of all energy. Charlotte usually spent her days in busy activity, but since returning from London a lassitude had descended on her and she was spending countless hours seated at the window, staring out and seeing nothing. It was as if the world had lost all its colour, all its joy. She even had no interest in reading, something she would once have thought impossible. When she did move from her chair, it was as if she was wandering around in a fog, unsure where she was going or what she was doing. Her brother and sister-in-law had tried to help, but nothing they did or said could bring her out of this despondent state.

She watched the gardener raking up the leaves, piling them up on to a wheelbarrow and pushing them up the path to be added to a fire, its plume of smoke rising from behind the trees. A maid entered the room to remove Charlotte's untouched afternoon tea.

The maid bobbed a curtsy, the tea tray in her hands. 'Will there be anything else, my lady?' she asked politely.

Charlotte shook her head and shame washed over her as the busy young woman departed. She had indulged herself for too long. The servants couldn't sit around moping every time they experienced an upset. They couldn't wallow in self-pity the way she was; they had no choice but to keep busy.

And that was exactly what Charlotte would do. It was time she pulled herself together and took some action. She couldn't make what Nicholas had done right, but she had to at least try to undo some of the damage.

She moved to her writing desk and took out a piece of paper, her pen and a bottle of ink. Nicholas was not the only one to have committed a great wrong. She, too, had benefitted from his cheating and that wrong had to be made right.

Unknowingly she had taken money from the Marquess of Boswick under false pretences. The hospital trust had no right to money that had been acquired in such a disgraceful manner. The cheques had already been cashed and building work had begun on the hospital conversion so there was no way that the cheques could be returned to the Marquess. But at the very least the man deserved a heartfelt apology from her.

She could only hope that Nicholas had at least made good on the money he had effectively stolen from the Marquess and had reimbursed him every last penny. She put pen to paper, expressing her regret at what had happened, and assuring the Marquess that if Nicholas had not returned the money then she was prepared to reimburse him. Charlotte was not sure how she would achieve this. The FitzRoys already had a mountain of debts that needed to be repaid, but Charlotte would find a way, she had to. She could not be part of such an appalling act of deception. She could only hope that the Marquess would give her time to find the money and would not expect work on the hospital to stop so the charity could pay back the money. It would break her heart even further if the people of the East End had to suffer because of Nicholas's dishonesty.

She signed the letter with yet another apology for her unwitting part in this deception and with a heavy heart sealed the envelope and fixed on a stamp. Instead of calling for the footman she decided to walk to the village and post the letter herself. It would give her something to do and stop her from returning to the seat by the window and her self-indulgent wallowing.

Hopefully the walk would also distract her overactive mind. Not that anything seemed capable of distracting her from thoughts of Nicholas. Nothing could stop images of him from whirling round in her mind, those unanswered questions from tormenting her.

She walked down the tree-lined driveway, going over and over everything that had happened between her and Nicholas and everything he had said. It didn't matter how many times she thought it through, how much she scrutinised every minute detail, she continued to feel an overwhelming sense of disbelief at what he had done.

She passed a gardener still hard at work. Despite her sorrow she forced herself to smile a friendly greeting as the man tipped his cloth cap at her.

She maintained that happy facade when she reached the village, smiling at the local people, going about their daily activities. Her ability to smile when inside she felt like crying surprised her, but no one else needed to be burdened by her own misery.

At the red pillar box she paused, the letter suspended in the slot. She hoped for the best, dropped the letter into the slot and immediately turned around to retrace her steps back to the house. The walk had done little to lift her mood, and she suspected it would be a long time before she would once again smile with genuine happiness, but despite that, she was determined to remain busy until she heard from the Marquess.

* * *

A week later Betsy came into Charlotte's private drawing room, carrying a letter on a silver tray bearing the Marquess of Boswick's crest. Charlotte ripped open the letter and quickly scanned the contents. It contained both good and bad news. The bad news was, the Marquess informed her, that Nicholas had acted like a complete cad and had not paid back the money he had all but stolen from him. The good news was the Marquess was indeed prepared to act like a gentleman. He had generously offered to overlook the debt and said the charity hospital could keep the money, despite, as he put it, the nefarious and underhand manner by which it was acquired.

Charlotte instantly put pen to paper. She wrote one letter to the Marquess, thanking him effusively for his generosity, his kindness and his forgiving heart. Then she wrote a letter to the East End Charity Hospital Trust's board. The Marquess might not want to be paid back, but she would ensure he would be rewarded in some way for his generosity. She entreated the board to place a prominent brass plaque on the hospital with the Marquess of Boswick's name on it, so his generosity towards the hospital would be honoured in perpetuity. It was the very least she could do for a man who had acted impeccably and shown that he at least was an upstanding, admirable gentleman.

Chapter Eighteen

The official unveiling of the plaque to honour the Marquess of Boswick's generous contribution to London's East End Charity Hospital was turning out to be a triumph.

Coloured bunting decorated the neighbourhood, strung from window to window, across the road, brightening up the drab narrow streets of brick terrace houses. The roads had been swept clean. Children's faces had been scrubbed and their hair brushed. A brass band was playing cheerful tunes and children were dancing in the streets. The locals, dressed in their finest Sunday best, were all out on the street to celebrate the momentous occasion and were taking full advantage of the free food spread out on tables covered in stiff white tablecloths.

The usually sombre area, where people struggled to eke out a subsistence living, had taken on a festive air. Even the weather had got into the spirit of the occasion and the spring sun was shining in a clear blue sky.

The Marquess, dressed formally in top hat and tails,

was looking as proud as Punch, his chest puffed up, his chin high, a satisfied smile on his face.

The board chairman signalled for the band to stop playing and for the noisy, bustling crowd to settle down. When he'd achieved a sufficient level of silence, he mounted the podium and made a speech thanking the Marquess for his generous support and commending him as a great man and an inspiration to all.

He then stood back to allow the smiling Marquess to pull a tasselled gold cord, which drew open the maroon velvet curtain and revealed a large brass plaque etched with the Marquess's name and expressing the appreciation of the board and the people of London's East End for his magnanimous contribution to the hospital.

The crowd burst into a spontaneous round of three cheers for the Marquess and the band struck up a celebratory tune. The chairman and his wife, and other board members, lined up to shake the Marquess's hand and express their appreciation. Journalists from several local, and even a few national, newspapers were in attendance and hovered around, anxious to interview the heroic patron who had so generously donated such a large amount of his money to help those less fortunate than himself.

Charlotte watched from the crowd. It couldn't have gone better and she was so pleased that today's commemoration would go some way to undoing the damage that Nicholas had done. Before the unveiling she had toured the hospital and was impressed to see the modern facilities. The Marquess's money had been well spent. The new hospital would provide free medical help to those who could not afford it and save countless people from unnecessary suffering. What the Marquess had done was highly commendable and Charlotte reminded herself that he had every right to bask in the repeated congratulations from the board, and the admiration of the local people and the wider public when they read their newspapers tomorrow morning.

Charlotte had once held a low opinion of the Marquess, but his generosity in allowing the hospital to keep his money changed all that. It no longer mattered that originally he'd no intention of donating money to the hospital. She did not care that when he had been told that Nicholas was giving his winnings to the charity he had sneered and said that people should be capable of looking after themselves. If they couldn't afford to pay for their own medical treatment, then it had to be due to their laziness or bad habits. At the time Charlotte had been tempted to point out to the Marquess that he was one of the laziest men she had ever met, having never worked a day in his life, preferring instead to dedicate himself solely to pleasure. But today he was a man worthy of respect and Charlotte wanted to let him know just how much she appreciated everything he had done.

Not only had he allowed the hospital to keep the funds, but he had never once mentioned that the money had been acquired through deception. He could have demanded the money back. Told the hospital and the public at large that it had been fraudulently acquired. He could have further dragged Nicholas's name through the mud, but he chose not to. For that, and much more, the Marquess deserved full credit.

Once the board members had finished heaping praise on the Marquess she would take the opportunity to thank him in person for all that he had done. The Marquess certainly appeared to be enjoying all the adulation. Charlotte couldn't stop herself from making an unkind comparison to a rooster as he strutted up and down the stage, his chest thrust out, his voice and laughter booming out above the noise of the crowd. Charlotte knew she was being unfair. The Marquess *should* feel proud of what he had done. He had saved the hospital and he had saved Nicholas from further degradation. He was entitled to a bit of strutting and to bask in the crowd's adulation.

The only people the Marquess seemed reluctant to accept praise from were the locals. As soon as one tried to approach him and express their thanks, he managed to turn his back and talk to someone else, leaving the poor man or woman standing with their unshaken hand outstretched. It seemed the Marquess's generosity didn't extend to actually mixing with the people he had helped.

But Charlotte refused to even criticise the man for his impolite behaviour. If he could show his generosity of spirit by letting the hospital keep his money and not revealing how it had been acquired, then she, too, could show some generosity of spirit and forgive him for what appeared to be otherwise unconscionable rudeness.

Charlotte waited till the journalists had finished their interviews and the adoring crowd around the

Marquess had started to thin out, then edged her way through the happy throng of local people enjoying themselves and tapped the Marquess lightly on the arm to get his attention.

He turned towards her, beaming with pride and wearing a joyous smile. He looked at Charlotte and his smile faltered slightly, before returning even wider and more self-satisfied. 'Lady Charlotte, it's a pleasure to see you again.'

'And it's a pleasure to see you, my lord. I just want to thank you again, in person. It's a wonderful thing that you've done, helping so many people who are less fortunate than yourself. Now the people of the East End will have somewhere to go when they are ill and can't afford the expenses of a doctor.'

The Marquess's lip curled with scorn. 'Well, as I've said before, they should fend for themselves and not expect to be supported by other people's money.'

That was not the response Charlotte had expected. It seemed his attitude to the poor had not moved in the slightest, despite his generosity. 'You don't agree with the philosophy of the hospital? Then why were you so willing to allow them to keep the money?'

He sneered at Charlotte and then resumed smiling as another member of the committee thanked him and shook his hand. 'You know very well why I couldn't ask for the money back,' he said out of the side of his mouth. 'Let's not pretend this is anything other than what it is. We both have reputations to preserve and I for one am not prepared to do anything to risk mine.'

Charlotte shook her head, not knowing what the Marquess was alluding to. 'Reputations? After today your reputation as a kind and generous man will be well known, but what has my reputation got to do with this?'

'Oh, for goodness' sake, just leave me alone, can't you? I sent that letter to Nicholas so your reputation is safe and that should be the end to it.'

Placing his hand on her shoulder, he moved her aside, puffed out his chest and moved off to once again be thanked by the chairman of the board, leaving Charlotte standing alone on the pavement, completely bewildered.

What had he written in his letter to Nicholas? What had her reputation got to do with anything? Surely he didn't think she had been working with Nicholas to cheat him out of the money? He must realise that wasn't so. And even if he did, surely he would want to ruin her reputation, just as he had done with Nicholas, not save it. And Nicholas knew she had nothing to do with the cheating, so what would he have promised the Marquess? It made no sense.

Charlotte shook her head slowly, trying to shake off the confusion. She didn't really care what the Marquess thought of her, or her reputation, but his behaviour was strange, to say the least. This had to have something to do with Nicholas's notice in the newspaper, but what Charlotte had no idea. There was only one thing for it, she had to find out exactly what the Marquess meant.

The band was still playing a happy tune. Couples were now dancing, the sound of their feet in wooden clogs loud on the cobbled street. It looked as though the street party would continue for some time. But the journalists had left and the board members were now talking to the Marquess in a more serious tone. Presumably they were trying to interest him in providing ongoing support for the hospital. Charlotte watched as the Marquess excused himself and headed towards his carriage, its shiny black elegance standing out against the backdrop of the drab, scruffy street.

A liveried footman was fully occupied shooing away the local children who seemed to think the carriage was part of the day's entertainment and were trying to climb up its wheels and on to the plush seats.

Charlotte rushed forward, cutting off the Marquess's progress and firmly took hold of his arm. He looked down at her fingers gripping his arm and sneered, 'That's hardly the behaviour of a lady, is it, Lady Charlotte, but I suppose accosting men in the street is something you're in the habit of doing.'

Charlotte ignored his barb. 'What promise did you make to Nicholas?'

His sneer turned decidedly salacious. 'You honestly don't expect me to believe that you don't know. After such a deal you'd think Kingsford would be expecting you to show your appreciation for what he'd done for you. I know I certainly would.'

She shook her head, trying to ignore the way he was looking at her, as if she was a tasty morsel that he was looking forward to eating. 'Well, you're wrong, he hasn't. So perhaps you'd like to enlighten me about this promise you made.'

'If you insist, Lady Charlotte,' he said with a nasty grin. 'My valet saw you outside in the middle of the night. And what a tale he had to tell.' He looked down at her chest and actually licked his lips. 'He got to see your duckies, said they were on display for all to see, and what's more, there was Kingsford, his hand up your dress, the lucky rascal.'

Charlotte's own hand left the Marquess's arm and shot to her mouth, but not before a loud gasp had escaped. The Marquess laughed loudly, enjoying her discomfort. 'Is that enlightening enough for you, Lady Charlotte? Or do you want me to go into more details about what my valet saw? It's quite an enjoyable story, I must say.'

Charlotte shook her head, unable to bring the thoughts whirling through her head into any order.

The Marquess laughed again. 'Oh, come, come, Lady Charlotte. No need to be coy now. Don't you want to hear all that the man had to say? I certainly found his description entertaining and rewarded the man handsomely for bringing me such useful intelligence.' The Marquess smirked and tapped his chin as if trying to recall. 'What else did he say? Oh, yes, now I remember. He said you were putting on quite a performance, panting, moaning and groaning. To use his words, you was carrying on like a right little strumpet.' He looked around at the local people, still dancing and enjoying their day out. 'No wonder you feel comfortable with the likes of them.' He looked back down at Charlotte. 'After all, your behaviour was not unlike that of an East End whore.'

For possibly the first time in her life Charlotte was lost for words. She opened her mouth to tell the Marquess exactly what she thought of him, but no words came.

'I wonder what the good people on the charity hospital board would think if they knew what you got up to, not to mention the rest of society. But don't worry.' He laughed. 'This information is so valuable I made sure my valet kept it to himself. And as long as Kingsford doesn't spill the beans, as long as he keeps maintaining that he is a cheat and that I'm the better card player, you are safe. Although Kingsford's reputation is now in tatters, which is no less than the man deserves.'

'You blackmailed Nicholas?' Charlotte's voice came out in a strangled gasp. 'You made him print those lies in the newspaper so you wouldn't tell people what your valet saw? You're despicable, you're... you're...'

'Oh, don't be so melodramatic,' he growled. 'I ensured your reputation is safe. After how you had behaved, you should be thanking me, not standing there looking as though you've just been told I strangled your favourite pet. Maybe you should even give me a little taste of what you gave Kingsford, just to show your appreciation.'

Charlotte jumped back as if she'd been physically attacked, causing the Marquess to laugh louder.

'Now, if you'll excuse me, I want to get home as soon as possible so I can have a long bath and wash off the stink of these people.'

The Marquess pushed past her, forced his way through the dancing couples and climbed into his carriage. Without a backward glance he drove off, leaving a stunned Charlotte standing alone on the pavement.

Chapter Nineteen

Nicholas stared at the newspaper clutched tightly in his white-knuckled hands. Was the woman completely insane? Had she lost all sense of reason? Even for Charlotte, who seemed to enjoy shocking an easily shocked society, this was going too far.

He re-read the public notice, trying to absorb the full ramifications of the words.

Lady Charlotte FitzRoy, daughter of the late Duke of Knightsbrook and sister of the present Duke of Knightsbrook, categorically refutes the Marquess of Boswick's claim that Nicholas Richmond, the Duke of Kingsford, cheated at cards when at the Marquess's estate and makes the following statement:

'I was seated beside the Duke of Kingsford throughout the entire card game and give my assurance that at no time did the Duke cheat. I would also like to state for the record that the reason the Duke of Kingsford put a public no-

tice in this newspaper, claiming he had cheated, was because he was being blackmailed by the Marquess of Boswick.

'The Marquess was threatening to expose the fact that, during the party hosted at the Marquess's estate, the Duke and I behaved in a manner which the Marquess believed would ruin my reputation. The Marquess was exploiting society's unwritten rule that a woman who transgresses against the strictures regarding women's sexual behaviour will be shunned by society.

'Those unwritten rules dictate that while men can have mistresses, visit whorehouses, seduce servants and behave in any way they want, an unmarried woman has to maintain her chastity and all respectable women are expected to feign a dislike of sex.

'These are rules I abhor, rules that keep women in a state of subjection while giving complete freedom to men. And the Marquess's behaviour demonstrates how these rules can be used against women and, in this case, used to destroy the reputation of a good man.

'It is time that such ridiculous rules be thrown where they belong, in the dustbin of history.'

Nicholas rubbed his hand across his forehead. 'Oh, Charlotte, Charlotte...you don't understand what you have done.'

While he agreed with every word she said about how society treated women, she should not have said it, and not in such a public forum. Society would be scandalised. She would never live this down.

If she had made this pronouncement at a social event, there would have been a possibility of covering it up, but not now. Now all of England knew what had happened between them and there was no going back.

He placed the newspaper on the breakfast table and shook his head slowly. No, she should not have done it, but a small part of him couldn't help but admire her. She was a woman of such strong conviction and, ironically, while society might now despise her for what they consider her low morals, she had shown that she was an extremely moral woman. Her sense of morality and justice was so high she was prepared to sacrifice so much to undo a wrong, to sacrifice herself to save him and to defend her belief in what was right. How could he not be impressed by such a woman?

He looked back down at the folded newspaper. But she still should not have done it and, if she had consulted him before writing to the papers, he would have advised her against it and done everything he could to talk her out of it. Although talking Charlotte out of doing exactly what she wanted was never an easy task.

He had been so determined to make sure her reputation was protected and now, to save his reputation, she had destroyed her own. That was both admirable and extremely stupid, in equal measures. He would have survived society's disapproval—after all, he was a man and society was much more forgiving of a man who transgressed, particularly one with a title—but she would never survive this.

His fingers drummed out a rhythm on the newspaper as he contemplated how this damage could be undone. He had to save her. He had to ensure she was not ostracised from society.

His drumming fingers stilled. There was only one way that could be achieved. He would have to marry Charlotte FitzRoy.

He looked out of the window as he took in the full ramification of what he was thinking. Marriage was not what he wanted, but there was no other way. Being married to him would not entirely redeem Charlotte in society's eyes, but it would go some way to undoing the enormous damage she had done to herself with this notice.

It was not what he wanted, but what choice did he have? He owed it to Charlotte to do whatever it took to save her. After all, she wouldn't be in this position if it wasn't for him. If, as the Marquess had said, he had acted like a gentleman when they were alone together, then none of this would have happened. If he had kept his hands to himself the Marquess would not have been able to blackmail him, he would not have had to put the notice in the paper to save Charlotte's reputation and Charlotte would not have followed up by putting in a notice of her own to save his reputation. This was all his fault and it was up to him to undo the damage that he had created.

He slammed his fist down on the newspaper. Yes, he would have to marry Charlotte FitzRoy.

Now that he had made that decision there was no time to lose. He stood up from the breakfast table, strode into the corridor and called out to his valet. When the man appeared, Nicholas gave him instructions to pack a bag as quickly as possible so Nicholas could travel to Devon on the next available train.

He rushed up the stairs, followed by his valet. Nicholas would have to make all haste to undo this damage as soon as possible if Charlotte's good name was to be saved. He rubbed his chin. How long since he had shaved? He couldn't remember. That would not do, especially now that he was about to make a proposal of marriage. He halted halfway up the stairs, causing his valet to almost crash into him.

A proposal of marriage. He would be making a proposal. He would be married to Charlotte FitzRoy.

That was almost as difficult to comprehend as the notice she had placed in the newspaper. What would marriage to Charlotte be like? He had sworn he would never marry, but these were exceptional circumstances and they called for exceptional behaviour from him.

He resumed walking up the stairs. He would be married to Charlotte. He would wake up next to her every morning, would go to sleep every evening with her by his side. Was that such a bad prospect? He had to admit it was, in fact, a rather attractive idea.

He rushed into his bedroom and threw off his clothes as his valet removed the grey three-piece suit for Nicholas to wear on the journey. He attempted to help Nicholas dress, but there was no time for that. Nicholas instructed him to begin packing while he shaved, washed and dressed himself. He got a slight disapproving look from the valet for not letting him do his job properly, then the man jumped into action, pulling out shirts, cravats, day and evening suits.

'Pack my morning suit as well,' he called out to

his valet. He would need his morning suit to wear on his wedding day.

Nicholas paused and stared at himself in the looking glass, his lathered soap brush held against his cheek.

His wedding day.

He was to have a wedding day, followed by a wedding night. That alone was worth the sacrifice of becoming a married man. Nicholas smiled, lathered his face and ran the razor across his cheek. After their encounter at Boswick he knew that Charlotte had a passionate nature. In fact, everything she did she did with passion, including sending that letter to the newspapers. There was no doubt in his mind that their wedding night was going to be spectacular. And every other night and day in the future together.

He wiped the razor on the towel and continued shaving.

Their future together.

What would his future with Charlotte FitzRoy be like? Would their future include children? He hoped it did. Charlotte would make a wonderful mother. She was such a remarkable woman and she would make a remarkable mother to her children. His children. Their children.

He finished shaving and found he was whistling to himself. Perhaps this wasn't such a disaster after all. They would be married. They would have children, maybe even grandchildren and spend the rest of their lives together.

His only regret was that it had taken such a drastic action from Charlotte to make him see that marrying her was exactly what he wanted to do. What he had always wanted.

Yes, marrying was the best solution for this situation and one that was increasingly appealing for Nicholas. He just had to convince Charlotte that it was the best solution for her as well.

A loud scream resonated through Knightsbrook House. Charlotte cringed. She had been tempted to hide the newspapers from her mother, but she was going to find out eventually. It was better to get it over and done with.

'Charlotte, Charlotte, get down here immediately.' Her mother's uncharacteristically screeching voice carried from the breakfast room, down the hallways of Knightsbrook House, up the stairs and into Charlotte's bedroom.

Charlotte drew in a deep, resigned breath, left her room and headed towards her mother's strident cries. Dealing with her mother was inevitably going to be an ordeal, one Charlotte would rather not have to endure, but what's done was done and she stood by every word she had written. She had done the right thing, regardless of what her mother or anyone else thought.

She just had to get through her mother's tirade and keep reminding herself she had done nothing wrong. Society was wrong. The Marquess of Boswick was wrong. She was in the right and she had merely pointed out all those wrongs in an attempt to undo an injustice and to hopefully do something to change a society which was unfair, particularly to women. She had stuck to her principles and she would continue to do so, no matter how angry it made her mother.

She entered the breakfast room and the three people seated at the table turned towards her. Even the footman looked in her direction, curiosity etched on his usually expressionless face.

Her mother threw the newspaper at her, gasping as if unable to speak, her face crimson with rage. The pages fluttered to the floor and the footman bent down to retrieve them.

'Leave it, James,' her mother choked out. 'Leave us.'

The footman bowed, leaving the crumpled newspaper where it had landed, and exited the room.

Her mother continued to gasp, as if the words she wanted to say were stuck in her throat, choking her. Charlotte approached the table, but remained standing. Her brother stood up and even Alexander was looking at her with stern disapproval.

Only her sister-in-law appeared to have taken the public notice in her stride. Rosie sent her a small, sympathetic smile. 'Oh, Charlotte, you're so brave,' she said. 'But are you sure what you did was entirely sensible?'

'Sensible, sensible,' her mother squawked. 'Of course it wasn't sensible, nor was it brave. It's the most...the most... I don't even have the words to describe how utterly stupid you have been. You've ruined yourself. You've ruined this entire family. How could you?'

Alexander retrieved the newspaper from the floor and folded it up. 'The family has weathered worse things than this over the years, Mother,' he said, placing the paper on the table. 'Let's not overreact.'

'Overreact? *Overreact?* I believe I'm being the very definition of calm under the circumstances. Did you not read what your sister wrote? She admitted to… to…and not only did she admit to doing it, she went on to talk about men having mistresses and visiting whorehouses. Things no unmarried woman should even know about, never mind talk about, and in the newspaper of all places. Everyone will have read it. Oh, the shame, the shame.' Her mother closed her eyes tightly and placed her hands on the top of her head as if trying to hide from the world's disapproval.

'She does have a point, though, doesn't she?' Rosie said, picking up the paper and opening it to Charlotte's notice. 'There is one rule for men and one for women. It's completely unfair and it should be changed.'

Her mother looked at her daughter-in-law in horror and ripped the newspaper out of Rosie's hands. 'Who cares if it's fair or not, it's the way it is, and now my daughter will never marry. She'll never be able to hold her head up in public again. The door of every respectable home will be closed to her. She'll never be invited to another ball, ever again.'

'Well, that's one good thing to come out of this, I suppose,' Charlotte said, causing her mother to send a teaspoon flying past her ear, clattering to the floor behind her.

'There's no need to provoke your mother further,' Alexander said quietly, looking in the direction of the abandoned spoon. 'You don't want to give her apoplexy.'

Charlotte looked at her gasping, crimson-faced mother and realised he was right. As tempting as it was, it would be unfair to provoke her mother further. She was suffering enough and she only meant what was best for Charlotte, even if she was completely deluded over what was really in Charlotte's best interests.

'There is, perhaps, a way out of this,' Alexander said, pulling out a chair for Charlotte so she could sit down.

'Yes, yes, you're right,' her mother said before Alexander could continue. 'We could have her committed.' Her mother nodded frantically, her eyes darting from Charlotte to Alexander, as if it was she who had lost her mind. 'Yes, that would explain it all away. We could say that Charlotte went completely mad. She didn't know what she was doing or what she was saying because she was insane. We could even threaten to sue the newspaper for printing the rantings of an unfortunate, mad woman.'

Charlotte's sympathy for her mother's suffering dissolved instantly. Society's opinion meant so much to her that she would rather see her daughter incarcerated in one of the notoriously cruel asylums than face their scorn.

'I do not mean that, Mother,' Alexander said. 'I mean the Duke of Kingsford could do the decent thing and marry my sister.'

'No, that will not be happening,' Charlotte said, springing to her feet, causing her chair to overturn and clatter to the floor. 'That will not be happening,' she repeated, in a louder voice.

Her mother also stood up. 'You're right, Alexander. If we can't get her committed, then he will have to marry her.'

'No, that will not be happening,' Charlotte said again, her voice becoming strained. 'We've already discussed this, Mother. The Duke and I will not be getting married.'

Her mother slammed her hand hard on the table. 'You have no choice. Your foolish notice in the paper has changed everything,' she yelled. 'You will be marrying the Duke, whether or not you or the Duke want to, and the sooner the better.'

Today was the first time in Charlotte's life she had heard her mother raise her voice. It was yet another rule that her mother believed only applied to women. Men could shout as much as they liked, but polite, well-brought-up ladies did not raise their voices, no matter what the provocation.

'And he has no choice. He has to do the decent thing and marry you,' her mother continued in an even louder voice. Charlotte had often been reprimanded for behaving in a manner that her mother described as being like a fishwife. Charlotte was tempted to point out to her mother that right now she was showing decidedly fishwife-like tendencies, but she was sure that would come under her brother's definition of provoking her mother.

'After an escapade like this the only way anyone in this family is going to be able to hold their head up in society is if you marry Nicholas.' Her mother sat down, still staring at Charlotte with unconcealed rage. 'The Duke will know this as well. And if you don't do it to save your own reputation, or the good name and respectable position of this family, then do it to save his. After all, you've destroyed that as well.' She crossed her arms as if that was the final word on the subject.

It was Charlotte's turn to thump the table. 'If you read my letter properly, Mother, you'd know that a man's reputation can survive just about anything, even taking a young woman's so-called virtue.'

Her mother thumped her fist on the table and stared at Charlotte. 'You will be marrying him.'

Charlotte stared back at her with equally unflinching eyes.

'Alexander,' the Dowager screeched, turning her attention to her son. 'Talk some sense into this stupid girl.'

'It would solve this problem, Charlotte,' Alexander said. 'And it would redeem you in the eyes of society.'

'That's up to Charlotte and the Duke,' Rosie said quietly, placing her hand on Alexander's arm. 'After all, marriage is for life and Charlotte should only marry a man she is in love with.'

Alexander sat down and gently patted his wife's hand. 'Yes, you're right, my dear.' He turned and looked at Charlotte. 'If you don't love this man, then obviously you should not be expected to marry him.'

'Has my entire family gone completely insane?' her mother screamed out, grabbing the paper and ripping it into pieces. 'Why are you all talking about love? So what if she doesn't love Nicholas? So what if he doesn't love her? None of that matters. She must marry him to save this family.'

'I will not be marrying anyone,' Charlotte said emphatically. 'And I most certainly will not be marrying Nicholas Richmond.' She sat down and crossed her arms to signal it was her words, not her mother's, that were to be the final ones on this matter.

Chapter Twenty

Being horsewhipped was a definite possibility. He might even be run out of town and told never to darken the doorstep of Knightsbrook House again, but these were outcomes Nicholas would have to deal with if they eventuated. He jumped down from the carriage, looked up at the FitzRoys' three-storey ancestral home, then rushed up the steps. He paused at the top, his hand raised, about to knock on the solid oak door. Over the centuries, how many other men had stood where he was standing now and taken a moment to contemplate their fate? The FitzRoy family had been one of the leading powers in Devon since medieval times. They had once ruled the local area as if it was their own private fiefdom and would have had almost complete control over the lives of all those who lived on their land. Their fortune had taken a major setback of late, due to the gambling habits of the father and grandfather, but they were still a force to be reckoned with. He doubted he was the first man to have fallen foul of the FitzRoy family; he just hoped they'd be merciful.

He pounded the brass knocker. The door was opened immediately and by the Dowager Duchess herself, not a footman. He tried to read her expression. It certainly did not suggest she had ordered the servants to bring out the horsewhips, the stocks or any other devices of punishment. She was smiling at him as if he was the one man in the world she most wanted to see.

At least her lips were smiling. The rest of her appearance contradicted that happy countenance. Her face was flushed, her upright posture was even more rigid than usual, and the smile did not reach her eyes, which were boring into his like a cold assassin staring down at a target.

'Nicholas, how wonderful of you to come so quickly. I assume you've read the papers and have come to propose to my daughter.'

Straight to the point as always.

'Yes, Duchess, I have.'

She nodded her approval, invited him in and stopped a passing maid carrying a feather duster. 'You, girl, arrange tea and sandwiches to be served in the drawing room and make sure a bedroom suite has been prepared for the Duke.'

She smiled back at Nicholas as the maid rushed off to do as she was commanded and instructed him to follow her into the drawing room.

'I take it you and the Duke of Knightsbrook have given your blessing for this marriage,' Nicholas asked as the Dowager sat down on the chaise longue and indicated that Nicholas take a seat.

'Yes, we have and I think we should have the banns read at our local church this Sunday. Then we should have the wedding here at Knightsbrook House as soon as possible. I think a quiet wedding would be for the best, just immediate family, rather than inviting a large number of guests.'

Nicholas nodded. This was so much better than being horsewhipped. 'And Charlotte, is she in agreement with this marriage and with rushing the arrangements?'

'Well, it's not ideal. Every young woman wants her engagement to be long enough to give her dressmaker time to make a suitably ornate wedding gown and, under normal circumstances, Charlotte would want as many people as possible to witness her happy day, but these circumstances are not exactly normal so needs must prevail.' The smile wavered, then became just as broad and just as artificial as before.

Nicholas could see why the Dowager would be wavering. Having a suitable gown made? Wanting as many people as possible to witness her happy day? That did not sound like Charlotte. Was she really happy with this arrangement? He doubted it. And there was only one way to find out. 'As I have your blessing perhaps I should now talk to Charlotte herself.'

'Oh, there's plenty of time for that, have your tea first.' She vigorously rang the brass bell on the side table, to encourage the servants to hurry up. The door opened, but instead of a maid bearing a tea tray, Charlotte entered.

Nicholas stood up and smiled at her. Unlike her mother, there were no contradictions in Charlotte's body language. She was angry. Her pretty face was pinched in disapproval as she stared at her mother through narrowed eyes. She was dressed in her usual style, with a plain skirt and blouse, and unadorned with jewellery. Her hair was pulled back in a tight, simple bun at the nape of her neck. Yet, despite this, and her angry expression, the woman he intended to marry still looked beautiful.

'I suppose my mother has told you that you have to marry me.'

Just like her mother, she was straight to the point.

She sat down, sent her mother one more disparaging look, then turned to him. Her face softened slightly. 'Nicholas. I'm so sorry about all of this. I knew deep down that you weren't a cheat and I can't thank you enough for that notice you placed in the newspaper. But you did not need to do it. You should have called the Marquess's bluff. After all, I've told you often enough that I care nothing for what society thinks of me.'

Her mother huffed an exaggerated sigh. 'You've made that clear enough.'

Charlotte shook her head, her eyes once again narrowing into an icy glare. Instead of the expected argument with the Dowager, Charlotte turned back to him. 'But I thank you, Nicholas, for the gesture. You thought you were doing the right thing, even though it was misguided. You shouldn't have let the Marquess blackmail you and attempt to ruin your reputation.'

Another loud huff came from the Dowager. 'Misguided, misguided, you call him misguided. I think you should look at your own behaviour, my girl, before you start criticising anyone else's. And as for ruined reputations, well…' The Dowager huffed again, even louder.

He saw Charlotte's jaw tighten and she took in a few deep breaths. 'But despite what my mother has no doubt been saying to you, I still have no intention of marrying. Even more so now. I will not let the foolish rules of society force you or me into doing something that neither of us wants. They can gossip and act as outraged as they like, it won't cause me to abandon my principles.' She sat back in her seat as if there was nothing more that needed to be said.

Nicholas held up his hand to stop the Dowager from once again chastising her daughter. 'Charlotte, I am…'

The door opened and a maid and a footman entered, the maid carrying a tray of sandwiches and small cakes, the footman a tray bearing the tea. Before the interruption Nicholas was about to inform Charlotte that he was not being forced into anything, but he needed to talk to her. He had no intention of proposing marriage in front of the Dowager. He needed to get her alone.

As the tea was being served, he watched the exchange of irritated looks between the Dowager and Charlotte. It was obvious that Charlotte had been subjected to some sustained bullying from her mother over the topic of getting married and, stubborn as she was, this would have only made her more resistant to the idea. If he was to win her over, he would have to adopt some tactical behaviour. At least the serving of tea was giving him time to think of how he was to do that.

'Your mother has made her opinions very clear on what course we should now follow,' Nicholas said as diplomatically as he could when the maid and footman left.

Charlotte huffed her disapproval, in a manner not unlike her mother. 'And yet no one cares what I think, do they? Well, Nicholas, if you came here to propose, then I'm afraid you've had a wasted journey because I don't want to marry you or anyone.'

She lifted her teacup to her lips, then returned it to the saucer, untouched. 'Not that I don't appreciate what you did for me, because I do.' She looked down at her teacup, then back up at him. 'I really do. It was so honourable, one could almost say heroic, to sacrifice yourself like that for me.' Her voice had softened, giving Nicholas hope.

'It was no more than you deserve,' he said in an equally soft voice.

'See, the man's honourable, heroic, you said so yourself. What more could you want? For goodness' sake, marry him and be done with this matter,' the Dowager barked out.

Charlotte's jaw instantly tightened and she crossed her arms in defiance. Nothing was going to be achieved while they were in the Dowager's company. He needed to get Charlotte alone so they could talk without her overbearing presence.

'I will not be getting married just to satisfy the demands of society and to conform to their stupid rules, rules that are designed for one thing only: to keep women in their place.'

The Dowager frowned at Charlotte. 'This is no time for one of your political rants. That's what got you into this disastrous situation in the first place. Even you must be able to realise that once you put that notice in the newspaper you would have no choice but to get married. Now you are going to have to marry Nicholas whether you want to or not. It's as simple as that.'

'I do have a choice. It's not as if Nicholas is going to kidnap me and marry me against my will.'

Nicholas smiled at an image of him carrying a kicking and screaming Charlotte up the aisle over his shoulder. She frowned at him and he pulled his face into a more serious expression. 'No, certainly not. Women may have few rights, but at least they now have to give consent, rather than being forced into marriage.'

Charlotte nodded her agreement.

'More's the pity,' the Dowager mumbled, causing the return of Charlotte's frown.

This was getting them nowhere. 'Perhaps Charlotte and I should take a stroll round the garden,' he said to the Dowager. 'If you'd like to send for Charlotte's lady's maid to chaperon.'

The Dowager exhaled loudly. 'It's a bit late to care about you two being chaperoned, isn't it? Go on, go on.' She waved her hands towards the door. 'Go for a nice stroll round the estate and don't come back until you've convinced that wilful girl to marry you.'

* * *

'I'm not marrying you, so don't even waste your breath asking,' Charlotte said the moment the oak doors closed behind them.

'I think you've made that perfectly clear.' He offered her his arm. She paused for a moment, then took it and they strolled down the stairs, along the gravel path and towards the lake.

Nicholas kept his counsel while he thought things through. How do you convince a woman that she should marry you, even though she doesn't want to? Only yesterday he was also opposed to marriage, but now he knew it was the best outcome for both of them. But how was he to convince Charlotte? It was a situation he would have once thought impossible. There were young women up and down the country who would go to just about any lengths to be married to the Duke of Kingsford, to have the title of Duchess of Kingsford and all the wealth and privileges that came with it. But he had to go and fall in love with the one woman in England who had no interest in marrying him.

Love.

Nicholas almost stumbled, causing a concerned Charlotte to look up at him. He touched her hand in reassurance and continued walking. He was in love with Charlotte FitzRoy. That explained everything, that strange euphoria that came over him whenever he was in her presence and that overwhelming sense of absence that consumed him when they were apart. It was all making sense now. He was in love with Charlotte FitzRoy. Deep down he was sure he had known for a long time that what he was feeling was love, but had just refused to admit it to himself.

But would even a declaration of love be enough to convince Charlotte to marry him? He smiled to himself. The Dowager had said Charlotte was wilful and that was definitely true. It was another quality he adored about her. But it meant if they were to marry, there would be no way he could convince her that it was a sensible idea. Even a declaration of love was unlikely to work. If they were to marry, there was only one way it was going to happen. Charlotte was going to have to come to that conclusion herself.

'You said I shouldn't have put that notice in the newspaper, but I could say the same thing to you. You said I was being honourable, even heroic, but those terms more aptly apply to you. What made you do it?'

Charlotte drew in a deep breath and exhaled slowly. 'When I put that notice in the newspaper I did not mean to compromise you further. I did not want you to think you had to marry me. You have to believe that I merely wanted to let everyone know that you are not a cheat.'

'I know that and I doubt if there's anyone in England that even remembers that several months ago the main conversation topic was my cheating. Now all anyone will be talking about is Charlotte FitzRoy and her outrageous pronouncement.'

She looked up at him, defiance in her eyes. 'Well, hopefully they'll also be talking about society's hypocrisy. Everyone knows that many men have mistresses, but no one talks about it. And as for frequenting whorehouses, you just have to listen to what some of the working girls in the East End have to say. So many of them have clients that they describe as posh gents. Those men can carry on like that, yet at the same time young women are expected to remain virgins until they marry.'

Nicholas could only nod his agreement. 'And I admire the way you are so outspoken. It's something I've always admired about you.'

She stopped walking and looked up at him, her eyebrows raised, her head tilted in question. 'You have?'

He nodded. 'I remember the first time we met. It was one of the first balls of the Season. You were only eighteen and I walked in while you were reprimanding the Duke of Cadmont, a man old enough to be your father, over the way he had spoken to his valet. The man was staring at you like a fish out of water, his mouth opening and shutting, unable to form any words. I doubt if anyone had ever spoken to him like that before and certainly not a young, unmarried woman.' Nicholas laughed at the memory. Perhaps it was then that he had started to fall in love with the fiery Charlotte FitzRoy. He had certainly been impressed and knew that she was a young woman he wanted to get to know better.

She continued walking slowly down the path. 'Oh, well, he deserved it. You should have heard what he said to his servant, and his tone of voice, it was appalling. The servant was in no position to defend himself, so someone had to.'

'I think it was at that moment I knew just how special you were and that I would never be good enough for you.'

Charlotte stopped walking and looked up at him. 'Why on earth would you think that? You were always the most handsome man at every ball I attended, the most charming, and your notoriety gave you a certain appeal among all the debutantes. I was surprised you paid me any attention whatsoever.'

That was certainly not how Nicholas remembered their early encounters. 'If I remember correctly,' and Nicholas was sure that he did, 'you didn't tell me I was charming or handsome. Didn't you describe me as dim-witted with no conversation worth mentioning?'

'Oh, that. I've explained that. I was angry with you. You had rejected me and I was lashing out.' She looked up at him, her eyes beseeching. 'I've never considered you dim-witted, Nicholas. You're one of the wittiest men I know and the only one who makes me laugh. And as for your conversation, of course I've always enjoyed talking to you. I would hardly have all but thrown myself at some dull-witted man who I couldn't talk to.'

'Really? From memory...' Nicholas tilted up his head and looked skywards as if trying to recall. 'You told me there was only one thing that you were interested in and it wasn't my conversation.'

He was pleased to see, despite everything that had happened between them, she was still capable of blushing, but she laughed to cover her embarrassment. 'Well, there was that as well, but it wasn't just that. And while we're reminiscing, if you remember correctly you rejected me outright back then.'

He stopped and took hold of her hands. 'You're wrong, Charlotte. I would never reject you. I told you

I would not make love to you because it would ruin your marriage chances. You knew that I had no intention of marrying you or anyone else. I'm sorry if I gave you the impression that it was you I didn't want. That simply wasn't true. I wanted you, I still do. It's just that at that time I didn't want marriage.'

She looked down at her hands, then back up at Nicholas. 'You never gave me the wrong impression. I knew you wouldn't marry me then and that was not what I wanted either. It's still not what I want. I don't want to marry you or any other man.' She gently pulled her hands from his, took his arm and resumed walking. 'And I especially don't want to marry now just because it's what society expects of a so-called ruined woman. I will not marry just to redeem my reputation.'

'What do you want, Charlotte?'

She looked up at him and bit her top lip in a gesture that on anyone else would suggest shyness, but Charlotte had never been shy about saying what she wanted. 'I still want you, Nicholas. I just don't want to marry you.'

Nicholas fought hard not to react to her suggestion. There was no denying how much he wanted her, but he wanted more. He wanted her to be his wife. He didn't just want to make love to the woman he loved, he wanted to spend his life with her, to share every moment with her, to face and overcome every challenge with her.

She smiled slightly. 'There's one good thing that has come out of all this.'

Nicholas held his breath. Finally, she had come to

the realisation that marriage would be a good idea. It would save her reputation and mean they could spend the rest of their lives together, they could raise a family together, watch their grandchildren grow up.

'Now that I'm a ruined woman there's nothing to stop us from making love. You can't say you won't take my virginity because it will ruin my chance of making a good marriage. No one wants to marry me now, Nicholas.' She gave a little laugh. 'No one wants a ruined woman.'

Nicholas drew in a deep breath, held it for a moment, then exhaled slowly to try to calm the rampaging desire that was coursing through his body. Nothing would give him more pleasure than to take this highly desirable woman to a discreet place right now and satisfy the need for her that was consuming him, his mind and his body. Desperately trying to ignore the evidence of his desire, straining in his breeches, that her words had invoked, he attempted to think of something, anything, that would quash his desire. But with Charlotte standing so close that her feminine scent was overwhelming him, her silky skin mere inches away from his touch, her beautiful body on offer for him to satisfy his pounding need for her, his mind was incapable of thinking of anything other than how much he wanted her.

She smiled up at him, sensing his dilemma. 'Society already condemns me for what I wrote in the newspaper. As far as society is concerned, I couldn't get more sullied. So there's nothing to stop us now. Nicholas, I don't want to be your wife, but I could become...' she bit her bottom lip again '... I could become your mistress.'

He drew in another deep breath, and looked out to the horizon, away from temptation.

'No, Charlotte, you're wrong. You said no one wants to marry you, but one man does. I want to marry you. I do.' He drew in a deep breath so he would not waver in what he was about to say. 'And if I take your virginity it will be on our wedding night, no other time.'

'Really? Are you serious?'

He looked down at her and fought to keep his voice steady. 'I'm deadly serious. If you want me to make love to you, then you're going to have to marry me.'

Chapter Twenty-One

Charlotte was unsure which was making her angrier, being blackmailed or being rejected. All she knew was she was furious. Furious at Nicholas, furious at her mother and furious at society for having these ridiculous rules about what a woman could or could not do.

Not so long ago, they had combined forces against her mother to save them from being coerced into marriage. Now it seemed Nicholas was on her mother's side, on society's side and most definitely not on *her* side.

'If that's how you feel, then there's nothing more to be said.' She turned abruptly and stomped back to the house, all the way muttering about the unfairness of the world and her disappointment in Nicholas for finally succumbing and conforming to what society demanded of them.

She passed her mother and Rosie, talking quietly together in the hallway. They stopped talking the moment they saw her. Presumably they were gossiping about her, just as the rest of society would. Well, damn them, and damn society.

Her mother stood in front of her, trying to bar her progress. 'Well?' she asked. 'Should I contact the vicar and tell him to read the banns this Sunday?'

'You most certainly will not. Not this Sunday. Not ever,' she called out as she stormed past them and ran up the stairs.

Throwing herself on her bed, Charlotte was horrified to find that tears had gathered in her eyes. Whether they were tears of anger, of frustration or embarrassment at once again being turned down by Nicholas she was unsure. All she knew was she had never felt more devastated or more confused. Nicholas knew how she felt about the institution of marriage. He knew she saw it as yet another way to control women. How could he possibly think that she would change just because other people would now be talking about her? Let them talk. She would still stick to her principles.

A knock on the door made her wipe away her tears. She stood up and brushed down her skirt so she could assume a semblance of being under control. Her mother no doubt wanted to lecture her again on why she had to marry Nicholas, to tell her one more time why she had to save the family from ignominy. She would not let her mother see her in this state. She needed to be composed if she was to fend off another tirade from that insufferable, stubborn woman.

She braced herself and opened the door. But it wasn't her mother. Rosie was standing at the door, concern etched on her face. She stood back to let her sister-in-law enter.

'I suppose you've come to lecture me about why I have to marry Nicholas. Well, you'll be wasting your breath. I'm not getting married and that's that.' Charlotte threw herself down on a wing chair beside the bay window.

'You know me better than that,' Rosie said, seating herself in the chair opposite Charlotte. 'I've just come to see if you're all right. You looked so distressed when you rushed past us. Did Nicholas say or do something to upset you?'

'Yes, he did. That man is the limit.'

Rosie said nothing, just nodded her head and waited.

'I knew my mother wouldn't be on my side, but I thought Nicholas would be. I thought he would agree with me that we should not be forced into marriage, but he's just as bad as everyone else.'

'So he asked to marry you?'

Charlotte shook her head.

Rosie drew her eyebrows together in confusion. 'So he didn't ask you to marry him.'

Charlotte gritted her teeth together and drew in a deep breath before answering, 'He said he wouldn't make love to me unless I married him. The man is trying to blackmail me into marrying him. It's unforgivable.'

To her horror she saw the edges of Rosie's lips move into a smile before she adopted a more serious look. 'What do you mean? Are you saying you didn't actually make love to him when you were at Boswick? That was the impression I got from the notice in the newspaper. It was certainly the impression your mother got and presumably everyone who has read it. If nothing happened, then why did you say it did?'

'What the Marquess's valet actually saw us doing was still enough for the Marquess to blackmail Nicholas, but we didn't actually make love.' She looked out of the window. 'Nicholas rejected me then as well. He keeps rejecting me, it's just so infuriating.' She looked down briefly, then back up at Rosie. 'And humiliating.'

Rosie tilted her head to one side. 'It doesn't sound like a rejection to me. If he had rejected you completely, then the valet would have seen nothing. The Marquess wouldn't have blackmailed the Duke. He wouldn't have put his notice in the paper. You wouldn't have put your notice in the newspaper. None of this would have happened.'

'I know that.' Her anger started to ebb. If it wasn't for her, Nicholas would not have been put in a compromising position. But that still didn't excuse him for trying to blackmail her. She grasped on to that spark of anger and allowed it to reignite. 'You're right, he didn't reject me entirely, but he didn't do as I asked when we were alone together at Boswick. And he's done it again, he rejected me again just now.'

Rosie raised her eyebrows in question, but said nothing.

'Well, I suppose it wasn't exactly a rejection today,' she said in answer to the unasked question. 'He did say he'd make love to me on our wedding night, but that's just blackmail, isn't it? He's trying to make me go against my principles.'

Charlotte looked at Rosie, imploring her to agree, to see that she was right.

'No, he didn't reject you, Charlotte. It appears to me that it was the other way around.'

'It is not. I've never rejected Nicholas,' Charlotte said, her outrage evident in her raised voice.

'You told him that all you want is for him to make love to you, but you rejected the idea of marrying him. Does that mean all you want from Nicholas is to make love to you? Nothing else?'

Charlotte looked at her sister-in-law and tried to take in what she was saying. 'Well, no, not exactly, but I don't want to marry him.'

'Why not?'

'I'm surprised you have to ask me that. I've said often enough why I don't believe in marriage. I don't see why a woman should have to surrender all her rights over to a man. A marriage is not an equal partnership and I will not allow a man, any man, even Nicholas, to have control over me. I do not want to become some man's possession. I don't want a marriage where a man can do whatever he wants and I just have to tolerate it. I do not want to be like my mother.'

'My marriage isn't like that.'

'Yes, but you're married to Alexander. He's a good man and he loves you.'

Rosie said nothing.

'Oh, all right. Yes, Nicholas is an honourable man

as well and I can't imagine him ever treating me as if I was anything other than his equal.'

Rosie laughed lightly. 'And I can't imagine you allowing anyone to ever treat you that way either.'

Charlotte nodded her agreement.

'But if you don't love Nicholas then you shouldn't marry him.'

Charlotte shrugged, unsure what to say.

'Do you love him, Charlotte?'

She bit her bottom lip. No one had ever asked her that before. Her mother had never mentioned love when demanding that Charlotte get married. Did she love Nicholas? 'Well, I admire him. That's for certain.' She looked out the window. 'That notice he placed in the newspaper was so brave. I was so sure it couldn't be true when I read that he had confessed to cheating at cards. It wasn't like him at all. I went down to London to confront him, but he did not deny it.'

She looked back at Rosie. 'He would have known that if I had found out the truth I would have confronted the Marquess and the Marquess would have revealed what happened. He did it all for me, sacrificed himself for me. It was misguided, but it was very brave and for that I admire him terribly.'

'But do you love him?'

'Well, he is handsome.' She smiled at Rosie. 'The first time I saw him I couldn't believe that a man could look so good. He was so sophisticated, so manly and I just loved his blond hair and his blue eyes. I'd never seen a shade of blue so deep and that wonderful smile of his.' She smiled again, remembering how he looked when she had seen him at her first ball, during her first

Season. From that moment on there was only Nicholas. She hadn't noticed any other man at that ball, or any other social event she attended that Season.

'And every time I've seen him since that first day, he just seems to get more and more handsome. When I'm in his company all I want to do is touch him, to kiss him. I seem to lose all sense of reason, which is why I keep throwing myself at him.' She looked back out the window. 'Even though he keeps rejecting me.'

'He didn't reject you today. He offered to marry you. But you still haven't answered my question. Do you love him?'

She looked back at Rosie and bit her bottom lip, to stop the words from escaping. Rosie raised her eyebrows and waited.

'Oh, all right. Yes, I love him. I've always loved him. Why else do you think I've saved myself for him? If all I really cared about was losing my virginity, then I just would have found someone else to do it, but once I'd met Nicholas, I knew it had to be him. If it wasn't him, it would be no one. From the moment I first saw him I've wanted him and only him.'

'So why don't you want to marry him?'

'Because I won't be bullied into it. Society demands women marry if they're to be considered respectable. My mother has tried to bully me into marriage and now Nicholas is doing the same.'

'So you're not going to marry him to teach society, your mother and now Nicholas a lesson. But what do you want? Do you want to be with Nicholas, the man you love?'

Charlotte went back to chewing her bottom lip as

she took in what her sister-in-law was saying. 'Yes,' she finally murmured quietly.

'Do you want to spend the rest of your life with him?'

Charlotte nodded, the fight seeping out of her like a deflating balloon.

'So you love him, you want to spend the rest of your life with him and he wants to marry you.' Rosie stood up and kissed Charlotte on the cheek. 'Well, I'll leave you alone to think about what you're going to do next.'

Charlotte turned towards the windows once Rosie had departed. The gardens, lake and farmlands became a blur as she contemplated this sudden realisation. She was in love with Nicholas, she wanted to spend the rest of her life with the man she loved, but did she want to marry him?

Chapter Twenty-Two

Having to admit she was wrong was something Charlotte was unfamiliar with. She was more used to pointing out why other people were wrong, why society was wrong, why the way women were treated was wrong.

She walked back down the stairs, rehearsing in her mind what she would say to Nicholas, although now that she had admitted that she was in love with him words seemed inadequate to express the full extent of how she was feeling. But one thing she knew for certain. He *was* the man she wanted to marry, the man she wanted to spend the rest of her life with, to wake up next to every morning, go to sleep beside every night, to grow old with.

The man she wanted to marry.

The man she loved.

She paused on the stairs and gripped the banister to fully take in those two simple statements that meant so much. Two statements that had turned her world upside down and made her see everything in a completely different light. She had let herself become blinded to what she really wanted, but now all had become clear.

Before her conversation with Rosie, Charlotte would have laughed if anyone had suggested she would actually want to get married. If anyone had been foolish enough to suggest it, she would have given them a lecture on the legal position of a woman in a marriage. She would have railed against how many of the marriages among the aristocracy were unhappy, with the woman usually being the unhappiest partner. But they were marriages that had been arranged for financial advantage or to advance the family's position in society. Whereas, she was in love with Nicholas. She wanted to marry the man she loved. She wanted to marry him for one simple reason: because she loved him.

She closed her eyes and gripped the banister more tightly. She loved Nicholas and she wanted to marry him. She was sure she would never tire of repeating those lovely words to herself.

Smiling, she continued walking down the stairs, along the hallway and out through the hall. He was sitting by the lake, where she had left him earlier.

And yet in that time so much had changed. Everything had changed.

Her heart began beating faster, with anticipation, with a touch of apprehension at what she was about to do, but mainly with the pure joy of seeing the man she loved. For a moment she paused, taking the opportunity to watch him before he saw her. He was staring out at the lake, absentmindedly tossing in pebbles, lost in his thoughts.

How could she not be in love with this man? He was the very epitome of masculine beauty. Strong, handsome and virile, but he was also brave, honourable, clever and witty. And this wonderful man had said he wanted to marry her. Now she was going to accept, but before she did, she was going to open up her heart to him, tell him how she truly felt about him. He deserved her honesty.

She drew in a deep breath and began walking down the steps. She had always thought that asking Nicholas to make love to her had been a risky thing to do because it had exposed her to humiliation and rejection. But now she was going to make herself even more vulnerable by telling him exactly how she felt about him. It was something she had to do. She had to be completely honest with him, just as she was now, finally, being completely honest with herself.

Now was not the time to close down and protect her heart. Now was not the time to tell herself lies. Now was the time to be completely honest with the man she loved.

She walked down the gravel path towards the lake. He looked around, saw her, smiled and stood up. Charlotte knew it was not actually possible, but she was sure his smile had made her heart melt within her chest.

'Nicholas,' she said softly as she approached him, loving the sound of his name. 'Nicholas,' she repeated just to hear its glorious sound one more time.

'Charlotte,' he replied, equally softly.

She looked up at him and reached out her hands. He took them and held them gently.

'I want to apologise to you, Nicholas.'

His eyebrows drew together and he looked at her sideways. 'Apologise? For what?'

'Oh, for everything—for being me, I suppose. For being stubborn, and wilful as my mother said, for losing my temper so quickly.'

Nicholas laughed, pulled her hands closer to his chest and held them against his heart. 'Never apologise for being who you are, Charlotte. You're perfect.'

She shook her head. 'I do need to apologise. I get so angry sometimes about the way society treats women, and all its stupid rules, that I let it consume me and it makes me angry with everyone, even those who don't deserve it, including you.'

He shook his head, still smiling. 'Your passion and commitment are just two of the qualities I love about you. Without them you wouldn't be you and that would be a tragedy.'

Love? Did he just say *love*? He did. Charlotte smiled, then tried to keep her face serious. Now was not the time to get distracted. Not until she had said what she wanted to say.

'I want to be honest with you.'

He raised an eyebrow, but said nothing.

She drew in a deep breath. 'When we first kissed, when I told you I wanted you to make love to me, I said I was never going to marry, but I still wanted to experience physical love between a man and a woman.'

He smiled, those striking blue eyes crinkling up at the corners. For a moment Charlotte allowed herself to be distracted, before reminding herself she needed to focus on what she was saying.

'Oh, I remember it well,' he said, with a light laugh.

'I knew you didn't want to marry and I claimed the same, but that wasn't entirely true. I had fallen in love with you. I wanted you to make love to me, but what I really wanted was for you to love me. I just couldn't admit it to myself and I certainly couldn't admit it to you.' She drew in another deep breath. 'It wasn't just that I wanted to experience physical love, I wanted to experience it with you. That was why I have remained a virgin. It was you, and only you, that I wanted to make love to.'

He looked down into her eyes, his face soft and loving. 'And I have a confession to make as well. Five years ago, I also fell in love, with a beautiful, spirited young woman.'

Charlotte gave a small gasp at this admission.

'I've loved you from the moment I saw you giving Cadmont a dressing-down. It was as if I had been struck by lightning, I was so entranced by you. You were so magnificent, beautiful, fiery and impassioned. But I knew I would never be good enough for you. You were clever and passionate, not to mention the most beautiful woman I had ever seen. When you said you wanted me to make love to you I said no, not just because of society's rules, but because I wanted your love, not just your body.'

He sent her a teasing smile. 'Although I certainly wanted that as well.' His words caused her heart to quiver in the most delicious manner.

'But what I really wanted was for you to love me and I thought that was an impossibility. How could a woman like you ever love a man like me, who, as you said, was just a rake, only good for one thing?'

Charlotte tried to interrupt, to tell him how wrong he was, but when he lifted her hands to his lips and gently kissed her fingers, she momentarily lost the ability to talk.

'When I left for Europe I was sure I could never have your love,' he continued, her hands still held close to his lips. 'While we were apart I thought about you every single day. I had put a physical distance between us to try to put you out of my mind, but I failed dismally.'

He kissed her hand once again, then held them close to his heart. 'Charlotte. I love you. I want to marry you, not because I want to save your reputation. Not because I care a damn what society thinks or expects, but because I love you. All the time I was in Europe I tried to deny it. I tried to deny it when I saw you again, but it was impossible to deny something so powerful. I love everything about you, your mind, your soul, your passion, your everything.'

He loved her.

Charlotte could hardly believe what she was hearing. Nicholas Richmond, the wonderful, handsome, honourable, brave Nicholas Richmond had just said he loved her.

She bit the edge of her lip. 'So, do you still want to marry me, because I really, really want to marry you.'

He smiled at her. 'Oh, yes, I want to marry you with all my heart, but let me do this properly so we have something to tell our children and our grandchildren.'

Children? Grandchildren? Charlotte would one

day be the mother of Nicholas's children. She did not think it was possible to feel such happiness. She knew she was smiling like a fool, bubbling over with joy, but she didn't care.

Nicholas released one of her hands and dropped to one knee. 'Charlotte FitzRoy, will you do me the immense honour of consenting to be my wife? I promise I will love, honour and cherish you for the rest of my life. If you marry me, it will make me the happiest man alive. I've always loved you, Charlotte. It has always been only you. I want to spend the rest of my life with you. To devote myself to you. Will you marry me?'

Charlotte fought to pull her smiling face into a stern expression. 'I'll say yes on one condition.'

'Anything you want, it's yours.'

'That you do as you promise and take away my dratted virtue on our wedding night.'

Nicholas threw back his head and laughed. 'That is one promise I'll be more than happy to keep.'

'Then I accept, but only if you kiss me. Right now.'

He laughed again as he stood up. 'Happy to oblige.' He pulled her towards him. When his lips touched hers, this time, instead of melting, Charlotte was sure she was about to explode with happiness. As his strong arms wrapped around her, she moulded herself into his body and kissed him back, letting him know with her kisses, just as she had with her words, how much she loved him.

He deepened the kiss and only one doubt remained—would they really be able to wait until their wedding night to consummate their love?

Epilogue

It was just a kiss. Just one kiss.

Through a fog of desire Charlotte heard the vicar coughing and spluttering. Reluctantly she pulled back from kissing her husband and looked at the embarrassed vicar, pulling at his collar and blushing from his neck up to his forehead.

When the vicar had said *you may kiss the bride* at the end of the wedding service, he obviously hadn't expected them to kiss with such passion. But how could she kiss Nicholas in any other way? As soon as her lips touched his, fire burst within her, consuming her, consuming the two of them.

She smiled conspiratorially at Nicholas, her husband, and he winked back.

Her husband, they were now husband and wife, joined together as one.

That kiss had sealed it. It was much more than just a kiss. It marked the beginning of their life together as husband and wife. It was an expression of their love and passion for each other and it signalled what was to come later that night.

Nicholas took her hand and gave it a gentle squeeze as they turned and walked out of the small country church. Local people were gathered at the entrance. They cheered and threw flower petals as Nicholas and Charlotte emerged, followed by their family members and a few invited guests.

The guest list had been restricted to those who had commended rather than condemned Charlotte for the notice she had placed in the newspaper. She had been surprised at how many people had written to her, saying they agreed with everything she had said. The members of the charity trust board had sent her a letter telling her the plaque thanking the Marquess of Boswick had been removed. They had also written a letter to the newspapers that had reported on the unveiling, telling them that they had been deceived by the Marquess and they had nothing but contempt for the man's behaviour. The last Charlotte had heard of the Marquess was that he had closed up his houses, packed his bags and headed off to parts unknown, possibly in Europe, possibly in the Americas.

The chairman of the hospital charity had also told Charlotte how impressed they were with her bravery and the letter had been signed by all members of the board. She had also received letters from numerous women's groups thanking her for drawing public attention to the inequalities between men and women and asking her if she would join their organisations to fight for greater equality for women.

Nicholas had read the letters with as much interest

as she had and had declared that, with the two of them working together, it wouldn't be long before women had the vote and complete equality with men. Charlotte thought he was being perhaps a bit too optimistic about what the two of them could achieve, but was excited that her husband had as much passion for her causes as she did.

On the doorstep of the church Nicholas kissed her again, causing a resounding cheer to erupt from all those watching. Charlotte wanted this kiss to go on for ever, wished she could stay in Nicholas's arms for ever, but they had a wedding breakfast to get through, before they could spend their first night together as husband and wife.

Nicholas had insisted they wait until their wedding night, something she had objected to, but Nicholas was resolute. He had, at least, partly conceded and given her some delicious samplings of what the night would be like, the memory of which caused her body to react in a manner not appropriate when they were still on church grounds.

Reluctantly breaking from the kiss, she looked up at Nicholas and they smiled at each other. They had waited over five years and tonight they had a lot of time to make up for.

* * * * *

*If you enjoyed this story, be sure to read
the previous books in Eva Shepherd's
Breaking the Marriage Rules miniseries*

**Beguiling the Duke
Awakening the Duchess
Aspirations of a Lady's Maid**